Hawaiian Hurricane

by

Laney Kaye

The Spirit of Ohana Cruise Ship,
Book One

The Wild Rose Press, Inc.
PO Box 708
Adams Basin, NY 14410-0708
Visit us at www.thewildrosepress.com

Publishing History
First Edition, 2024
Trade Paperback ISBN 978-1-5092-5435-4
Digital ISBN 978-1-5092-5436-1
Previously Published by CrossWorlds Publishing 2019

The Spirit of Ohana Cruise Ship, Book One
Published in the United States of America

Dedication

For Taylor
Who believes I'm The Little Engine That Could

Chapter One

Sara

The storm-driven waves foamed far below me, the occasional mountainous whitecap forcing my retreat from the guardrail. Though the wind tugged at my ponytail and whipped escaped strands across my face, the pelting rain had eased. My fifth stint on the Hawaiian cruise ship, *The Spirit of Ohana*, and we'd run into a rare hurricane. Which perhaps proved the old sea-faring lore that a woman aboard a ship brought bad luck—though I shared the jinx label with a third of the other crew members and half of the fifteen hundred passengers.

The ship surged up and over a wave, and I clutched the rail, choking off a squeal as we bottomed out with a thud that quivered through the reinforced steel hull. An adrenaline rush chased the flash of fear, and I braced my legs to ride out the rock and roll. Eyes squinted against the salt spray, I gazed across the dark ocean toward the invisible coast.

Kept busy in the cabins picking up wet towels and making uncountable beds—well, not exactly uncountable, I knew precisely how many sheets I had to tuck and how much time to allocate to cleaning other people's toilets—I'd missed the highlight of the Big Island passage, an evening viewing of the Kilauea volcano bleeding lava down the black cliffs. But in any case, the orange-red ooze of demon vomit, hissing with evil anger as it reached the sea, was a little too end-of-the-worldish for my taste. I was more a Na Pali coast kind of girl, the miles of emerald-green cliffs, waterfalls, and hidden valleys of the unreachable, untouched land calling me to embrace my new freedom.

I tucked a strand of tangled hair behind my ear, grinned as it immediately escaped, and licked the tang of salt from my lips as I turned my face into the wind. Last year I'd have huddled in the lush interior of the cruise ship—in fact, with a stateroom and butler service, I'd probably never even have stepped out onto the deck. Most certainly not during a hurricane. But things had changed. I'd changed.

My stomach rumbled, and I swiped mist from the face of my watch and tilted it toward the muted yellow glow of a deck light. A little early yet to turn down the last of the beds before I took a dinner break. Whether dining in Michelin-starred restaurants in London, months of pot noodles while working in the Solomons, or the endless buffets aboard *The Spirit of Ohana*, I never had a problem with the *Eat* part of the new mantra I'd decided to live by.

Despite a flirtation with Buddhism, I was having more trouble with *Pray*. Begging favors from a flavor-of-the-week deity didn't sit well.

Love, however… I drummed my fingertips on the rail. I'd settle for sex. Working in close confines with the ship's entertainment director had, well, stirred my juices. Not that a cocktail of lust did me much good. Jay flirted outrageously—and I'd quickly learned that my ten-day roster on the ship required packing twenty pairs of panties—but our employer had a strict *No Fraternization* policy.

And despite my current life, my legal training meant I was all about the rules.

As I reluctantly retreated to the scant shelter of the dripping metal walls of the ship, a flash of white strobed against the murky, churning ocean. Orca! I lunged back to the rail, squinting into the storm. There it was, a patch of light surfing the dark waves. A dead whale?

The ocean surged, bringing the carcass closer. No, not a whale. A small yacht. The rain hurled needle-sharp flurries, and I rubbed my eyes one at a time so I didn't lose sight of the dismasted wreckage, a burgundy sail slicking the ocean like blood. The boat must have slipped its moorings in the hurricane.

I glanced toward the storm doors that sectioned the rain-lashed deck from a plush, carpeted passage twenty feet away. My induction handbook probably had an obscure section directing me to report shipping hazards, but by the time I found my way to the bridge, surely the wreck would have sunk safely out of the way?

The yacht crested another wave. *What the hell?* The sudden pounding of blood in my ears competed with the thunder rolling across the sky. A person huddled in the bottom of the vessel.

No, not a person. Fishing nets. Or the sail, torn from its restraints. Or old clothes, rags. Anything but— The bundle rolled as the yacht hit a trough. White flesh gleamed stark against the night.

Shit. In fact, triple shit. I scanned the deck of *The Spirit*. Why wasn't there some kind of smash-and-sound-the-alarm device? Trains had them, and it wasn't like they risked running into shipwrecks.

A hand rose feebly from the hull of the yacht.

Alive. Crap. That was bad. Well, good. But bad.

I raked my hands through my hair, tugging a decision from my brain. By the time I found help, the yacht would be swallowed by the ocean. Already it plunged and bucked fifty, maybe a hundred feet away, beyond the bubble of security created by the lights of *The Spirit.*

A hundred feet. I could do that. The pool at home was sixty feet, and until the last few months, I'd swum twenty-five laps, morning and night. Of course, the pool didn't have a wave machine churning out skyscraper-sized breakers or a population of the myriad stingy, bitey things that no doubt inhabited this part of Oceania.

I shucked my leather lace-ups and my jacket. The life preserver was tricky to wrest from its mounting—I'd be putting in a report on *that* failure—but eventually, with the chunk of plastic under one arm, I clambered onto the bottom rung of the guardrail.

Stupid movies. Who could forget that actress who had looked windswept and poignant on the bow of her ship? But I was vibing clinging gargoyle rather than regal figurehead.

As *The Spirit's* storm door clanged against the metal wall, I dropped my foot back to the deck, quivering in cowardly relief. The cavalry had arrived. Or the Marines or coast guard or whoever, I didn't much care as long as the responsibility for rescuing the occupant of the yacht was no longer mine.

But instead of framing some great uniformed hunk, the butter-yellow light from the passageway created a halo around my roommate, Melanie. One hundred pounds of sweet-but-useless blonde and about as far from assistant-rescuer material as it was possible to get.

"Mel!" As she struggled toward me, bent double against the bluster, I realized that if she blew away—which seemed entirely possible and fairly probable—I'd be responsible for two deaths. I waved her back, the rushing wind filling my cheeks. "Go get help."

With the life preserver clamped under my arm more firmly than a handbag in Ho Chi Minh City, I pulled myself back up on the railing. My toes scrabbled against the plexiglass sheet. Why did they make these things so hard to climb, anyway?

Oh yeah, so nobody climbed them.

Throwing one leg over the top, I straddled the fence. Then lurched forward, my cheek crushed against the rail as I clung to it like a baby koala. The liner plunged. A surge of vertigo yanked my stomach into my mouth, and I squeezed my eyes shut. The wind shrieked, gleeful salty fingers trying to tug me from my precarious perch.

What was I thinking? This was a totally shit idea. I was a lawyer—or at least, I had been until a few months ago—and that really should rule me out as either a hero or an idiot.

I forced my eyes open, assessing the black maw of the ocean about—*no*. I didn't want to calculate how many feet below me. Even from the lowest deck, slamming into those waves was going to hurt like a slap from a frozen fish.

Melanie struggled closer, probably thinking I was planning to top myself—though I clutched the life preserver with the same desperation I'd clung to a donut the week I tried intermittent fasting.

The yacht had disappeared into the gloom. Even if I sounded the alarm now, finding the stricken craft would be impossible. I was out of both time and choices.

I was right—hitting the water did hurt. And screaming while submerged was another less-than-stellar idea.

Fortunately, the combination of the life preserver and my inherited personal flotation device—*thanks for the boobs, Mum*—propelled me back to the surface with gut-wrenching speed.

My head emerged into a world of darkness and towering waves, and I coughed and spluttered, the salt burning hotter than a dragon's indigestion.

Waves crested and crashed down, pummeling my flesh into a trough that might have been forged from steel.

I could barely open my eyes against the salt sting, and I'd taken onboard enough water to kill a camel. Without doubt, this was the stupidest move of my life. Even dumber than saying "I do" before I was twenty.

The Spirit of Ohana steadily chugged away, a disappearing city.

They'd turn. They had to. Once they understood Melanie's breathless plea, the captain would order the engines thrust into reverse.

And run over me. Chop me into shark bait.

Or worse, if I kept floundering around out here, they'd have to rescue *me*.

Despite my prowess in the pool, with one arm wrapped around the buoy, I was swimming like a damaged frog…which immediately made me think of Paris and the wonderful meals I'd enjoyed there.

Wait, was my life was flashing before my eyes?

The yacht loomed from the darkness as though the ferryman had come to carry me across the Styx. Upper-body strength had never been my thing, and now I carried twenty extra pounds. Okay, maybe thirty. How was I supposed to drag my waterlogged body aboard the towering hull?

A cable trailed the boat like an anchored snake, and I swapped my death grip on the life preserver for the frayed rope. Planted my sock-clad feet against the hull and leaned back to walk up the side.

Yeah, not even the coolest comic character could pull that off without a green screen.

The cable bit into my palms as I rode out the push and shove of the lesser waves, waiting for the next crest.

The invisible force built, tugging at my legs, pulsing like electricity, alive and growing until suddenly the wave was beneath me, pummeling me against the timbers. With nowhere else to go, the energy exploded upward, lifting me like a skyrocket. My shoulder slammed into the side of the boat, and I flung my other arm over the gunwale, clinging like a damaged starfish as the receding water tried to suck me back into the depths.

My fingernails dug into the wood. Screw saving the occupant of the crippled yacht; my own chance of survival also lay in that hull. A search party would have no hope of locating a solo swimmer in the inky ocean, but the yacht would have lights and beacons. I needed to get aboard and signal for rescue.

The next wave crashed over my head, but I clung to the boat. As the water drove down on me like a pile driver, pain screamed through my elbow and shoulder, almost overshadowing the flaring sting in the cheek that had smashed against the hull. It had to be bleeding.

Burley for the sharks.

The thought galvanized me. The next wave powered

up beneath me, and I used it to fling one leg over the gunwale. With my breasts hampering my attempt to slither elegantly over the ledge, my blouse ripped open as the buttons gouged into the wood. If *The Spirit* returned now, they'd probably bring harpoons to bear.

The yacht plunged almost vertical, then slammed into the trough. The impact launched me into the air, flying for a graceful moment until I hit the floor of the boat with a squeal.

Well, not exactly the floor. Something slightly softer but no warmer.

Strong arms wrapped around me, as though I was rescued rather than the rescuer, and for a moment I was tempted to lie there and revel in the comparative safety. Then a wave crashed over the boat, the water swirling around me. Which meant the body beneath mine must be close to submerged. Not drowning the person I'd set out to rescue would probably be a good idea.

The body mumbled. I clambered to my knees, rocking precariously as I bent closer to catch the words. A male voice. Instinctively, I clutched my ripped blouse closed. Because obviously, a random boob flash was totally my biggest issue right now. "EPIRB?" I echoed, probably sounding like some washed-up seabird twittering away.

"Seat."

I crawled across the wildly bucking deck, locating the locker beneath a bench. I'd done something to my shoulder, something bad, but fear dulled the pain.

I scrabbled open the latch and rummaged in the cupboard blindly. Located an emergency beacon. Activated it. At least that was straightforward. I wouldn't have been surprised to find it came with an instruction book. In Swedish. With a hex key. It was turning out to be that kind of day. Or that kind of life, really.

Using the flashing LED from the beacon, I shuffled back across the deck on my knees.

Maybe I had been better off without the light, because now I could see that my fellow passenger lay in a brine-thinned pool of blood. The sea kept adding to the volume, yet a deep gash on his forehead oozed enough to turn that water pink. He was as pale as a corpse, and I couldn't tell whether he was still breathing. The water lapped over his face, yet he didn't splutter or move. According to the mandatory first aid training, to which I'd paid somewhat half-assed attention, that probably was not a great sign.

I should bail to stop the craft from sinking, but my limbs were jelly. Instead I inched toward my fellow passenger. My right arm refused to work, and my ribs felt like they shoved through what should have been pretty decent padding. But pain proved I was still alive, right?

Wedging the left side of my body partly under his, I then lifted the sailor's shoulders above the water level, cushioning his head against my chest. He probably shouldn't be moved, but I needed to protect him…and I wanted some company, because this darn sure felt like it was racking up to be the last few minutes of my life. "Can you hear me?"

Eyes greener than the Wall of Tears in Maui flashed open, blinking against the torrential rain that sought to help the wild ocean drown us. The sailor slowly lifted one hand and stroked the sodden hair from my face, his words barely audible above the crashing ocean. "Why are you here?"

Chapter Two

Rick

The vagaries of upper-crust, eccentric parents meant being rescued from a watery grave by the employees of a cruise ship wasn't the most embarrassing thing to ever happen to me, although perhaps impressively close. There had been the time that Vanessa Cottesloe-Meyer declared her undying devotion. Possibly unrelated, but I'd promptly been sick all over her fancy red-soled shoes. No thirteen-year-old should even have access to shoes that cost more than the GDP of a small nation.

The two decades since had cemented my dislike of both fancy shoes and women with double-barreled surnames.

Fortunately, my memory of the more recent humiliation was patchy. I did recall I'd been crewing a yacht alone, gleeful at the thought of Mother's lemon-sucking disapproval when she found out. Which, of course, she would the moment Marty realized I'd given him the slip. He would have had a trace on my platinum credit card. In fact, the bodyguard had probably been on my tail before I'd even reached the southeastern coast of Big Island.

Other than that, my memories were scattered, featuring nightmarish flashes of the sinuous red-orange ooze of Kilauea melting purple dusk-shadowed cliffs, and mountainous waves crashing down upon my boat.

And breasts. I had a very clear recollection of ample, soft breasts.

Apparently an odd but by no means unpleasant side effect of the great whack to my head from the splintering mast, which I now remembered.

The white ceiling above me swirled in and out of focus. I sucked in a breath, winced as my lungs protested, and made an effort to concentrate on the pressure cuff a white-coated medic wrapped around my upper arm.

He leaned over me and flashed a light into my eyes. "Ah, reactive pupils. That's better." He swapped the light for a square of gauze and dabbed at my head. The fabric came away covered in blood. "Looks like you're going to sport a scar from this one. I'll have to pop in some stitches. Still, could have been worse."

Hardly. Mother would have conniptions, her precious son scarred like a common street brawler. The thought of her wrath brought a quick grin to my lips. She was only ever happy when she was unhappy, so my sojourn in Hawaii should have her bordering on ecstatic. Cautiously, I edged a hand up to my jaw. Felt like I'd been hit by a lorry. Loaded with gravel.

Squinting at the silver name badge on the doctor's white jacket worked—*Michaels*. I jerked my chin at the fresh gauze pad he wielded. "What's that, doc?"

"Rubbing alcohol."

"Uh-uh." I shook my head as decisively as the pirouetting world would allow. I'd played college rugby and knew to avoid that stuff like the plague.

Michaels blew between pursed lips. "The amount of salt you've had washing over your wounds, you'll barely notice the sting of a little alcohol."

"Not happening," I replied, my tone firmer than I felt. In fact, that was the only thing that seemed solid. The room was vague and misty around the edges, and my spinning head lent a surreal aspect to my jellied limbs. The sight of unicorns galloping over rainbow bridges wouldn't seem abnormal right about now. I tried to force my brain into order. "Aren't you supposed to offer me a slug of rum and a rope to bite on?"

"Whatever your experiences, this isn't the Queen's Navy, you know," the doctor said over his shoulder as he rummaged through a metal cabinet. He uncapped a dark-tinted bottle and wafted it under my nose. "Iodine's your other choice."

My eyes watered, sinuses smarting like I'd thrown back a shot of tequila. Hadn't touched the stuff since Guanajuato, Mexico, where an investigation into the overexploitation of the underground aquifers had led to far too long of a night spent in a cantina. "Perfect. Or as close as it'll get." Sadly, unlike tequila, it wouldn't give the kick I craved. No, on second thoughts, my head really didn't need a kick.

Michaels laid the yellow-stained gauze on my forehead, then turned to a side table. "As you're conscious, I'll need your identity and consent before I do the suturing." He waved a waterlogged wallet in my direction.

My hand shot to my pocket. *Damn.* Where my pocket would have been if I wasn't as naked as an eel beneath the thin sheet.

The wallet splodged onto the steel side bench, and the doctor poised a pen over his notepad. "Can you tell me your name?"

"Sure." The word came out gravelly rather than

droll.

Michaels tapped his pen on the page. "Care to share?"

I could claim someone else's identity. Say I'd picked up the incriminating wallet on a beach, and invent an alternate life. Except that kind of thing wasn't so easy, in reality. Marty would be all over it. "Richard Winchester." The doctor hadn't asked my title, so I could omit that.

"And do you recall what happened?"

Sure. I'd been running away. Temporarily. "Boating mishap." A storm. Snapped mast. And— I jerked into sitting position. *And a mermaid.*

Oh yeah, great. Nothing wrong with my head. Unicorns *and* mermaids.

"Steady on there. You'll be dizzy." The doctor still held his pen poised for my revelations.

But there *had* been a mermaid, a black-tailed woman who'd slithered into my boat at the height of the storm. I frowned. No, not a tail. Black pants. And a white blouse. I distinctly recalled a white blouse because, despite the swirling darkness that crowded my mind, I remembered the soft comfort as she'd slipped beneath me, ample breasts cushioning my head. The waves had turned to chop, and the yacht bucked and yawed furiously. Light had bathed us, voices growing loud as the massive bulk of a ship blocked the few stars in the sky. I'd tried to cling to the mermaid and refused to be strapped in a litter and lifted aboard the rescue vessel until someone assured me she'd also be taken onto the ship.

Then where was she? "There was a mer—girl." Yeah, best not get the doc to order a psych evaluation straight away. The tabloids would have a field day with that.

Michaels held the notepad and pen toward me. "Sign and date, please." He scrutinized my tight scrawl, as though he could verify it as real, and then took a needle and length of suture from a plastic tray. "You may be more comfortable if you lie back while I do this."

I moved back onto the hard pillow. Had he even heard me?

The gauze tugged as he peeled it from my forehead, my grinding teeth almost obscuring his words. "And you mean Sara, one of the cabin stewards." Needle poised, he raised his eyebrows when I didn't respond. "The girl who rescued you."

"She what?" The blurted words didn't exactly announce my Oxford education. But rescued me? Not quite how I remembered it. In fact— Whoa, no! I cupped my groin. Obviously, it would be more appropriate if I didn't recall the hard thrust of her nipples against my chest until I had control of my reactions. But rescue? Even in my semiconscious state, her embrace as the motion of the boat rhythmically ground us together had definitely felt more raunchy than rescue.

Minty breath washed over me as the doctor leaned forward with the needle, then paused as the ship rolled. To register within a ship this size, the hurricane must still rage fierce. "Sure. Sara spotted your yacht, grabbed a buoy, and dived in after you. Bloody mad. But she is our token Aussie, so what can you expect? Probably been wrestling crocs since she was a kid."

My head hurt too much to discern whether the doctor teased or actually believed all the nonsense about Australians being brought up rough and tough. Though, if the woman had jumped into a hurricane...she had to be certifiable. Shame.

No, not a shame at all. Despite my surge of deluded interest, obviously brought on by the crack to my head, her crazy meant I wouldn't have to add her to the list of women I strove to avoid.

"No, you don't." Michaels jostled my shoulder until I dragged heavy lids open. "Can't have you drifting off until I'm sure there's no concussion. Let me finish this last stitch, then we'll get you up and about."

I groaned. "You have to be kidding." The unicorns had moved to stomping on my head. Nasty beasties.

The door to the left of the stretcher bed opened with a whisper of wood on linoleum, and Michaels turned to speak to someone. "Take the identity from Mr. Winchester's wallet to the captain, please. Let him know our unexpected guest is conscious."

"Rick. Just Rick." The farther I could distance myself from the surname, the better.

"Sure," the doctor replied easily. "I'm guessing your phone will be unserviceable. Is there someone you'd like us to contact on your behalf?"

State-of-the-art, waterproof to forty-thousand leagues, my phone would be fine. I should make the call myself, but the thought of the instant recriminations made me feel like a school kid up before the head teacher. "Try the phone. Passcode's 4116. You're looking for Martin Robbins. Just let him know I'm fine." Damn, I didn't feel fine. "Please," I added. Yeah, ever the British gentleman. Even with my head cleaved in two.

Michaels pressed tape over my stitches. "You didn't fare as bad as Sara, for all your exposure."

My gut clenched. Some bloody gentleman. The

15

mermaid getting injured hadn't even occurred to me. "She's hurt?"

The doctor lifted an "about time you thought to ask" eyebrow. "A few grazes. Dislocated shoulder. Hell of a bruise to her ribs. She's in the treatment room next door."

I swung my legs from the bed. Grabbed at the sheet, which tried to slide away as a white-coated woman entered the room. She paused in the doorway, staring at me with big eyes. Damn, I knew that look.

She didn't take her gaze from me. "Dr. Michaels, could I see you in the corridor for a moment?"

I'd been sprung. As Michaels stepped out, I glanced around the room, like locating my chinos would enable me to flee the scene.

Not a hope. Michaels already blocked the doorway, his body language absurdly deferential. No doubt he'd readily hand over that tot of rum now. "Oh, ah, I'm sorry. I didn't immediately realize who you were, Mr….ah, sir… I'm not sure what I should…"

I groaned. "Rick. Just Rick is fine." This was how it went, every bloody time. I never got to be normal.

"Sure," the doctor agreed, avoiding calling me anything at all. "Could you excuse me for a moment while I speak with the captain?"

Like he needed my permission. I waved a hand, staring at my feet. The skin was wrinkled, white from waterlogging, with salt caked in a visible crust. I craved a hot shower.

Michaels moved into a cubicle off the treatment room, his voice too low to make out actual words as he used the shipboard phone.

He returned to the room in a flurry of movement, fussing over the dressing on my head. Nervous. "Yes, that should be fine. Not too much swelling, though I suspect it may look worse tomorrow."

I slid him an apologetic grin. Poor sod would discover whether his stitching made the grade once the photos hit the news and Mother saw them. Maybe I should warn him up front? Mother's negative rating predictable, she'd want plastic surgeons involved.

Well, she could take a flying leap on that one. We were about fifteen years past her having any sway in my life.

Yeah, right. The presence of the thick ream of papers in my Waikiki suite punctured that particular delusion. I suppressed another groan. Damn, I was a long way from free. Between Mother's concern for the family name and Marty's paid concern for my welfare, I was probably more controlled than any blue blood of far higher birth. But if I wanted this last transaction to pass through seamlessly, I had to be seen to be playing Mother's game. Between them, Elizabeth and Marty had me by the balls. A particularly unpleasant mental picture, when thinking of one's mother.

Michaels handed me burgundy striped pajamas, bearing what I assumed to be the ship's logo on the breast pocket. *The Spirit of Ohana.* Ohana was one of the few Hawaiian words I knew, so I translated. *The Spirit of Family.* Ironic, given the tangent of my wandering thoughts.

Michaels ducked his chin, clearing his throat as he turned his back. "As we won't make landfall in Honolulu until early morning, the captain has had the premier stateroom prepared for your convenience."

I thrust my legs into the pants, then slid from the bed to hike them up. Plenty wide enough in the waist, but cut for midgets. Or for normal-height people, perhaps. Few off-the-rack garments fit my frame.

I snorted. Hell, how would I know? When had I last made an attempt to purchase something that wasn't tailored? No, even that wasn't the whole truth; when had I last purchased an item of clothing, period? I had a stylist and a buyer. Barely had to dress myself.

I plucked at the pajama pants. Thin cotton, not fine linen. I liked them. Suddenly, very much. "Okay, let's do this."

Michaels passed me my waterlogged wallet, and I squeezed the leather, droplets forming on my fingers.

I waved the incriminating evidence at him. "Can we keep this quiet?"

He nodded. "Of course, sir." Another knock sounded. Busier than Waterloo station, down here. Michaels opened the door, revealing a suit-clad man who would challenge me for height, with shoulders to balance. "This is Jay Edwards, *The Spirit of Ohana's* entertainment director. He'll accompany you to the stateroom."

"Your chariot awaits, sir." The newcomer nodded at the wheelchair that leaned against his thighs.

I staggered over and lowered myself. "How fast can you move? I don't much relish being a spectacle." Like I wasn't accustomed to it.

"This end of the ship's relatively quiet, sir. We keep the lively stuff in the bars toward the bow."

The chair lurched from the hard flooring into the carpeted hallway. "You can cut the 'sir' crap. It's Rick." I rubbed my forehead, flinching as the edge of the bandage peeled up under my fingertips. "Do you know a cabin steward called Sara?"

Far above me, my chauffeur chuckled. "Do I know Sara?" His tone seemed to hold a good deal of suggestiveness. "Everyone knows our favorite Aussie."

"So the mermaid's a party kid?" I said, slurring a little as my head throbbed. So much for my brief fantasy, but the fact remained that Sara had risked her life for mine. "Could you have her sent to my room, please?" Best to make the requisite expressions of gratitude before the no doubt inebriated Aussie discovered who I was and developed a sudden attachment to me. To my title.

Chapter Three

Sara

"You okay to walk, mate?"

Yanks using the Australianism always struck me as hilarious. I shot a glance up at Jay. "Are you offering to carry me?" Because he could say yes anytime he wanted.

For once, the laughter dropped from his voice. "You know I would." Then he grinned, re-establishing our senior/junior employee role. "Do anything for one of my best crew members."

"Good, then you can get me out of this." I jerked my chin toward the end of the corridor.

"No can do. Rick's a very proper British gentleman, probably needs to swear his undying gratitude for you throwing yourself into the middle of a hurricane to rescue him. Reckon you're going to be stuck with him now."

I tugged at the sling supporting my arm. "What? I've only got to strip the cabins, then I'm off for two days as soon as we dock."

"The Chinese say that when you save a life, you become responsible for it. Looks like you've *dived* into trouble."

"Lucky none of us are Chinese, then," I muttered. A cheating ex-husband controlling our joint finances was enough for any girl to deal with. I halted as Jay turned into a corridor cordoned off with a burgundy tasseled rope, an ornately lettered sign marked *Private* swinging in the breeze of our passage. "You have to be kidding. There are cabins available on my level. What's the deal with the executive suite?"

A soft chime on the PA system interrupted, and we both paused. A reminder the poolside bar was closed due to the weather—which meant the pool had formed a mini tsunami and emptied itself over the deck.

"Captain's orders. But I'm sure if I leave the two of you alone for a few minutes, you can find out why." Jay raised his eyebrows suggestively.

"You wouldn't believe on how many levels I'm not interested." Yet the memory of the guy's hard body beneath mine in the bottom of the tossing boat brought heat to my cheeks. I straightened the fresh uniform blouse I'd struggled into. "Last chance for you to be my knight in shining armor and rescue me."

Jay swiped a key card. Lowered his voice. "I'm not in the habit of checking out guys, but I think you may not require rescuing." He swung the door open. "Mr. Winchester?"

I stepped into the entry foyer, glancing around curiously. Executive suites were not on the cleaning roster for junior stewards, and though my almost-ex-husband and I had traveled extensively, we'd not done a cruise. Simon insisted they required far too much interaction with socially unacceptable guests.

As I'd shared a cabin with Melanie for the last two months, even the standard cabins had begun to appear generous. But this suite, fully appointed with an open-plan dining room and a stainless-steel kitchen, was the size of a small apartment and on par with any of the best hotels Simon demanded we stay in. An entire wall of glass doors opened onto a balcony, which overlooked the dark ocean. Another lightly smoked double-glass door sectioned off a bedroom with a bed as big as my cabin. The linen would have to be custom made.

Jay ushered me forward, gesturing to the burgundy leather sofa in the recessed lounge.

I pushed back. "I'm not going to sit down," I muttered, hyper-aware of my bedraggled appearance. Scraping up a decent ponytail with one arm out of use had been nearly impossible. I swiped a hand over my hair, brushing the graze on my cheek. Shit, I'd forgotten that. I'd look like a train wreck. Not that it mattered. All I wanted was to get out of here and grab a hot shower and a few hours' sleep before I did my final room service.

"Ah, Mr. Winchester." Jay straightened alongside me.

"Rick," the guy who approached growled. A little taller than Jay, he looked nowhere near as friendly. Not that I did more than glance at his face, which seemed oddly familiar. He wore striped pajama pants. And nothing else. Well, unless the towel he rubbed his dark hair with counted.

That hair lay slightly long against his neck, probably because of the weight of the water that clung to the tips. Not that I was concentrating on the length of his hair, anyway. It simply provided my eyes an excuse to follow the journey of a lucky drip. Pendulously trembling until it became bloated and fell heavily from his hair to his shoulder, the water then trickled horizontally along his collarbone for a few inches before plunging straight into the valley between his pecs, then undulating over well-defined abs. His muscles didn't bulge like Jay's—which I'd checked out thoroughly on our hours off, spent at one of the many beaches—but the guy was cut. Hard and lean, he brought to mind a strung bow. Lithe, powerful, dangerous. Like he didn't work out, but *worked*.

And I *really* needed to look away from that drip now, because it was about to slide across his flat stomach and disappear into the fine trail of hair that led down to…yup. There it went. Below the edge of the pants slung low around his hips.

The silence of the room impinged, and I looked up. The guy's eyes were locked on me. Oh. Crap. I'd totally missed the introductions.

I sent Jay an imploring glance. To his credit, he kept a straight face—though I knew he'd shit-stir me later—and repeated the introduction. "Sara, meet Rick Winchester. Rick, this is Sara Grant, one of the best crew under me."

I snorted, trying to swallow my laughter. Jay never missed an opportunity. "I believe I've pointed out that I'm not under you, Jay."

He strode toward the kitchen. "As I was explaining to Rick, that depends entirely on how many rules I can persuade you to break."

The heat shot up my neck, stinging when it reached the graze. Jay was incorrigible, but here? Still, if he wasn't self-conscious in the other man's presence, why should I be?

I fake-scowled across the room as he took champagne from the fridge. "You're full of it, Jay. I've only a couple of weeks of contract left, so you're the one with a career to risk. We both know you're all talk."

Jay clapped a hand to his heart. "Ah, wounded. Not

so much a mermaid as a siren, Rick. Watch out, she'll lure you in, then wreck you."

Mermaid? What was he talking about?

I switched my gaze toward the semi-clad man. He had to wonder what we were bantering about, though a tiny smile played at the corners of his lips, his posture at ease.

"I'm in housekeeping. Jay's the entertainment director. Not my supervisor," I explained. Not knowing where to look made it hard to talk. Well, I knew where I *wanted* to look, but it would be inappropriate.

Jay sighed loudly. "Much as I'd love to order you around."

"Uh-uh." I wagged a finger at him. "That's a whole different story. Told you I'm not into that. Not until I get to know you better, anyway." What the hell had gotten into me? Not only had I never had any such conversation with him, but I wasn't into dom. That'd been more Simon's thing, both in and out of the bedroom, and it left me cold. Yet something about Rick's presence compelled me to perform, to catch his attention.

Ridiculous. The guy had spoken, like, one word.

I pretended not to watch Rick's butt shift beneath the pajamas as he crossed to the wet bar and took crystalware from the cabinet. Only two stemmed glasses. He moved with casual grace, like a big cat. Sure in his space.

He assessed me over the glasses for a long moment before he spoke, his tone as assured as his movements. "I suspect Jay would be happy to find a place for you as part of his entertainment…division."

My knees weakened. Wordplay? My absolute kryptonite. What Rick said was, technically, perfectly correct. Yet with a mere pause, he managed to inflect the words with such insinuation my breathing quickened. I shifted to nonchalantly lean my weight on one hip, trying to ignore the various other body parts that had instantly responded to his implication.

Jay nodded. "I keep saying I'd love to squeeze her in."

Calling on every ounce of my acting ability to remain cool, I gave the massive cruise director a slow burn, from his shaved head to those basketballer-sized feet, then returned my gaze to his midsection, deliberately lingering on his groin. Shook my head with feigned regret. "I'm quite sure I'd be the one *squeezing* you in, Jay." Though I directed my words at my co-worker, they weren't for his benefit. Something about Rick had me on edge, creating a wild electricity coursing my veins that made me reckless.

And rules and reckless never mix well.

The half-naked man grinned, the bandage across his forehead giving him a piratical look. His accent lent his words a sexy directness, as though his request was a politely veiled command. "Tell you what, Jay, I'm starving. Maybe I was actually adrift for days, not hours. I do recall there was a soccer ball I became unacceptably friendly with before I forced it to walk the plank. Could you *go* ask the kitchens"—he stressed the direction—"if there's any chance of rustling up some food? Perhaps something to accompany this champagne."

Jay wiped a hand across his face, probably hiding a smile; the glass-fronted fridge was stocked with the makings of supper for about twenty people, including cheeses and cold cuts. Fruit sat in an etched crystal bowl. Room service was on call.

Rick was smooth. Too smooth. I needed to back things off a notch or two. Problem was parts of me were way too invested in the moment and not the least interested in backing off. Specifically, my nipples. Hard as pebbles, they angled toward Rick's naked torso like Cupid's arrows.

"Certainly, sir." Jay winked at me as he passed, headed to the ship's kitchens on a pointless mission, and I folded my arms across my chest, hiding the evidence.

Maybe too late, as Rick watched me for a long moment, as though weighing up his next move.

I took a deep breath and turned away slightly, hoping to deflect his attention as I gestured at the opulent surrounds. "You've clearly landed on your feet."

One of his dark eyebrows quirked, and he tilted his head a little, as though he didn't understand. The familiar ease with which he dropped an embroidered hand towel over the bottle of champagne, sinews in his forearms cording as he eased the cork free without an ostentatious noise, clinched my suspicion; he was accustomed to the finer things in life.

Entitled ass. If I needed to find a ploy to calm my raging hormones, that knowledge would do it. I didn't want another moneyed, pretentious wanker in my life, no matter how briefly.

He poured two glasses, handed me one, and clinked them together. "To ships that pass in the night. Or in this case, and more fortuitously for me, did not pass."

I stared at the trail of golden bubbles in my glass. Though I hadn't had a drink in eleven months—as part of my new commitment to living a simpler life after months of working for the Public Solicitor's Office in the Solomon Islands while living in a tiny two-meter square room—surely, one sip wouldn't ruin that undertaking? I returned the toast. "To strangers in the night."

The bubbles felt good going down.

Going down. Not words I should even think, in my current state. I gulped again. Holy hell, how could the guy smell so good? A couple of thousand other people were also using the complimentary toiletries provided in the en suites. He should smell just the same as them, not like…like…God, probably like testosterone. How hard up was I? Left alone in a room for five minutes with a vaguely attractive man—okay, he rated a damn sight hotter than that, but anyway. I was thirty. A professional attorney. Knew how to conduct myself.

And my panties were soaked. What the heck?

It was the pain meds the doc gave me. I'd unthinkingly mixed the drugs with alcohol. Okay, so it was only the tiniest sip, and only seconds ago. But still, technically, anything I did now wasn't my fault.

Rick hadn't stepped back after moving in to propose the toast. "Would you care to sit?"

Uh-huh. On his lap.

I glanced at the lounge room. No. If we moved there, he'd probably take the leather tub, and then I wouldn't be able to smell him. "No. I like it standing up." Yeah, the word choice was accidental. Not.

Fine lines feathered from the corners of Rick's eyes, and I tried to find another focus. Incredibly difficult, with an almost-naked man standing four inches away. Clearly, he knew nothing about personal space. And that was just fine.

"Whatever you prefer. So why the desire to get wet?" He paused for a heartbeat, as though gauging my reaction. No doubt a blush. "I mean, what possessed you to leap into the ocean?"

"Guess I was hoping for a Maui moment."

He didn't reply, merely lifted one of those immaculately groomed eyebrows as I sipped at my champagne. Groomed, I had to keep that in mind. Sign of a narcissist.

Or, possibly, of a guy who paid a little attention to manscaping and personal hygiene. Not automatically a bad trait, even given the amount of time and money Simon spent on his own pursuit of beauty. *Damn it.*

Plus, Rick's eyebrows were potentially naturally perfect, just like the shadow of stubble that shone blue-black through his pale skin. Stuck in the ocean, he couldn't have deliberately grown it out to that precise so-sexy length, yet there it was, like a testosterone-etched come-fuck-me signal. Airbrushed perfection to make a grown woman drool. Well, wet in one fashion or another, anyway.

I took another gulp of champagne. Time to get my mind out of the gutter—actually, my focus was already about three feet above the gutter, given Rick's height. Okay, I'd keep the exchange businesslike. Professional. Practice the three C's.

Cum, cock, cunnilingus?

No! What the hell was wrong with my mind? Concision, coherence, clarity.

I jerked back, trying to distance myself from my own wildly rampaging imagination. My bandaged shoulder jostled a marble pillar, and I gasped, champagne slopping over the rim of my glass.

A crease appeared between Rick's eyes, and he quickly closed the distance I'd managed to put between us. "The doctor said you've dislocated your shoulder."

"Doc exaggerates. It's a strain." Seriously, was this cabin airtight or something? The oxygen seemed to be mighty thin, and none of it was getting to my brain.

His fingertips grazed my collarbone. I probably should have done a few more buttons up on my blouse, per uniform regulation. But the damn things were hard to close left-handed. Besides, the way my chest seemed to swell with the extra blood pounding through my veins right now, I needed all the room I could get.

His fingers stole beneath my lapel, exposing the lilac tint of a fresh bruise. "I am so sorry."

My lips trembled, but not because his touch hurt.

He bent closer, his breath warm against my neck. Glanced at me for permission before he peeled the fabric aside, examining the bruise with all the interest of a professional. "That looks awful."

My knees sagged at the low throb of his voice. But it was pure reaction, had to be. To near death, not near manliness. "Can't say that's the best response I've ever had from a guy peering inside my shirt. May be the most memorable, though."

He straightened, looking a little abashed. "Oh yes. Sorry. I was referring to the bruise. The damage I caused." His thumb slipped inside my shirt, brushing the lace trim of my bra. "Certainly not anything else."

Dammit, he definitely would not have taken the single seat in the lounge, and my knees said I definitely needed to be sitting down. I swallowed, praying he couldn't hear the dry-mouthed click of my tongue. "I hope that's not your best pickup line." My breath fluttered nervously, the words jerky.

Rick's gaze shifted to my face. Without breaking contact, he placed his champagne flute on the marble side table, took my glass, and slid it alongside. Then he cupped the unbruised side of my face, his callused palm firm against my cheek. Odd. He had the hands of a laborer but the suave air of someone else entirely. Not that I'd picked up that vibe from his borrowed clothes. Striped pajama pants yelled plumber as loudly as they yelled professional.

His thumb brushed across my lower lip, a trail of tantalizing friction that left the tip of my tongue instinctively chasing his movement. His focus was glued to my mouth, and his words were a low rumble of desire. "Do I need a pickup line?"

I should feel insulted at his arrogance, thinking I'd so easily fall into his arms. But the only thing I was feeling were his hands, one caressing my face, the other teasing the edge of my bra. Hell no, he didn't need any line. I'd pegged him as a cocky, entitled bastard, but right now I couldn't care less about my snap assessment. For the first time in months, I felt totally alive.

His mouth descended slowly, barely touching mine, testing the reception.

I leaned in. Flickered my tongue across his lips, tasting and teasing. Champagne and salt, an aphrodisiac mix to spin my senses.

I'd forgotten what it was like to kiss someone out of pure desire. Not the *bye-have-a-good-day* or *pick-you-up-at-the-airport* type of peck on the cheek that barely rated as more than an air kiss, but a totally involved, *I-want-to-devour-you*, uninhibited snog.

Rick's hand moved to the outside of my shirt, palming the swell of my left breast, his fingers searching for my nipple. No prize for locating the hard nub, it wasn't exactly timidly hiding, but trying to thrust over the top of my balconette bra. My lower lip between his teeth, he tugged gently and simultaneously rolled my nipple between his finger and thumb.

I yelped as the tingle shot straight from my breast to my loins, my clit pulsing with need. His hands were still on the outside of my clothes, yet tension coiled in my belly, the pressure between my legs heavy and pouted and *longing*.

Damn. Sure, it had been a long time, but this was ridiculous.

Rick released my tormented lip, kissing it in seeming apology. His tongue probed, not entering, seducing. One hand slid up into my damp hair, and he loosened the band of my ponytail. His fingers cradled my head, holding my mouth to his. But still not kissing me deep, not like I wanted. Teasing instead, teasing until I could scream my need to have him thrust into my mouth, hot and hard and wet.

I pressed closer, my breasts crushed against his naked chest, my fingers digging into his taut biceps. Heat radiated from his body, and I moaned.

His tongue darted into my mouth. Flicked at the tip of my tongue, fast and light. And, fuck, he was playing it like he'd play my clit.

Withdrew. Plunged back in.

The hand in my hair held me willingly captive as he fucked my mouth with his tongue, his other hand wedged between our fused bodies, finger and thumb expertly rolling my nipple in the perfect rhythm, bringing me to the edge.

My head swam with the seductive taste of him and the knowledge that he was going to bring me to orgasm with little more than a kiss. I wanted it so badly I could already feel the dizzy swirl of anticipation curling in my belly, the pulsing between my swollen, slippery folds, the breathlessness that left me dizzy. Five more seconds and he'd kiss me to a climax.

But the rules. There were rules.

So hard to bring them to mind, with the breath sawing in my throat and blood pounding in my ears as desire throbbed in my loins.

What the hell were the rules?

I was married. That was the rule.

Chapter Four

Sara

Yeah, married. The most important rule. I had to focus on that. Not on the hard body pressed up against mine, his mouth stealing the oxygen from my own.

I should think about Simon, instead.

Simon, who was doubtless cheating on me right now, following a pattern he'd set years ago. A pattern I'd permitted with my silence, condoned if not encouraged. The last time I'd spoken with him as my husband—rather than as someone who was holding the purse strings to our joint accounts—had been almost a year ago, to check why he hadn't arrived at Honiara Airport. The suggestion to meet to celebrate the end of my placement in the Solomons and our anniversary—despite the fact we'd not celebrated in seven years—had been his.

Give us a chance to reconnect, he'd said.

We could go and visit the orphanages, he'd said.

Maybe that'd stop me banging on about having a baby, he'd said.

Lied through his perfectly veneered teeth, he had.

His non-arrival on the flight from Australia hadn't been even close to a surprise. He'd always said third world countries were undeserving of either his time or his tourist dollar.

Though I'd known where he'd be, I'd phoned anyway. To check he was still alive—so I could kill him.

Not literally. That would definitely be against the rules.

In our luxurious Sydney apartment, Simon had pitched his voice to drown out the soft background music. Dire Straits' "Romeo and Juliet." "Sorry, Sara. Last-minute trial. Been run off my feet."

The narrow camp bed in my bare room tipped as I jerked the phone from my head, staring at it. *Exhibit A of one philandering husband's deception, Your Honor.* Did Simon think me an idiot? Last-minute trials in our shared profession were a logistical implausibility. I mashed the phone back to my ear like I could squeeze the truth from it.

The susurration of Simon's crew-cut gray hair brushed the mouthpiece as he turned away, murmuring something, his words muffled by a rustle of linen. *One-thousand-count Egyptian cotton bedsheets.* Then his voice boomed again. "I tried to call, but your cell was out of range."

The quickly stifled giggle in the background of the call proved his lie. Most likely his probably just-out-of-diapers PA, Emma. No forty-year-old man needed a vacuous blonde nineteen-year-old assistant. Not unless he could afford a Viagra addiction.

Of course, Simon could afford any drugs he fancied.

I didn't feel angry. Not then, anyway. Just tired. So tired, I didn't think before I spoke. "Simon, maybe we need to talk about a divorce."

Silence for a moment, then Simon's measured, professional tone, betraying neither shock nor regret. His best court performance to date, or finally some honesty?

"Sure, we can take a break, if you think it best."

Best? Hell no, I didn't think it best. Best would be not having wasted twelve years of my life.

I didn't reply. Staring at my hand, I willed each of the fingers to slowly unclench, white flesh turning back to pink. Winced at the flash of gold from my wedding band.

"Let's stay friends, though," he said.

"Go fuck yourself," I said. Well, no, I didn't. But I should have. Thing was, he had nubile Emma doing all the fucking he required—which left me with no reason to rush back to Australia.

But still, divorce had been my suggestion, not his. It wasn't like Simon had slammed the door on our relationship. And perhaps I shouldn't either. Maybe, after having spent a couple more months volunteering at an orphanage in the Solomons, and then taking the menial job aboard the *Ohana* to prove to myself that I wasn't constrained by my experience and training— although I'd come to realize that cleaning toilets and practicing law did have some similarities—I should be done with my sulking. See what I could salvage from our twelve years together.

Rick's lips moved to the side of my neck, his stubble grazing my flesh, an exquisite mixture of pleasure and pain. I moaned and tipped my head back, giving him access.

Intelligent, qualified, self-confident, I didn't *need* my husband. The question was, did I still *want* him? Except the question was irrelevant. Though it was impossible to think rationally while another man's kisses drove me crazy, the law was clear; I'd promised myself to one man.

I pulled from Rick's grasp and took several wobbly steps back, putting the marble pillar between us.

Chest heaving, Rick eyed me questioningly but didn't pursue. "All right?"

I nodded, too busy trying to control my breathing to respond. Hell. Yes. So much more than all right. But also, all wrong.

He handed me the glass of champagne, apparently oblivious to the tenting of his loose pajama pants.

If only I could master that level of indifference. Instead, my heart thumped fit to burst out of my chest. Or at least, enough to explode my boobs out of the way-too-tight bra. It had been my favorite bra, too, but now I resented the barrier it had formed between my aching nipple and Rick's fingers. Because, if we'd been skin to skin, I'd have gotten off before my brain interfered. Apologizing to myself for what I'd done would be far easier than trying to justify what it was I wanted to do.

Champagne bottle and glass in hand, Rick nudged his chin toward the recessed lounge. "We might be more comfortable in there." Spoken like he invited a regular guest to take a seat, not someone he'd spent a torrid few minutes tongue-fucking.

"Sure." The word came out as a croak. Fitting, given I might add to the slimy amphibian impression by sliding right off the leather seat. At the very least, I'd leave a damp mark. Celibacy had created a dam, and now my spillway overflowed like a waterfall.

Rick sat next to me on the generous leather lounge, close, but not quite touching. "As I was saying," he continued smoothly, "what exactly were your intentions when you decided to throw yourself into a hurricane?"

I shrugged, then wished I hadn't as pain speared

through my shoulder. "I didn't think it through. Saw your hand move and realized that if *The Spirit of Ohana* continued, we'd lose you in the night. Jumping overboard seemed the only option."

The crystal sang as he circled his finger around the top of his glass. "Weren't you terrified?"

"I'm pretty sure I peed myself, but fortunately, there was plenty of water to disguise the fact."

The side of his mouth lifted. I should focus somewhere else. Except most everywhere else seemed naked.

He leaned forward and refilled my glass on the table, then handed it to me. "I believe I read that attracts sharks."

I had to stop drinking. For one thing, I had work in a few hours. But more importantly, alcohol would lower my resistance. Cause me to forget the rules, be seduced by the fact that Rick chose to talk instead of flouncing off like a sulky child—or a senior partner in a law firm—in the face of my rejection. Which did *not* mean I needed to edge closer to him. Or long for the touch of his hand on my breast. Or to feel his lips again.

I shifted on the seat, sort-of-accidentally drawing the crotch of my panties tighter. "I heard that the combination of heat and bodily fluids attract all sorts of animals." Damn, what was it about this man that made me unable to control myself? He wasn't even my type.

Actually, given that I'd married a wealthy, articulate, handsome man, Rick was most definitely my type. But I sure as hell didn't need to make the same kind of mistake twice, so he was not my *new* type. However, while the combination of drugs and alcohol played havoc with the analytical portion of my brain, the effect would soon wear off. In the meantime, what harm could there be in capitalizing on my lack of inhibition and enjoying the thrill of a little flirtation? Providing I set boundaries, I'd be fine.

Rick's thigh nudged mine, and his pupils dilated. He understood the game was back on. "Indeed. Heat and moisture. You risked attracting the most unpredictable of beasts."

If he stared any longer, he'd find moisture all right. I splayed my left hand, casually covering the apex of my thighs. Yeah, because sticking a hand over my crotch to hide a damp patch was sure to look casual. "Unpredictable often holds an element of excitement."

"If it happens to be excitement you're looking for," he replied. His hand brushed my thigh.

There. That's where I should draw the boundary. No touching. I licked my lips and tried to focus my mind on the game. "I was more afraid of what was circling beneath my feet than excited. I was never so relieved as when I hauled myself into your boat."

His stubble was a bluish blur, only inches from my face. "And I was never so happy as when you landed on top of me."

I brought my glass up between us, though the sling holding my arm already created a barrier. I sipped desperately at the drink. Because alcohol was known for its grounding effect, right? "Uh, yeah, sorry about that. Not my most graceful move."

"Not graceful? With an injured shoulder? I'd rate your landing a ten."

"I managed to stick the dismount, huh?" My pulse fluttered wildly as Rick's fingertips stroked down the side of my neck.

Out of bounds.

But really, people touched all the time. That wasn't so bad. Was it?

His voice dropped octaves. "Gymnastics? That brings all kinds of images to mind. Mostly involving you and rigid poles."

"Interesting word association." Yeah, like my mind hadn't totally gone there. "Dismount has more of an equine association for me."

His hot breath shivered up my neck. "I'm not surprised. I do seem to recall, with the boat bucking on those waves, you rode me rather like I was a horse."

I tried to look outraged, but with the fear of imminent death removed, the memory of being astride his hard body seemed far more erotic than embarrassing. "I did not. Besides, I prefer to ride bareback."

"Godiva fashion?" His lips curled, his face almost too close now for me to register the movement. "That's an image I'll be happy to keep in mind."

"Is that so?" Screw the witty repartee. His lips found the sensitive spot just beneath my ear, his tongue darting out to massage it. Then his teeth nibbled gently at my earlobe, his heavy breath wet and ticklish in my ear. He played me so well; who even needed a G-spot?

One hand moved to my knee, then slid up my thigh as he kissed along the line of my jaw.

I had to stop him. Now. He'd scaled the Berlin Wall.

He took my glass and placed it on the table. Fingers on my shirt, he did a far more dexterous job of opening the buttons one-handed than I'd done of closing them. His lips shifted to mine and pressed insistently against what I wanted to pretend was a firmly closed seam. Damn, he knew how to kiss. He didn't stay in the one spot, didn't drown me in spit, but moved around, teasing, tasting, sampling. Keeping me on edge, wanting more, barely able to breathe, but happy to suffocate.

Apparently, he also needed air. He broke away, his dark hair mussed where my fingers had somehow tangled in it. "You taste so good."

"All that salt. And a near-death experience supposedly enhances your appetite." That was it; we were both overwrought, caught up in the euphoria of survival. I'd be back to my rational self soon.

His mouth traced a series of tiny nips and licks to my ear, each touch winding me tighter. "Well, I'm so hungry this is well worth dying a thousand times over for."

Okay, so rationality probably wasn't going to kick in soon enough. I had to analyze the situation. If I made out with Rick just a little—*ahh!* The option of *just a little* passed as he peeled open the front of my blouse, his stubble thrillingly abrasive as he kissed the hollow at the base of my throat.

If I made out with Rick—*period.* No qualification on the duration or extent—would that make me square with Simon? Maybe then I could return to my husband and no longer resent his infidelity. Was this, in fact, what Simon had intended when he repeatedly suggested via email that I take time out to find myself?

Or was I simply trying to justify what I wanted?

Rick's fingers slid inside my bra.

I tensed, yet my back arched, my breast thrust into his hand. He tugged the fabric down, exposing me. Smoothed his hand over the white orb, weighing it in his palm.

His thumb glided over my aching nipple, and he

stared with rapt attention as the bud doubled in size. "Amazing."

No. He shouldn't speak. On-the-spot negotiations weren't my forte, so I couldn't think straight if he spoke. I wound my fingers into his hair and tugged his mouth back to mine, my tongue hot and urgent. Maybe I should stop analyzing, just react. The guy was hot as all fuck and totally up for it, judging by the state of his pants.

He kissed me back, tempering my ferocity with a deep, lingering embrace, and then bent to lay a trail of kisses down my chest and over the curve of my breast.

Oh fuck, so close to my nipple. The rules, did I need any rules? Did I even want to go back to my husband? Was there any point, beyond familiarity? Friends shipped us as *Sira*, a legal power couple, but we'd not truly been a couple for years. I hadn't missed Simon in eleven months; I'd only missed the sex. And even if I leveled that score, my husband would still be a self-centered tosser.

But didn't I have some kind of obligation to try and save my marriage?

I pulled at Rick's hair, tugging his head up before his questing mouth reached my nipple. Because then I'd be truly lost. "No…"

"No?"

"I have to work tomorrow. Today. In a few hours." Kind of like the old *I'm not allowed to date* excuse from high school. Pathetic, but handy.

"No," he repeated, but more of a groan this time. "Bugger work. Call in sick."

I tried to ease from his grasp. "No work, no money."

"Don't worry about the money. I'll make it right."

My skin shrank from his touch. I slammed a hand

into his shoulder, shoving him away as I lurched from the lounge. Sudden anger pitched my voice low and dangerous. "What the hell?"

Chapter Five

Sara

The arrogant prick. Because I worked a menial job, I should be thrilled to screw him for the cash? Maybe consider myself lucky?

"Wait, Sara! What's wrong?" Rick was half off the lounge as I fumbled with my buttons. Couldn't do the damn things up one-handed. "Sara, stay. Jay's bringing food, remember?"

I tugged my shirt closed, squaring off with him, cold fury replacing the molten lava of seconds earlier. "You'll wine and dine me, so then I owe you for dinner? No thanks. Completely lost my appetite." For everything.

My exit wasn't as smooth as I'd have liked. Flat lace-ups slipping on the highly polished tiles, I had to let go of my shirt to grapple single-handedly with the doorknob, ignoring Rick's protests behind me.

Predictably, Jay stood in the corridor, balancing a platter as he reached to swipe his key card.

Open shirt clutched in one hand, I tried to brush past him.

"Sara, are you okay?"

"Fine. Mr. Monopoly is all yours, though."

"Wait." Jay tumbled the tray to the floor, ignoring the food that tipped onto the carpet, and lunged to grab my good arm. "Sara, wait up. Did he do something?"

I furiously blinked back tears of mortification. I was too old to be caught out by this kind of shit. Or at least, I should be. "Nothing at all. Just a rich wanker."

He scowled, his fists bunched as he shifted from one foot to the other, as though he couldn't decide whether to detain me or rush in and beat up Rick Winchester. "Let me shove this in the door, and I'll walk you back to your quarters."

Stiffening my spine, I shook my head. "Don't worry about it. But if you happen to know of any hookers on this cruise, your mate in there's after one. I'm sure he'll be happy to tip you. But I'm not for hire, so I'm heading to bed. Alone. I'm beat and got to be up in a few hours." My tone sounded a damn sight perkier than I felt, not betraying the seething anger and…belittlement?…that churned inside me. How the heck had I managed to— well, not fall for, but stumble a little in the direction of— a clone of Simon?

"Work?" Jay nudged his chin toward my sling. "Didn't Doc give you the day off?"

"Light duties." The roster required all the cabins to be stripped, the linen and toiletries piled in the corridor for the reset crew to deal with over the two-day docking. We had an ongoing competition to see who could service their cabins and disembark the fastest, to maximize their brief R&R. Doc *had* given me the day off, but then Melanie would have to cover for me and lose precious time ashore. I'd persuaded the doctor to compromise with a certificate for light duties.

"I'll catch you later on, Jay. Got to crash." I couldn't wait to put distance between myself and the pompous ass in the stateroom.

My lips tight, I strode along the corridor, still

fumbling my buttons closed. Anger adding speed, I thundered down multiple flights of stairs, into another corridor, and turned a corner. Stumbled. Not over my own feet, for a change, but over a man, huddled on the floor. "Sorry," I gasped, my palm slamming the door he leaned against as I regained my balance.

"My fault." He glanced up, pulling his legs in closer to his chest, his eyes tinged with red.

Drunk. I scooted around him and walked a few more steps. My pace slowed. I should call security. With a sigh, I reached for my phone.

Which lay at the bottom of the ocean.

Fantastic. Seriously, could this day get any worse? I needed to ignore the drunk and get myself to bed. Pretend I wasn't going to lie awake, horny as hell and fuming, for what was left of the night.

But rules. The handbook made it clear customer safety and comfort should be paramount.

I retraced my steps.

The guy sat with his head pressed to his knees, arms wrapped around them, his pose screaming misery.

Yeah, well, maybe I should just take the piece of carpet alongside him. "Are you locked out, sir?"

He looked up, pulling his face into a poor semblance of a smile. Blond-streaked hair in a military cut. Handsome, but not done any favors by the sorrow etched across his features. "No. I'm waiting for someone."

His words unslurred, he wasn't drunk. I bobbed my head and left quickly. Right now, I didn't need to take onboard anyone else's distress.

Melanie snored in her bed, so I stripped in the dark and crawled under the covers of my own narrow bunk. I lay staring at the ceiling, lit by the emergency exit light.

The pitching of the boat, more noticeable here close to the waterline at the bow, reminded me of the mountainous waves I'd faced earlier.

And what that had led to.

I grunted and rolled over, staring at the wall. The graze on my cheek pressed into the pillow, so I flipped to my back again, hand idly flopping against my breast. Then not so idly. Could I recreate the sensations Rick had aroused, the tingle that shot straight to my core, the excitement that had bubbled within me at his touch?

Nope.

Apparently not without his mouth.

Jerk. Hopefully, he had blue balls right about now. Though more likely he'd simply have found someone else to purchase for his sexual pleasure.

Damn. I didn't need to be thinking of that pleasure. Or of his taut, ripped body pressed against mine. And I most definitely did not need to think of the hidden promise that tented his pajamas. Pajamas were ridiculous, anyway. Well, ridiculous, or sexy. Somehow, he'd managed to pull them off.

Ha, I wished he'd pulled them off.

My mind back in the gutter, no, make that lower, *in the sewers*, I shot a glance across the room at Melanie. She muttered in her sleep and then went back to snoring. My hand slid over my breast again, then across the soft mound of my stomach. And lower. Even nuns masturbated, right? It didn't count as breaking the unwritten vow of celibacy in my *Eat Pray Love* quest.

Damn that man. No, correction, damn all men. And damn the fact that I was actually right-handed, but with that arm in a sling, even frigging myself was monumentally difficult. Fingers working furiously in my slick folds, I brought myself to a silent climax, my teeth gritted and head pushed back into the pillow as I imagined Rick's hard body tensed over me, plunging into me.

And despite working up a light sweat, still I couldn't sleep. Instead, I replayed Rick's clever innuendo and improved on my own not-so-brilliant repartee. The fact that he'd proven himself an egotistical tosser, infatuated with the power of his money, didn't seem to diminish my desire so much as make me long to punish him. In all kinds of ways.

Which he probably wouldn't actually dislike.

Ugh.

I rolled over again and pounded my pillow into submission. If I had to lie awake thinking about arrogant men, focusing on the one I'd left at home would be more useful. Only a few days remained until the end of the month, and the orphanage I'd worked for in the Solomon Islands was counting on my donation. Although I couldn't log in to our bank account from the unsecured onboard service, I'd directed—no, I had *requested*, as one never directed Simon—to transfer several thousand dollars. Much as the kids craved affection, only money had any real power to help them. Simon was right about that much; money was king. Just not the way he used it.

But for the last two weeks, my texts and emails to him had gone unanswered. After months of surprisingly civil emails where he urged me to take the time I needed to sort out what I truly wanted from life—and I pretended to be unaware of his latest affair—he'd gone to ground. Or more like, gone under the covers. Between Emma's taut, tanned thighs.

Chapter Six

Rick

I shoved the two champagne glasses onto the stone countertop and poured a slug of whiskey instead.

Hated sodding champagne, a girl's drink.

Where the hell had I gone wrong with Sara? I couldn't deny the instant physical attraction—she'd knocked me off my feet when she appeared in my room. Soft and curvy in all the right places, nothing like the anorexic celery stalks who chased me. But then, when she dished back to Jay as good as she got, she'd about done me in. Articulate, intelligent, and funny. She was some package. And those magnificent breasts that had pressed up against me in the boat, like she was an erotic angel sent to rescue me, well, the sight of them had damn near made me come undone. I'd just needed to get that fiery little volcano of a nipple in my mouth. And I'd been damn close—maybe too close, considering my vow to stay away from women for a few months—until she'd flared like a firecracker on Guy Fawkes Night and totally shut me down.

And I didn't bloody know why.

A tap on the door and the scratch of a key card in the lock jerked my head up, and relief washed through me. I shouldn't feel so glad that she'd brought her crazy back, but I'd analyze that later.

The door opened, and my gut lurched as the entertainment director entered, his face cut with a scowl, head swinging from side to side as he checked out the room, like he expected to find evidence of my cock-up. Lucky some of that evidence had subsided beneath my pajamas.

I dragged a hand down my face. I'd seen enough angry boyfriends to know where this was headed. "She lit out."

Jay eyed me coldly. "Yeah. I saw her in the hall. Seems there was a…misunderstanding?"

Clearly, if he were not on paid time, rather stronger words would have been used. I poured another inch into my tumbler, dosed a second glass, and pushed it toward him. "I offered to fix up her lost wages, and she gave me a right bollocking, then hightailed it out of here."

He took the glass and rolled it between his palms, staring hard at me. "Wages? Is that exactly how you phrased your, ah, offer?"

With no distraction, or rather, no *pleasant* distraction, the wound on my head was beginning to hurt like a bitch. "Yeah. Wages. Pay. Money. Something along those lines. Why?"

His grin spread as slowly as an oil slick. "You maybe should have picked up an English-to-Aussie translation dictionary. Seems you insulted her by intimating she was, ah, available for hire."

"Hire? You mean as…" I slammed the glass down. "Bloody hell, no! I meant I'd make good on her lost wages because she's unable to work. It's the least I can do, considering she was injured saving my worthless arse."

"That's not how she interpreted it." Jay tossed back

the whiskey.

The git could afford to look smug; he had no competition now. Sod it, the evening had seemed so promising. I'd avoided death and picked up, to boot. Not that picking up ever proved difficult, but this was the first time I'd felt a flare of…intrigue? That was it. Sara was different. A tad older than the girls who customarily briefly caught my attention, she was definitely all woman. And not just in those curves which so comfortably fit my hands, evidence of a woman who knew how to enjoy all life had to offer instead of fainting with desire at the sight of a lettuce leaf, but in her forthright mannerisms, her lack of artifice. Not to mention the hot-as-hell way she flirted, using her clever mouth to turn me on. Hell. That mouth. The thought was enough to make me as hard as a rock. Again.

I moved behind the bar, hiding the evidence. "So I'll, ah, talk to her in the morning. Explain. Apologize." Why did it sound as though I asked for Jay's permission or guidance?

"You won't catch her. The ship is docked for forty-eight hours, and housekeeping work from first light to clear the cabins so they can spend the weekend on land."

My fingers drumming the bench, I gazed into my glass like I could read the leaves.

Despite how long I stared, I could think of only one way around this. "I need to speak with the captain." I hated pulling the *I'm someone special* card, probably hadn't done so for close on ten years, but the opulent cabin proved I'd already lost my hard-won anonymity. Being outed had to come with some privilege.

Jay seemed to recall our roles and straightened, setting aside the tumbler, his face unreadable. "I'm not certain if he's available right now, but I'll inquire."

I harbored no illusion as to the captain's availability. As Jay left, I made my way to the bedroom and retrieved my phone. Dropped onto the massive bed and stared at the blank screen a long moment. *Phones.* I hadn't even gotten Sara's number.

But the captain could be relied on to furnish it.

Frustration rumbled out of me in a growl, and I toggled the on button. Nothing like a dressing-down from Marty to reset my priorities.

Amazingly, the phone didn't explode with the number of notifications flashing onscreen. At a glance, they all seemed to be from Marty. No point opening the early voicemails, the latest would give me a better measure of how close the man was to a coronary.

Stress always thickened Marty's accent with the strains of the Liverpool slums, though, intimately familiar with the bodyguard's history, I knew he hailed from nowhere near there. His last voicemail practically unintelligible, the tone said it all. Marty was far from impressed.

My finger hovered over the call button. Almost two a.m. I probably shouldn't bother him. Except the last call had only been thirty minutes ago. About when I'd been kissing Sara, my fingers on the hot button of her incredibly erect nipple, my mouth so close… Damn, I wanted back there. But why? Since I'd reached about fifteen, there'd been no shortage of boobs for me to paw. I'd given up dating over the last few months because a man could only take so many naked breasts thrust in his face.

Well, no, that wasn't quite true; I'd never actually *tire* of any portion of the female anatomy. But having every sexual favor available for the taking detracted from the excitement of the hunt, the thrill of conquest.

Sara had been different. Her eagerness had seemed…natural. Lusty. I tapped the phone against my chin. Was she even aware of who I was? Absolutely nothing in her demeanor suggested she felt in any way inferior. Not that I considered myself superior, far from it. But I'd become accustomed to—and annoyed by—the level of obsequiousness that colored my relationships. Had Sara seemed different because perhaps she actually desired *me*, not what I could provide?

Or was it because she'd proven herself principled? If I could move past my frustration at the misunderstanding, the cold, calm fury in her total shutdown of me was practically the sexiest thing I'd ever seen.

Unavailable, she became so much more desirable. Not that she'd been undesirable to start with. I'd been totally unprepared for the woman who invaded my suite—and apparently, my mind.

A knock at the door jerked the phone from my face, and I waited a heartbeat for someone to answer it. Damn, old habits died hard. No servants here.

I strode across the suite. Maybe Jay had talked some sense into Sara, though I wasn't entirely sure I trusted the guy. At first, it had seemed we might engage in some friendly rivalry over a conquest neither of us truly wanted. Now I'd happily kneecap him for the advantage.

Jay stood in the doorway, but unfortunately, no Sara. He dipped his chin, his jovial attitude exchanged for businesslike. "Mr. Winchester, Captain Raynalds."

The braid-bedecked officer alongside him nodded smartly, only a degree from saluting. "My pleasure, Mr.

Winchester."

I stood back, gesturing for them to enter. "Actually, given the circumstances of my being here, I believe the pleasure is all mine. And that's what I wish to discuss with you, Captain."

****

"Suppose I should be glad yer bloody alive." Marty's gruff tone didn't hide the relief that leaked through his words.

"Never better," I replied, shifting the phone away from my bruised head. My words were possibly true, now that I had a plan. "Listen, Marty, be as pissed as you like tomorrow, but I need you to do something. I've got to get some kip now, I'm absolutely knackered, but I need you to get a car and be at the dock by five a.m. sharp." That'd give me about three hours' sleep—though, with Sara on my brain, I'd be lucky to get three minutes. "Passengers aren't permitted to disembark until seven, but the captain's agreed to let me off early so we can get away without too much fanfare."

"Good of him," Marty grunted sourly.

I could just about hear him toting up the cost of the captain's gesture, whether it be in money or favors to be claimed.

"Unfortunately, Captain Raynalds had already alerted his stakeholders that they'd picked me up. Hopefully, as I only had my wallet for ID, they may have chosen not to go public without confirmation. Snoop around, see how much information's leaked."

"Yer tellin' me how to do my job now, lad?"

Nearly thirty-four and Marty still called me lad. "Wouldn't dare, Marty, and you can roast my bollocks over it—but tomorrow, not now. Listen. Laundry's already cleaned my clothes, so just bring me some runners. And be prepared for a long wait."

"Wait? Why? You said five. I'll be there at five."

I straightened the edge of the bedcover. Scratched at the back of my neck. "We're waiting for someone else."

"Do you care to fill me in? Y'know, as the head of your security and all."

"Actually, no. No, I do not. I'll see you in the car in a few hours."

I disconnected the call and lay on my back, staring at the ceiling. Feeling the emptiness of the huge bed. Alone was no way to celebrate a narrow escape with my life, but I didn't feel much like drinking or partying. What I wanted was some clever talk from that cheeky mouth. I wanted to fall asleep with my aching head cushioned on a soft breast.

Though, with those breasts anywhere near me, sleep was the last thing I'd be doing.

Damn, just the thought of Sara had me hard again. I dropped a hand to my ridiculous pajamas and rubbed at the aching bulge.

Okay, rubbing wasn't doing an ounce of good. All I could think of was Sara lying astride me in the boat, all wet and warm. After risking her own life to save mine. Lord, what I wouldn't give to thank her properly. And to discover if she was as eminently squeezable all over as those magnificent breasts and the soft rounding of her belly had seemed to promise.

I palmed my cock, wiping the pre-cum from the tip down the shaft, pretending the wetness was her mouth.

Hadn't done that since I was a teen. Hadn't needed to. Always a willing hand or mouth nearby, always a pair of legs ready to spread.

I fisted faster. Actually, I didn't want Sara to go down on me. I wanted to bury my face between her thighs, clasp those buttocks I felt quite certain would be every bit as superb as her breasts, and hold her to me as I plunged my tongue deep into her center. I wanted to make her come on my tongue, shaking and quivering. Damn, I wanted to thank her for my life, in every way I could imagine.

I let go of my cock and rolled over, stuffing my face into the pillow. Refused to hump the mattress like a juvenile.

But only because tomorrow I'd persuade Sara to allow me to apologize. In the best way I knew how.

Chapter Seven

Rick

I took the stairs three at a time, eager to get off the boat before I was detained. Seemed I wasn't the only one. A young woman stood at the desk in the main lobby, a backpack and suitcase leaning against her legs.

The night clerk rubbed bleary eyes as he addressed her. "Miss, disembarkation doesn't commence until seven. You've another two hours, and you're entitled to breakfast before you leave."

The woman clenched her hands on the polished counter. "But the ship is docked, and I have a meeting I must get to."

Valid excuse, but the tears thick in her voice gave her away—holiday remorse, escaping an unwanted lover. For a moment, I was tempted to suggest she accompany me. But my life was already complicated enough. I headed to the disembarkation door.

The captain waited there, all white suit and gold frogging, like he belonged in the navy. "Good morning, Mr. Winchester. I trust you slept well?"

If sleeping well included bending my rigid dick in half against the mattress all night, unable to banish the desire for a woman I'd only met for a few minutes, then, sure. "Absolutely, Captain. Were you able to make the necessary arrangements?"

"Of course, sir. *The Spirit of Ohana* is only too happy to cater to your requirements."

Predictable. "Excellent. Then I'll have my man contact you to arrange a press release later today."

The captain bobbed his head and proffered a hand. "I look forward to it. Bon voyage, Mr. Winchester. Should you ever choose to travel these waters in a more orthodox fashion, please don't hesitate to contact me directly."

"Of course." I strode toward the covered gangway, then paused, trying to sound nonchalant. "When you sail again, Captain, is Miss Grant rostered to sail with you?"

"I'm not aware of the housekeeping staff timetables, Mr. Winchester, but I'm more than happy to ascertain them for you. Perhaps I can convey those details to your man?"

"Perfect." I tugged the hood of the thin sweatshirt I'd purchased from the onboard store—opened solely for my shopping pleasure, as though there was any chance I'd grab anything other than the first thing that looked like it'd fit—low over my face, nodded to the captain, then strode along the empty tunnel that led to the just-waking portside terminus.

To face the music.

Sodding hell. Only a few vehicles dotted the lot, and Marty's car stood out like a dog's balls. Had the dock been full, still it would have stood out.

The early morning air held a hint of last night's rain, though it'd turn hot within a couple of hours before being relieved mid-morning by the freshening trade winds. But probably no more hurricanes. I jogged across the few feet of hardtop to the car. Didn't bother to peer through the darkly tinted windows as I cracked the door and threw the bag containing yesterday's tee and the pajamas inside, and then dropped heavily into the leather passenger seat. "I said get a car, not a damn hearse!"

Marty managed to further twist his permanently scrunched face. "Limousine. And you weren't exactly specific."

Hand on the dash, I leaned forward, anxiously surveying the doors of the port terminal, though it was hours early yet. My heart kicked as a woman appeared, but it was the girl from the foyer, minus her suitcase. At least she'd managed to escape. "I thought it pretty clear I wanted to blend."

An elephant had nothing on Marty's trumpeting snort. "Interesting way to go about it, lad. You care to explain why you're out to lose me my job? When I have a family to provide for, an' all."

"I don't actually believe that a dozen ferrets and three girlfriends, doubtless unaware of one another's existence, constitute a family on any legal census."

"Judgmental git."

I hid my grin. "Glorified nanny."

He lifted one shoulder. "Well, that might hurt, except you're the man-child who requires nannying." Triumph blazed across his face.

"*Requires* would seem an odd choice of word."

Scar tissue meant he could no longer lift either eyebrow, but the battered pugilist gave it a damn good shot. "Not from where I'm sitting. Didn't you just get yourself pulled out of the briny by some young thing about a tenth your size?"

Memory tugged an unwilling smile from my lips. "Touché. But how'd you know she's tiny?"

He scoffed. "Look at the size of you, lad. Unless she

was some bloody Amazon, it was a given."

I jerked my chin at the terminal where baggage handlers had started to filter into the long rectangular building, pausing to stare at our car on their way. "Before we draw any more attention, let's go dump this testament to self-indulgence and grab a cab."

Marty caressed the leather steering wheel. "What's wrong with this, then? You never complain at home. Well, okay, you carry on like a birthing cow, but we still use the limo or the four-wheel drive. And I can't drive a cab, anyway."

"So don't drive it, just hire it. You know, like a normal person. Come on, I don't want to get spotted sitting here like a penguin in the desert."

The engine ran so quietly I wasn't certain he'd started it until the car slid forward. My head of security's words drowned out any noise the motor might have made. "Well, anytime you want to start explaining, lad."

The breath I blew out bounced back from the closed window, and I shoved the hood from my head. "Same old, same old, Marty. You know how it is. I just wanted to *feel* something. Needed to disappear for a while."

"Aye, and you damn near accomplished it this time, from what I hear. Doctor said you gave yourself a nice belt on the noggin." He squinted at my forehead, the bruising no longer completely hidden by the adhesive tape. "I have a vested interest, more commonly known as a paycheck, in keeping you alive for the next two months."

"Two months? What, then you'll desert me? Aren't you supposed to forever remain as my curmudgeonly yet faithful companion?"

He peered across me as he pulled onto the main

highway into Waikiki. "Sod that, sunshine. I'm a bodyguard, not a damn Labrador. If you pull off this harebrained scheme, you'll be worth nothing, anyway. Then I'll go prostrate myself in front of social security and have myself a nice easy pension, instead of chasing after the likes of you."

"Worth nothing?" Flipping down the visor, I picked at the bandage on my forehead. The yellow iodine had to be making the bruising look worse than it was. I peeled the tape free. No. Wasn't the iodine. The bruise formed a purple lake around a good half-dozen stitches. "I think you may be overstating the case a little."

Sara's shoulder would look worse this morning. Poor thing. Yet I couldn't help wondering whether the bruise had spread from below the white curve of her shoulder, down onto the gorgeous rounding of her breast. The breast my hand had cupped, the fullness spilling over. That tantalizing nipple hard against my palm, begging for my mouth.

Damn. I coughed, shifting in the seat to adjust my crotch. Dragged my mind back to Marty. Who was definitely no substitute for memories of the erotic glimpses I'd had of Sara. "You may have to try out for Mother's dramatic society if old age is making you prone to such terribly un-British exaggeration."

He huffed at the unlikely scenario. "Well, I'm warning you now, lad, it'd be a hell of a pay raise needed to keep me. Thirty years of babysitting your lily-white arse are about twenty too many."

"I'd thank you to keep your eyes off my rear end." He had always been more of a dad to me than Father had, and my tone softened. "But you'll never need to rely on the government pension, Marty."

"I know that, lad," the bodyguard replied gruffly, one fist mashing at the squashed nose he swore was the result of a boxing match, but I suspected was more likely a bar fight. "Now, how about you spill the beans on just what it is we're up to, and let's see if we can't fix up your mess."

"It's not really a mess. I kind of screwed up with a girl."

The speed with which he whipped his head around would no doubt later come back to him with an arthritic kick. "A girl? Screwed up? What, pregnant? Who? Not some two-bit tart?"

"Whoa, slow down." I nudged my chin at the highway flashing in front of the windscreen, the car speeding up as Marty's angst hyped. "I didn't survive last night to become roadkill, thanks. Anyway, not that kind of screw up. The girl who pulled me out of the water. Like, literally. She jumped in the middle of that damn hurricane, swam to my yacht, and climbed aboard." I rubbed at my temples, unable to fathom what had been in her head. "I accidentally insulted her last night. I want to make good."

"How the hell could you insult a girl, lad? There's so many you should have had a word or two with, but I've told you before you're polite to a fault."

"I offered to pay her for sex."

"What the bloody hell? Well, that'll do it." He shook his head in disbelief. "Did the sea water addle yer brain?"

"Marty, watch the road, man!"

The guard glanced back at the near-empty road and dismissed its importance with a curt shake of his head. "What the hell, lad? Since when do you pay for sex? Why?"

"I don't, and I didn't intend my suggestion to come across like that." I ground my teeth together in frustration, trying not to replay my unfortunate choice of words the previous night. I'd backed off each time it seemed like maybe Sara had second thoughts; I'd tried to act the gentleman, letting her set the pace. Then a misplaced word or two had screwed me over. And now, thoughts of the woman consumed me.

Obviously, I needed to clear my conscience. "Thing is, I want to make it straight."

"So send her flowers."

"That's not going to cut it."

"Fine. Flowers *and* chocolate."

I chuckled. Marty's solutions always started with the obvious. Well, they pretty much ended there, too. But he had my back and would support whatever ludicrous scheme I came up with. The mound of papers waiting in my hotel suite bore witness. "Afraid it's going to take more than money to fix this one." A novel concept.

We headed down the straight carriageway of Ala Moana Boulevard, the industrial cement-block buildings and tropical weed-filled car parks giving way to lawned edges and swaying palms.

"So not some bit of crumpet we pay off quick before she gets attached?" Marty's tone shifted to lugubrious.

I'd have to come clean. When I noticed the gold band on Sara's finger, before I kissed her, it had been a relief. No need for me to fight the attraction I felt, she would put the brakes on, sooner or later. "There's no risk. She's married." Why didn't those words sound as comforting as I'd expected? "So no need for you to chase her off."

He sighed. "What is it with you and the married

ones?"

"I've explained it to you before. Safety. If they're married, they're up for a bit of fun on the side, but they aren't going to risk becoming attached. By the time they work out I'm an absolute bastard, they'll be right happy to go back to their husbands. Hell, I could probably start a new career as a marriage counselor."

"Huh. Pretty words, great concept. And how's it working out for you?"

I blew out an annoyed breath, drumming my fingers on my knees. Refrained from checking the time. No way Sara could have cleaned her cabins and made it off the ship yet. We'd only been gone fifteen minutes, so we hadn't missed her. "Okay, so it's only a theory, so far. I still surmise it has validity." He could lecture all he wanted about steering clear of married women. No way in hell was I taking that advice now. Odd Jay hadn't mentioned Sara's husband, though. She didn't exactly hide her wedding ring and sport instead the telltale indentation and paleness I'd noted on a number of women's left hands. Women I'd steered clear of. If they were undecided about their marital status, I was *very* decided. Not going there.

A rumble of disagreement dragged up from Marty's chest. "Well, lad, I conjecture they'd end up like the rest of your unintentional conquests. Not happy to return to another lover, whether they're married or otherwise."

Would that be so bad? I shook my head. What the bloody hell was I thinking? That knock on the noggin must have been a damned sight harder than I allowed for. Somehow, I'd flipped, in short order, from thanking a woman for saving my life, to wanting to give her a good rogering, to wondering if she'd leave her husband for me. Man, that was massively cocked up. And right now, I had zero room for cocked up. Or complications of any kind.

Explaining Sara to Mother would have been rather droll, though. "Mother, meet my girlfriend. She's an Aussie. A cleaner, actually. Oh, and she's married." With not a Camilla, Priscilla, or Drusilla in sight, and Sara's blood no doubt running fully red, Mother would have a fit of the vapors. Father, though? Father would love the story of a mermaid who leaped into my boat in the middle of a storm.

Would have loved it. Back when he could understand.

Sorrow loaded my chest, the burden I'd managed to shuck off for a few hours threatening to return. "So how is Father?"

Marty shrugged. "Same-same. How come you never ask about your mother?"

"Why? Nobody's thrown a bucket of water over her, have they? Broomstick's still in fine fettle?"

He looked confused for a moment, then snorted. "The wicked witch, huh?" He pulled his face back into a semblance of sternness. "Don't you think you should give her a break? You are planning on disrupting her life."

Not a reminder I needed. My jaw tensed with the familiar strain, and I turned to stare out of the window. "Hardly. She's not going to suffer. Fourteen rooms instead of thirty-two? I think I'm doing her a favor." A favor that would see my funds funneled to far more appropriate places than Mother's stable. Yet still, I hadn't been able to bring myself to sign the papers.

"If you manage to pull this off."

"Yeah. If."

He cut me a sideways glance as he navigated smoothly through the increasing traffic. "Second thoughts?"

"Second, third, and fourth, Marty. I don't want to hurt anyone. Especially Mother. But only money can fix the problems money causes."

"Wasn't your family's money that broke the world, lad."

An old argument, but Marty played devil's advocate, making certain I'd investigated the logic of my intent. Problem was, no matter how much thought I gave the plan, the effects of implementing it would not be limited to only myself. I gestured as the multilane highway gave over to Kalakaua Avenue, the narrower road more crowded, with high-end shops bordering each side. "There's a taxi rank. Dump the car. I want to get back to the dock."

The car slid smoothly to the curb. "A cab. Really, we're still going with that? Well, are you going to put your shoes on first, or do you plan on going hobo all day? What's with the thug look, anyway?"

I plucked the tight shirt from my chest. "Thug? I'll have you know this is expensive workout gear." And necessary, if I was to pull off the next part of my plan.

Chapter Eight

Sara

Melanie stood behind me, one fist clenching my hair as she brushed it up into a ponytail. I winced, and she screwed up her face in sympathy. "I'll give you a hand clearing your cabins this morning."

My wince had more to do with the hair pulling, but my shoulder was far more painful this morning than it had been the previous evening. I leaned forward to examine my face in the small mirror propped on our shared desk. At least the graze didn't look as bad as I'd feared. Like I'd fallen, not gone a round with a prizefighter. And it clearly hadn't been bad enough to deflect Rick's attentions last night. My stomach did a flip at the thought of him, and I scowled. Melanie's round blue eyes grew even larger, and I struggled to contain sudden laughter. "That wasn't for you. Just thinking of someone. No, don't worry about my rooms, Mel. Get yours done so you can get off."

"I don't have anything on until tonight. I'll help you, then we'll leave together."

Her words sounded oddly rehearsed, but lack of sleep probably addled my head. Well, lack of sleep and dehydration. All of my bodily fluids seemed to insist on accumulating somewhere below my waist and above my knees.

I puffed out a heavy breath and shifted in the low-backed chair.

She set aside the brush. "What is with you this morning? I've seen pregnant cats more settled. You took forever with the doc last night. I thought he'd decided to keep you in the medical bay. I fell asleep waiting to find out if you were okay."

"I wasn't with the doc." Damn, I hadn't meant to let that slip. Though why shouldn't I? I'd done nothing wrong. *Unfortunately.* "Jay and I were sent to Rick Winchester's cabin."

Yeah, I had nothing to be guilty about, yet I'd immediately thrown Jay under the bus so it wouldn't sound like I'd been alone with Rick. "You know they put him in the executive suite? How random is that?"

Instead of jumping on the gossip, Melanie spoke quickly. "Maybe that was the only room made up on short notice?"

Frowning, I leaned forward to pick up the pills the doc had given me. Downed them with a sip of water. "Yeah. Maybe."

"What's he like?"

"He, who?"

"You know, the guy you rescued. This Rick Winchester."

"Uh...damp." Nope, that was me. I stood, tucking my blouse into my black pants. "He's—I don't know—just a guy." I tried to shrug off the question, then relented and shot her a grin. "Actually, he's hot as hell. You remember the actor in that movie we caught last month?"

"You mean the chisel-jawed Adonis?" She did deer in headlights well, all eyes and surprise. "My ovaries sure do. Kaboom." Her hands pantomimed an explosion.

"Yeah, well, picture him, little bit darker, with a very proper Brit accent." That's why Rick had appeared vaguely familiar last night; I'd spent an inappropriate amount of time ogling his double in the movies. I pulled the sling over my arm but held up my finger to stop Melanie from interrupting. "He's got the look. But a total dick."

"Aww, no. Are you serious?"

I tugged open the door. "Yeah, serious. Typical. The bigger the dick, the bigger the dick."

We turned the corridor and headed for the central stairs. She danced in front of me, walking backward. "Wait, you saw his…"

The stairs had become steeper overnight. Evidently, swimming was not that fantastic as exercise. Damn, parts of me really hurt. In a serious way. "Figure of speech, Mel. I meant the more important, wealthy, good-looking, whatever, the more chance the guy will be a wanker. Point in case, Mr. Richard Winchester."

And I was done thinking about him.

Though maybe Mel was right to take me literally. The pajamas certainly raised a question. Or a flagpole. I hid a snigger.

Whoa! Done. Thinking. About. Him.

****

The last envelope tucked in my pocket, I cast a glance around the finished cabin. While tipping wasn't mandatory on the cruise, many travelers liked to maximize their chances of premium service. Not that I did anything different. Every kid got towel animals each day, regardless of their parents' generosity. Tips on the last day were always slim, though. There was no point tipping someone you'd never see again.

I squeezed the thin wad of envelopes. Definitely not enough in there to make my promised contribution to the orphanage. Not unless I'd unwittingly served some millionaire who considered twenty grand a reasonable tip. I pinched the bridge of my nose wearily. Even with Melanie's help, I was totally stuffed, my hands a little shaky, my emotions wound tight, constantly on the verge of easy tears. Daft. Yesterday's adventure, compounded by a sleepless night, had taken more out of me than seemed reasonable. Probably some kind of delayed reaction.

The knowledge that once I got ashore, I'd need to deal with the other aspects of my life seemed a looming cloud of dire proportions. Continuing to chase Simon to make the transfer was pointless, and in any case, there was the whole having unwillingly donated my phone to Davy Jones Locker issue to surmount. I'd have to use the public connection in the Backpacker's Hostel and shoot through the transfer from there. Bugger Simon and his concerns about financial cyber safety. He should have answered my emails. Hopefully, allowing for the time difference between here, Australia, and the Solomons, the money would still process before the deadline.

Once I'd dealt with that, I'd buy a new phone and call Simon. No, I'd FaceTime him. It'd be easier to read his expressions that way—and maybe seeing my husband after all these months would stir the guilt I should feel over my near infidelity. My husband's image might superimpose over the memory of Rick Winchester that refused to leave my mind, the recollection of the feel of his body that stirred all kinds of delicious things…and absolutely no guilt.

The cabin door banged open, and Melanie stuck her

head around the jamb. "I'm all done, you good?"

I nodded, tossing the last of the damp towels into the dirty linen sack. "You're a legend, Mel. I'd be here till the next trip if you'd not helped."

She grinned, pulling the band out of her long blonde ponytail and shaking her head. "Yay for loose hair for a couple of days, right?"

I freed my hair, running my fingers through the long curls. "Just yay for not having to stick my arms up over my head to put my hair up."

A sympathetic grimace twisted her pretty face. "Does your shoulder hurt an awful lot?"

"Worse than I thought it would." I forced a smile. "Nothing a couple of mai tais won't fix, though." As I'd sipped champagne the previous night, might as well do away with the whole abstinence part of my new-life philosophy. "Come on, let's get our gear and get off. We're probably the last housekeeping crew left aboard."

She glanced at her watch. "Yup. Okay."

We made our way back to our cabin far more slowly than we'd left. In truth, if I didn't need a decent internet connection so urgently, I'd stay aboard and go back to bed.

A quick tidy, our beds made, and Melanie trundled two pretty pink suitcases—which took up way more than her share of the cupboard space, though I never said anything—out into the corridor. I hefted my backpack, which contained most everything I traveled with, onto the bed. Flipped open the top flap and stroked a finger down the crumpled picture I'd taped there.

"Here, I'll carry it." Melanie paused with her hand on the bag strap. "Oh, what's the photo?"

I pulled the flap a little higher so she could see. "The

orphanage I worked at. These are the kids." The memory made me smile. "Cute little buggers, yeah?" In the photo, thirteen children clustered around me, each with a matching ear-splitting grin. Except for the tiny cherub on my knee, who gazed up at me with soulful eyes. *Sophia.* A tight knot formed in my chest at the memory of farewelling the children.

Melanie's hair brushed my face as she leaned in to look. "Well, cute if you like kids, I guess. Will you go back there?"

Take on another year of cold showers and deprivations? "I'd love to." Unfortunately, I'd have to clear it with Simon first. If I did return, it'd be to work in my professional capacity, volunteering for the law reform commission. Maybe leaving the islands had been the wrong thing to do, but I'd been terrified of allowing myself to fall into another rut of habit and convenience like I'd done with Simon. Not that much was convenient about the Solomon Islands, but still, I'd wanted to challenge myself and felt a need to keep moving.

But whether I returned or not, I had to get the promised money to the orphanage.

Melanie checked her watch again, and I closed my bag.

"Sorry, Mel. Daydreaming." I fended off her lunge for the backpack. "No, I can carry it. Just help me get it over my shoulder."

I regretted the bravado as soon as the webbing strap settled on my injured joint.

"Don't you need to put your arm back in the sling?" she asked anxiously.

"No. It's just bruised. Nothing wrong with it." I tucked the fabric sling, still hooked around my neck, out of sight. I would sure as heck be shoving my arm back in it once I was off the boat. Unsupported, it really hurt, but I didn't need her to make a fuss. "Do you have a hot date lined up or something?"

She had checked her watch yet again. "Uh, no, just time we were heading. Come on." That guilty, slightly furtive look again, which didn't sit well on her open face.

I frowned. Maybe she had a secret tryst organized. With Jay? Oh, come on, why did my mind leap to him? It wasn't like he was the only guy on the ship.

No, because Rick Winchester was also aboard.

If I had a free hand, I'd slap myself. I had a whole lot of more important things to think about than some sopping-wet, arrogant Brit.

Even though he was so freaking hot the water had probably steamed off him.

Damn.

Though I strode along the corridors, I was hard-pressed to keep pace with Melanie, who skipped ahead.

"Oh, hang on a moment." She held up a hand to pause me as we came to the final corridor, an arcade of fancy shops glittering in the artificial light like Christmas baubles. She dashed to the end of the arcade, opened the varnished wooden doors into the main foyer, peered through, and then pranced back to me. "Just wanted to make sure there wasn't a queue waiting to disembark. Hate standing in lines."

My fingers tightening on my bag strap, I hung back. Something didn't ring true about the way she was acting, but what on earth was it?

I shrugged off the concern. I needed to get over to the Backpackers Lodge, pronto, and sort my affairs. Ugh, *affair*. Poor choice of words.

Melanie pushed through the doors, holding one wide. The other door seemed to swing open of its own accord.

As I stepped through, a cheer went up. Dressed in full uniform, the entire crew formed a narrow aisle leading to the gangway. Instinctively, I stepped back, but someone snagged my elbow, and I jerked around.

Resplendent in dress whites, Jay grinned apologetically. "Sorry, mate. I know you're going to hate this, but we're under orders."

"What the hell, Jay?"

He slid the backpack from my shoulders, his eyes narrowing at my flinch. "Where's your sling? Here, put it back on." He adjusted the fabric, handed the pack to another crew member, and proffered his arm. "Care to walk with me?"

Chapter Nine

Sara

The rest of the crew gawked, leaning forward to watch us but not breaking the ranks that formed a corridor.

The blood rushed to my face, and I muttered furiously, "This is bullshit, Jay. Cut it out."

He closed his arm firmly, trapping my hand in the crook of his elbow against his hard bicep. "Only one way off this ship, Sara."

Well, that wasn't exactly true. I'd proved jumping overboard worked. And hurt.

As we passed through the funnel of crew members, cheers and applause rippled ahead of us, my stomach tightening with each wave. Jay guided me onto the planked walkway and down the short incline that led to a final section, tented with white fabric and bedecked with tropical flowers. From there, I knew a short tunnel led to the portside disembarkation hall.

But I wasn't permitted to escape.

In the marquee stood an older man, also white-suited but, denoted by the gold braid adorning his uniform, somewhat more important than Jay.

The entertainment director walked steadily toward him, drawing me along by keeping the pressure on my trapped hand. He halted in front of the dignified-looking man. "Captain Raynalds, may I present Miss Sara Grant, one of your stewards."

Holy crap. Though I'd seen the captain around, I'd never met him. Was I expected to salute or something?

Raynalds offered his hand, quickly swapping to present his left as he realized mine was incapacitated. "Miss Grant. I understand you are the crew member responsible for the rescue of Mr. Winchester."

That self-important, pompous ass had set this up to humiliate me? I snatched my hand back as quickly as I could, though Raynalds continued speaking.

"I'd like to thank you for your courageous act, which undoubtedly saved the life of a very fine young man."

Really? Were we thinking of the same person? Rick Winchester might be *fiiiiine*, but that probably wasn't the kind of *fine* Raynalds meant.

"On behalf of the owners, operators, and crew of *The Spirit of Ohana*, we're proud to call you part of our ohana. It gives me much pleasure to present you with this, from your shipboard family." He signaled, and one of the restaurant staff stepped forward, clutching a huge bunch of flowers.

I took them, ignoring incipient hay fever in favor of using the blooms to hide my flaming face. Shit, all the crew, desperate to get on shore for their brief leave period, had been held up for this. Another thing to blame Rick bloody Winchester for. I should have left him to drown.

The captain presented an envelope with a flourish. "And Mr. Winchester requested I personally see that you receive this."

The envelope, embossed with *The Spirit of Ohana*,

came from complimentary stationery in Rick's luxury suite. The handwriting had to be his, though. *Sara*, written in a dead-straight line, beautiful copperplate script. What a tosser. Though at least he'd spelled my name correctly, I usually picked up an H. I fumbled the envelope, awkwardly shoving it into my sling, the flowers cradled in the crook of my injured arm.

The captain stepped back and started applauding, a cue for the rest of the crew to clap frantically like sheer volume would buy them a leave pass. Fortunately, Jay took my arm again and guided me down the secondary corridor and into the port terminal.

"Well, that was horrible," I grumbled as he took my bag from the crew member who followed us out.

"Don't use past tense. It's not over yet," he cautioned.

I took a step back so I could look up at him. "What do you mean?"

He slung the bag over his shoulder and nodded toward the entry. "You'll see."

"Hell, Jay, I thought you were my friend."

As we exited the terminal, the cool trade wind pulled at my loose hair, obscuring my view. I tamed the hair and tucked it behind my ears—then wished I'd left well enough alone. Our passage was blocked by journalists, flashing cameras held above their heads, microphones thrust toward us.

I jerked to a halt, then drew back, but Jay kept a tight hold on my arm.

"Don't say anything to them. Not yet," he said.

Yet? What the hell was he talking about? I had no intention of saying anything, ever.

"Sara. Sara, where's Mr. Winchester?"

Hearing my name yelled by people I didn't know sounded odd. And how come Rick rated such formality?

Jay craned over the heads of the reporters, seeming to search for something.

A woman knocked my shoulder with her microphone. "Sara, were you and Mr. Winchester alone in the yacht for long? What did you talk about?"

As I gasped at the jolt of pain, Jay wrapped a protective arm around me. "No comment." His voice drew up from the soles of his feet, booming across the crowd of about twenty journalists. "There'll be a statement made by the company later." He lowered his voice, ducking to speak to me as the reporters jostled forward again. "This way. Come on, stay close."

I didn't need that last direction; I'd stick to him like a tick on a dog. Must have been a slow news day, but how the heck would I get past the reporters and over to the bus stop for my ride into town?

Jay guided me to the left where a handrail edged the wharf. Positioning me alongside the rail, he used his bulk to protect me from the crowd as he led me swiftly along the quay. About thirty feet away, another figure, features hidden beneath a hooded jacket, headed toward us.

I tried to swallow down the surge of panic that screwed my stomach into a tight knot. The crush, the noise, the shouted questions. I'd elected to practice company law precisely because I didn't like confrontation and didn't want to be bailed up on the steps of some courthouse and bombarded with questions. That's where Simon always shone, happy to take center stage. He'd draw himself up, waiting until a hush descended on the crowd, with all eyes focused on him. Happy to soak up every bit of the limelight.

I pressed even closer to Jay, wishing I could disappear, but any moment now the hooded figure would block our way, and we'd have to angle right, into the throng of reporters. Either that or jump the rail, into the sea.

Tempting.

Jay showed no signs of deviating, though, steadily plowing forward. He stopped just short of the menacing figure and held out my backpack. "Here you are, sir."

"I told you it's Rick."

Growled low enough that only me and Jay could hear, the voice was distinctive, nonetheless. Well, it didn't hurt that Rick gave his name, either, but I'd have recognized the deep rumble, the precision of the British accent, anyway. In fact, every part of my body recognized it.

My lips parted in an almost-silent groan. Well, moan, really. Seriously, did my hormones operate entirely independently of my brain? Because my brain was screaming, "C'mon, get us the hell out of this place," but my body was all "Ooh no, let's stand close to Rick. We like Rick."

I didn't have to make a choice, though, as Rick shouldered my pack, slid an arm around my waist, and pulled me from Jay. "This way, please, Sara. Let's get you out of here."

Dammit, did he really have to speak so close to my ear that my knees turned to jelly? *Entitled wanker*. I had to hang on to that thought. Though it was kind of hard, given his quaint, formal politeness, delivered in that oh-so-sexy accent. *Crap.* I cast a beseeching glance over my shoulder. How could Jay desert me?

The entertainment director threw a mock salute as

Rick led me away. "I'll catch up with you later. Give you a call, have drinks tonight."

Normally, I'd yank away from any guy who had the audacity to try and direct me, then slap him back into place. But if I did that now, where would I go? How would I even get through this ridiculous, inexplicable media horde? I had no choice but to fall into step with Rick as, hidden beneath his hood, he followed the narrow path along the waterfront.

As we moved away from the massive cruise liner towering above the dock, Jay strode back into the thick of the reporters. Standing with his legs spread, his face friendly and open, clearly inviting questions, he shot glances toward Rick and I a couple of times, as though he deliberately created a diversion and assessed our escape.

Rick guided me swiftly across the car park, seeming oblivious to the couple of reporters who scurried behind us, still panting questions.

"Here." He yanked open the rear door of a cab, waited until I was seated, still clutching my flowers, then closed the door and ducked around to the rear of the vehicle. Slammed my backpack into the open trunk, reappeared at the opposite passenger door, and slid into the back seat alongside me. "Okay, Marty, let's go."

I tightened my lips. Obnoxiously quick to make friends with the locals, on first-name terms with the cab driver, Rick probably thought it made him seem more approachable, a regular Joe. Well, he was dressed pretty average. I snuck a look sideways. Now that his hand wasn't so close to being in contact with my skin, assessing him was a little easier. Sneakers, chinos, and the hoodie. Maybe I'd read him wrong? Just because he knew how to open a champagne bottle and hadn't been thrown by the opulent surroundings of the premium suite, that didn't actually *confirm* him to be some rich tosser, did it? What had happened to my rigid belief in innocent until proven guilty? Hell, Rick could be a steward, like me, hence his familiarity with the suite.

Or maybe he was the fisherman that his roughened hands, caressing my skin last night, seemed to hint at?

Still, neither excused his attempt to buy me for sex.

Damn, I was so confused, and his nearness on the suddenly way-too-small bench seat was not helping my mental process. I had to cling to my righteous indignation, remember my fury, cut him down to size with a withering gaze... *Oh, but that size...* My gaze roamed over him as he leaned toward the front seat. He still smelled so good.

Nope, I was *not* thinking like that. *Focus.*

As the car pulled smoothly out of the park, I clipped my seat belt with a determined snap and turned to the driver to give directions. And froze. Two men sat in the front of the vehicle.

Alarm bells sounded in my head.

Abduction?

Rick caught my glance and gestured toward the front passenger seat. "This is Marty. My, uh, my partner."

The man in the front screwed toward me, his battered face twisted into something approximating a smile as he assessed me shrewdly from narrowed eyes. Finally, he nodded and stuck out a ham-like fist. "Pleased to meet you, Miss..." He stressed the last word.

For some reason, I was reluctant to offer him my left hand, the one with the gold band. Ridiculous, because I'd not hidden it from Rick. Or Jay. But something questioning lurked in this Marty's tone, as though he…what? Didn't believe I was married? What difference did it make to him?

I lifted my sling-clad arm, proving I couldn't shake hands. "Sorry. Marty, was it? Sara. Pleased to meet you." I met the challenge in his eyes square on, refusing to back down. The guy looked like a fighter, but I'd handled bullies before. The slick business types were the ones I had trouble with. Types like Simon.

Marty nodded slowly, then his face split in a grin. "Can see where you get the mermaid bit from, lad. Lucky you were there for my boy, Sara."

With the smile both the man's countenance and tone changed, and I relaxed.

"Oh, you're Rick's dad?" No, wait. Hadn't Rick said partner? Did he mean life partner? My smile wobbled. Shit, I'd put my foot square in it. Waded in it, in fact, and walked it all back indoors, to boot.

Marty shrugged. "May as well be his dad. Someone's gotta pull the lad out of trouble. Looks like it was you, this time."

Rick cleared his throat. "Sara, where can I drop you?"

The pronoun seemed odd, given there were four of us in the vehicle, and Rick wasn't the one doing the driving. "Uh, Backpackers in Waikiki." I gave the address from memory. I always stayed in the same place, and they even held some of my larger items in storage, those I couldn't fit in my shared cabin.

"Sure." Rick seemed to lose interest in my conversation and tugged a phone from his hoodie pocket. His fingers flew across the screen.

In the front seat, Marty grunted and pulled out his own phone.

Great company, these guys.

About thirty seconds later, Marty spoke to the driver. "Pull over when you can. I've a call to make. No reception in here."

The driver frowned and pointed at the phone in a cradle on the dash. "There's reception. Always reception along this strip."

Marty repeated slowly. "There's no reception." Though his words weren't intimidating, his tone sent a shiver through me. So cold and commanding, the man oozed inarguable authority.

The driver pulled the cab to the side of the road, and Marty clambered out. Rick watched him for a second. Scowled at the driver. Fingers drumming on his thigh, he compressed and released his lips, as though he debated whether to speak.

I needed to look out of the window, at the view. Not at the view *in* the cab, though it was undeniably mighty fine. Yet it proved kind of impossible to pull my eyes from the strong profile, and Rick seemed completely unaware of my perusal, focused on his phone screen again.

Okay, so if I was going to stare, I should at least speak. One of us should have some manners. Except I was still pissed with him, right? About…something or other.

No, that wasn't right. A strong, intelligent woman, I wasn't about to let a little eye candy overrule my outrage. Even if that eye candy was pretty much a stick of rock. An all-day sucker.

Holy hell, where was my brain taking me? I needed

to wind down the window. Even with the air conditioning shifting strands of hair around my face, it was growing awfully close in here.

As I pulled at the neck of my shirt, trying to allow a little air to creep into the lava pool, Rick's gaze settled on me.

"About last night—" Again, he glanced at the driver, as though it mattered if his words were overheard. He lowered his voice and leaned a little closer. Pinned me with his green eyes, like I was a butterfly mounted on a board.

Yeah, spread open like a butterfly, with him doing the mounting, that's what I wanted.

Shit. Focus. I'd missed half his words because the blood pounded so hard in my head. *Pounded. Hard.* Seriously, did everything need to have a double meaning? I shifted damply on the seat. Rubbed a hand across my forehead, frowning as I tried to concentrate.

Rick drew back, probably thinking my scowl was directed at him. "I'm sorry, I didn't intend for you..." He raked a hand through his hair. "What I said last night, you took it the wrong way."

I hiked an eyebrow. Simon's quasi-apologies always came with a twist that made the issue my fault.

Rick held up a hand, palm out, in instant surrender. "No, that is, *I* got it wrong. I didn't mean what I said."

Aw, c'mon Universe, hot as hell *and* he got it? Totally unfair edge. His uncertainty intriguing, I feigned innocence. "Oh, so you didn't want to have sex with me?"

He winced and glanced at the driver again. Yeah, sure, the driver's ears were practically flapping, but no doubt he'd seen and heard worse.

"No, I—"

Marty lowered himself back into the car with much wheezing and puffing.

"Sorted?" Like a coin flip, Rick changed back to confident.

"Sorted," Marty affirmed. He waggled one stubby finger at the road, indicating the driver should continue.

Rick settled back into his corner, apparently forgetting our half-conversation. "Is the Backpackers Lodge any good?"

"Far nicer than some places I've stayed." Damn, why had Marty interrupted? Now Rick kept his gaze on the road. Rigidly. Like he knew I checked him out, but permitted it. Well, I didn't need his permission for anything, but there was no harm in looking. I dropped my voice so I'd have an excuse to lean an inch closer. "At least it has hot water."

His head jerked around. "You usually stay in places without hot water?"

His appalled tone nearly made me laugh. Perhaps he could imagine nothing worse than a little discomfort. I'd have been tempted to lay the story on a bit thick, just to see his reaction, but there was no need. Accommodation in the Solomons had been basic, and I was actually kind of proud I'd toughed it out. "Without even running water, never mind hot. Though I wouldn't say 'usually.' "

Damn, there was that honesty thing again. Way to ruin a good story. I'd sounded hardcore for a second, but now Rick would peg me as just another privileged white female, complaining about first world problems. Not that I wanted to give him any details about my life, but I had to retrieve the situation. "I did a nine-month placement in the Solomon Islands. Living conditions aren't great there at the best of times, but I went over shortly after the earthquake, which took out a lot of the infrastructure."

"A placement?" The bewilderment on his face was almost cartoonish. "As a steward?"

No reason to tell him everything. I'd skip the first six months, where I'd volunteered my legal knowledge to assist the hard-pressed Public Solicitor's Office. "A volunteer at an orphanage."

"Ah. Interesting." To his credit, he actually did sound interested. "Are a large number of children institutionalized?"

"It depends—"

My reply was cut off by the cabbie. "Backpackers."

"Ah. Right." Rick's single-word, single-syllable replies sounded terribly British. But was that disappointment that crossed his face as he glanced across me to the Polynesian hut façade of the multistory building?

Despite my training and experience, I found the guy impossible to read. But it made no difference. Regardless of what his face did or did not reveal, I was better off out of there. "Well, thanks for the ride." I turned to the cab driver. "What's the fare?"

Rick stopped me as I reached for the money belt beneath my shirt. His hand lingered, fingertips brushing the flesh I'd bared. "I'll get it. Least I can do. And I still need the taxi, anyway. I'll carry your backpack in."

He exited his side of the vehicle, and I almost fell from mine as the door I leaned against opened. I jerked around to find Marty offering his hand to help me out. It seemed he could move disconcertingly fast and quietly when he wanted to. Or when my attention was elsewhere.

Rick spoke over my head as he hauled my backpack from the trunk. "Definitely all good, Marty?"

Marty huffed. "Said it was, didn't I, lad?"

Rick grinned as though accustomed to the man's surliness. "Right. After you, Sara."

I should tell him I'd manage just fine from here, but carrying the backpack down the ship's corridor had hurt more than I cared to admit. The pain meds the doc had given me to take this morning were definitely wearing off, both my bruised ribs and shoulder aching enough to set my teeth on edge. Carrying the ridiculous bouquet represented about the extent of my ability right now.

I led the way into the foyer of the lodge and smiled at the familiar face behind the counter. "Hi, Maryam. Back again, like a bad penny. Single, please."

Maryam slowly brushed dark hair behind her ear, adjusting the flower that held it in place, as she assessed Rick. "Single?" Her question loaded, she paused, as if I'd change my mind. Then she huffed. "I have got to have words with you, girl."

She turned to a pegboard behind her. "Oh." Her hair swayed across her back as she glanced from side to side. Then she swiveled back to the counter. Crossed to the computer screen and stared intently, occasionally tapping at keys. "Wow. I'm so sorry, Sara, but we're fully booked for the next two nights."

"What?" I stared at her in disbelief. The strenuous exercise yesterday, the sleepless night, and the growing pain all weighing heavier by the second, I had to get my room. I needed to make the transfer. It was already later than I'd calculated on it being, thanks to my slow work and the embarrassing affair on the ship. It had to be well after lunchtime.

As if to reinforce my calculation, my stomach roiled. Or maybe that was an aftereffect of the meds, because I felt decidedly sick. Probably hadn't been the best idea, taking them on an empty stomach. "But my gear, Maryam. It's in your storage." Like that guaranteed me a room. Stupid. Why hadn't I thought to book?

Probably because, in three months, I'd not needed to.

Maryam still stared at her computer screen, as though she couldn't believe the bookings, either. "I'm so sorry, Sara. I've never known us to be booked out before. There must be some kind of festival or something in town. No idea what, though, I've heard nothing." She gave the screen one final perusal and then shook her head, the scent of her frangipani bloom wafting over me. "I'll, ah, I'll get the key to the storage room for you."

She turned from the screen, snatched an A4 printed map from the counter, and circled two locations. "Listen, there's another decent backpackers here, and one here. But don't stay at these." Highlighter swapped for a pen, she ran a line through several listings on the bottom of the page. She pushed both the paper and a key across the counter, her attention distracted as a large group blew in the door, talking loudly in German and trailing sand and wet snorkeling equipment across the floor. "Ugh, you have to be kidding me. Hey. Hey, you guys!" She waved her arm at the group, then glanced hurriedly back at me. "You can get your own gear, right? I need to make sure they don't dump that wet stuff in the dorms."

"Sure." I reached for the key and paper, but Rick palmed them.

"Lead on. We'll grab your things and hit the next

place."

I nodded, suddenly glad he was there. Which was ridiculous. I'd managed perfectly well on my own for months.

Chapter Ten

Rick

I grabbed the key and scrap of paper Maryam handed over. Tried to sound casual, instead of unchivalrously gleeful. "I'll put your pack in the car, then we'll grab your stuff from storage, okay?"

Sara gazed up at me. Blue eyes, a blaze of emerald splashed like a firework from her left pupil. Shades of the Hawaiian ocean. How was it I'd noticed her wedding ring, but not her eyes?

She reached for the paper but then winced and cut the movement short. "Okay. Thanks." Instead, her hand slid beneath the sling to rub at her ribs. Or stroke them. Rhythmically.

I dragged my eyes away from the hypnotically alluring movement. Bloody hell, I'd not even asked how she felt this morning. Not really had an opportunity. My own head throbbed, but according to the doc, she'd been beaten up worse. I couldn't let her stay in a backpackers; she needed to be somewhere decent. Somewhere a doctor would come and check her over. I'd long ago discovered that, given adequate financial encouragement, practitioners made house calls regardless of the country.

I strode to the doorway and waved Marty over, almost afraid that if I gave Sara too much space, she'd bolt. Not that I had any reason to care if she did, but I believed in paying my debts.

As I handed the bulging backpack to Marty, I also slipped him the page containing the numbers of the other two hostels the receptionist recommended. "The marked ones. Same again."

He rolled his eyes but lumbered out.

The storeroom key swinging from my index finger, I turned back to Sara. "Right. Let's grab your gear and check you into the other backpackers, huh?"

She glanced up at the clock above the desk, chewing on her lip. "Yeah…okay."

Made sense she didn't want to spend her few hours of leave trawling from one hotel to the next. The quicker I got this bit sorted, the better off she'd be. Oh, and the quicker I'd have discharged my obligation. Yeah. That's totally where my focus was.

The two cases and a backpack I shifted out of the locked cage suggested Sara believed in traveling light. Or perhaps the luggage represented all her worldly belongings. Who knew?

She knelt to unzip one of the cases I'd dragged out, struggling single-handedly to release the padlock.

I dropped to my knees alongside her. "Can I help you with that?" As I reached for the bag, my hand covered hers. Nothing abnormal in that. I probably touched other people's hands a dozen times a day, just never noticed the slight charge of electricity the contact gave off.

So why the hell did I notice now?

Sara cut her eyes sideways at me, a smirk playing at the corner of her mouth. "Are you good with zips?"

Bloody hell, every time that smart little mouth gave

me a bit of lip, I wanted more. Okay, so this was definitely abnormal. Fortunately, my brain was accustomed to working independently of my testosterone-driven regions. "I'm generally better with hooks and eyes, but I'll give it a try." Good, pretty smooth. She'd never realize how damn messed up her maybe-teasing had me.

Sara's smirk spread to a grin, openly challenging me to best her in the wordplay. "When it gets a bit stiff, I find it works better if I give it a good firm tug."

Best her? Lord, I wanted to put her over my knee and spank her. But I needed to stay kneeling for a moment or two, or my cover would be blown. Of course, if I stood right now, that sassy mouth would be level—no. Not supposed to be thinking like that. I owed Sara a favor, whether she wanted to take it or not.

Yet I couldn't shut off the part of my mind that needed to know if her teasing meant she'd forgiven my faux pas of the previous evening. And if she had, was that an invitation to take up where we'd left off? With her breast more than adequately filling my hand, her mouth hot against mine.

Sara extricated a brightly printed, sarong-wrapped bundle from the luggage I unzipped. She unwound the cloth and pulled free a laptop, the lid decorated with sparkly stickers, some places up to an eighth of an inch thick with the adhesives. She caught my expression. "The kids at the orphanage. I took them trinkets and stickers." Her nails a natural pink, like the sunset hues of seashells, she caressed the computer case. "And they insisted on giving them back. Stuck on here, so I'd remember each kid."

Her voice held a note of sadness, and I was almost

certain her lip trembled. I was certainly staring closely enough to find out. "That's all you need?" I zipped the case and signaled Marty to load both bags into the trunk.

Sara nodded, the melancholy reaching her eyes now, turning them into the deep, mysterious, mountain waterfall pools of the hinterland, instead of sparkling like the ocean. "Yeah, I have to take care of something." She looked up at the clock again and then clambered to her feet, the bouquet of flowers she'd carried now wedged between the computer and her chest.

First time I'd ever wanted to be a flower.

I shook my head in irritation. None of that tripe. I needed to maintain focus, give my business my full attention, the plan so monumental I couldn't afford a misstep, a lapse in concentration. Sure, I owed Sara a couple of nights at a decent hotel as a thank you and as an apology for my words the previous evening. Nothing more than that.

The fact that the accommodation would ultimately be in the same hotel as my suite was simply exemplary time management. I couldn't be running from one end of town to the other to check up on her for two days.

As we pulled up at the next backpacker's, I stayed Marty with a raised hand. "Don't take the luggage out yet. We'll check in first." I had an odd feeling the lodge would be all booked out. Marty would be out of a job if it wasn't.

"Sure, sure, snap your fingers when you want me to haul it," he muttered, settling back in his seat.

I stood alongside Sara in the queue, the passage of other tourists causing me to occasionally brush against her. Just to be polite, rather than bump into them, that was.

Three guys in front of us, their Australian accents distinct against the more melodious American and Hawaiian tones, caught my attention. My jaw tightened as I looked down at Sara, wondering if she'd noticed. Would she speak with them, eager for a taste of home? A jolt of possessiveness flashed through me.

She seemed distracted, though, neither returning my gaze nor paying any attention to the other tourists. Her fingers tapped a tattoo on the computer case, faster and faster as we approached the counter. Funny, drumming fingers were my go-to agitated move.

She didn't wait for the receptionist's greeting. "Do you have a room? Single? Dorm? Anything?"

The receptionist heaved a bored sigh. "Sign's up at the front. All full. Mahalo."

"Mahalo," I echoed, pausing for Sara to do the same. Instead, she glanced at the digital clock and calendar at her elbow on the desk.

As she swiveled toward me, she blinked quickly and then lowered long lashes to hide her eyes. "Seems someone's having a huge party this weekend. My invite must still be in the mail." Her lips lifted, but the smile was mirthless. "You know, you don't have to hang around. I can sort my own accommodation."

So she said, yet she looked paler by the minute. "It's fine. Come on." I guided her back to the car, refusing to meet Marty's accusing stare. "We'll get lucky at the next one," I lied. Sod it. Now I kind of felt guilty. But why? I was doing the woman a favor, but I couldn't openly offer the accommodation, or she'd take it the wrong way and read a trade I didn't mean to imply into the offer of an upgrade.

Sara closed her eyes as the car cornered sharply, a

grimace pulling the corners of her mouth down. Bloody hell, this wasn't the way I'd seen the day going.

I leaned close. "Sara? Are you okay?"

Her eyes flashed open, and she smiled, but her lips were rimmed with white. "Yeah, just a little tired. Guess I got a bit too much stimulation last night."

She had me by the balls. Even though she looked increasingly exhausted, slight purple shadowing her beautiful eyes—no, her blue-green eyes, that's what I'd meant to think—even so, she toyed with me, like a lazy cat holding a mouse between its paws, knowing the animal couldn't escape.

Maybe I didn't want to escape.

I swallowed hard and cleared my throat. "Can't say I slept too well myself."

She sat up a little straighter, seeming energized. "Getting wet seems to interfere with sleep patterns."

The cab pulled in to the curb before I had a chance to answer. Just as well, as I had absolutely nothing. Mainly because all the blood in my body had rushed well below my brain.

I climbed out slowly into the shade of a huge palm tree, allowing Marty to duck around and get Sara's door while I took a half-dozen deep breaths, trying to find some self-control. Shoved my hands into the pockets of my chinos, trying to hide the way the damned fabric tented. Definitely should not have gone commando today.

Sara left the flowers in the car but still clutched her laptop as she made resolutely toward the check-in desk. I hung back, knowing the response she'd get. She spoke with the clerk, then her shoulders slumped. As I moved alongside, she put her laptop on the counter and touched a hand to her temple, eyes momentarily closed.

"Okay." She pinched at the bridge of her nose. "Do you have the time, please?"

The check-in clerk glanced at his computer screen. "A little after two, miss."

"Shit." Sara's hand covered her eyes. Her fingers trembled and fluttered away as she brushed the graze on her cheek. She took a deep breath. I knew because I saw the rise of her chest. Not that I was looking.

Hell of a reaction for not getting a room. "Sara? What's wrong?"

She startled, as though she'd forgotten my presence. "Nothing. Just, I have to get something done." She turned back to the receptionist. "Do you have an internet password I can log on with?"

"I'm sorry, miss." The man truly did sound apologetic. "But the passwords are for guests only."

"I'll pay for a room," Sara blurted. "I don't need the actual room, just a secure connection for half an hour. Please, it's important."

The receptionist looked apologetic. "I'm afraid all the codes are linked to specific rooms and metered, so I can't help you."

"Okay, okay." Her fingertips drummed on the laptop. "Where's the nearest coffee shop? With Wi-Fi?"

"A café connection won't be secure," I cut in. "You said you needed security, right?" Hell, she had her lips mashed together, chewing on the seam. She looked truly distressed. But the internet thing wasn't really my fault. And I could fix it easily enough. "Listen, my hotel's not far away. I have a suite, unlimited internet. Just come and use that. We'll organize you a room there, too."

She frowned, but I wasn't certain if it was directed

at me, or if she was distracted by her thoughts, her eyes intent on mine, but her mind clearly elsewhere.

"I don't need a room, but if I could quickly use your internet, I'd be grateful."

"No need for gratitude." Yeah, really no need, because I'd proven myself an absolute ass. I hadn't given a moment's thought to the possibility of Sara being in a rush to do something, but had solely focused on my plan to get her into my hotel. Bloody hell.

I ushered her to the car and nodded to Marty. Damn, this should've been a moment of triumph, proving to my head of security how well the plan had worked from the moment I'd texted him instructions to ring through and book out the first backpackers' hostel. "Take us home, Marty."

Though it took the cab only minutes to traverse the remaining blocks and pull up in front of Outrigger Waikiki, Sara became more agitated by the second. She shoved her left hand through her hair several times, her lips moving soundlessly as though she rehearsed a conversation, then gnawed on her thumbnail, knuckles gleaming white on her clenched fist.

I tucked the laptop under my arm and took her elbow to lead her into the foyer. "Marty will sort the bags."

She seemed distracted and uncaring of what happened to her scant belongings. The lift whisked us to the top level where I had the Diamond Head Oceanfront Suite. Far from the most luxurious place I'd ever stayed, but the views of the beach and the extinct volcano of Diamond Head were superb, and the large suite still offered far more in terms of both comfort and space than I required.

Though I knew getting Marty to book anything

lesser would be impossible, I had a new hankering to try a backpacker's lodge.

Sara didn't even glance around the room, seemingly indifferent to the lavish surrounds. Of course, the premium suites she serviced on *The Spirit of Ohana* paralleled this room, so she had no reason to be impressed.

She took the laptop from me and settled it on the rolled oak desk, then flipped it open. Glanced up from beneath the dark curls that cascaded across her face as she leaned over. "Your password?"

I located the card on a glass side table and passed it to her, then gently nudged a leather upholstered chair into the backs of her knees.

Her fingers flying across the keys, she sank into the chair slowly, staring at the screen as she waited for a connection. She sighed, and her shoulders eased.

"I'll, uh, I'll be over here." I pointed toward the sun-drenched window. Damn, I should've set up her room first so she could log on from there. Though my suite was large, it probably still looked like I was trying to pry into whatever she was doing on the computer.

She flashed me a smile, the nervousness that'd surrounded her for the last hour seeming to dissipate. "Sure. I'll be out of your way in a minute."

I didn't want her to go.

The realization was as sharp as it was ridiculous. I knew nothing about her. Except that she was married and worked on a cruise liner. Rocked the most awesome body I'd ever seen. And had a smart mouth that entranced and titillated me, with lips that tasted like the finest liqueur. *Hell.* How could I find a way to persuade her to stay for a while?

She inhaled sharply, and I jerked around, although I'd been watching her reflection in the window rather than the enormous expanse of white sand and blue ocean spread before me. "Something wrong?"

She half stood, folding one leg beneath her on the chair as she punched frantically at the keys. Pulled her injured arm out of the sling and used both hands on the keyboard. "No. Oh no, he wouldn't." The words were half whispered, and she collapsed into the seat, leg still curled under her.

Bugger the not-looking-like-I-was-prying thing. I crossed the room quickly and crouched alongside the desk so my face was level with hers. "Sara, what's wrong?"

This time, when she tried to blink them away, the tears spilled down her cheeks. Still staring at the computer screen, she seemed not to notice. But I sure as hell did. Each tear was a kick in my bruised gut. What the hell had I done?

"I'm locked out of my bank account," she said.

Despite her tears, relief surged through me. At least this wasn't an issue I'd caused. "Wrong password? Can you reset it?"

"Not wrong. Locked out."

Ah, that'd be something to do with overdrawing or not paying bills. Neither things I had any familiarity with, but it happened. So I heard. Easily fixed. Well, easily fixed, if I could find the words that didn't give her cause to rip me to shreds, anyway. "Don't let it worry you. I can spot you some money until you sort it." There, that sounded perfectly casual, a totally throwaway line. Something anyone would do for a friend, never mind for the woman who'd saved their life. A woman who, disheveled and pale, still stirred my cock in the most inappropriate manner. *Damn.* I shifted a little to hide the evidence.

"No. The bastard's locked me out." The words seemed to jerk her back to the present. "My husband changed the account passwords."

I winced at her mention of a husband. Stupid, I'd told Marty that Sara being married worked for me, right? But her easy admission made it clear she didn't intend for there to be anything between us. "So…call him?" Great, now I was offering marriage advice.

"I lost my phone. In any case, he's not taking my calls."

"Okay. Well, I'm sure we can sort this with the bank on Monday." I wasn't sure of any such thing, but it seemed the right thing to say.

Sara flicked her gaze up to me. "You don't understand. I need twenty thousand dollars. Today."

Chapter Eleven

Sara

As Rick took a half-step back, I realized it probably sounded like I'd propositioned him. How much would I have to put out for twenty grand?

Heck, half an hour ago, I'd have considered paying Rick for his time. But now...shit, now I was destitute. My head pounded, my shoulder and ribs ached, and I'd embarrassed myself by bawling in front of a complete stranger. I stared blankly at the computer screen, waiting for inspiration.

No, not inspiration. Intelligent, practical, independent, I'd work this out. I only needed to apply logic, and that was my forte. "He can't lock me out of my own account. It's either-to-sign but still joint finances. I'll call the bank. What time is it?"

Rick rotated his wrist, a silver-link watch catching the light of one of the soft room lamps set in every corner and nook. "A little after two thirty."

I flicked my fingers up, doing the conversion. Shit. Hawaii was almost a full day behind, so it'd be near midday Sunday in Sydney. I'd never get on to a bank.

I startled as Rick cleared his throat. "Ah, you said your...husband won't take your calls?"

He seemed to have a little trouble spitting out Simon's title. "No. Goes to voicemail and he doesn't call back."

"So assuming he is avoiding you, if you call from a different number, there's a chance he'll pick up?"

I stared at him. How had I not thought of that? Using a cell phone had become such second nature I'd forgotten other options existed.

Rick gestured at the cream phone on the desk. "Zero for reception. They'll give you the country code. Unless you know it?"

My hand hovered over the phone. "Reception will itemize the account, won't they? I'll repay you."

He looked at me for a long moment, as though he wanted to say more. "Sure."

Still my hand hovered, unwilling to pick up the phone. I didn't want to speak to Simon. Actually, I didn't want to ever hear his voice again. How had I not realized that before?

"I'll, uh—" Rick waved at the door to the suite. "I'll give you some privacy."

"No, don't go!" What the hell? I was suddenly afraid of being alone with my husband's voice? So I begged some stranger to stay? I was losing my marbles. "I mean, you don't have to go. I'll only be a minute." I faced the phone, then turned back to him, trying not to sound too pathetic. "You don't happen to have any aspirin, do you?"

He scanned the room, as though there'd be a packet lying around on one of the immaculate surfaces. "No. I'll call down to room service and have them bring some up."

His fingers brushed mine as he reached for the phone, and I jerked back, sticking my trembling hand under my thigh. Anyone would think I'd not been touched by a man for months. Well, I hadn't. Not until last night. God, last night. Why the hell had I thought I should hold back for Simon? Oh yeah, that was right. Rules.

As Rick hung up, I snatched the phone before I could change my mind. I needed to discuss those rules with my husband, find out just how many he was breaking and how many he expected me to bend. I punched in all the codes, then his number. Held my breath as his phone rang twice. "Simon? Don't hang up, it's me. I know you've probably been trying to call, but I lost my phone." One of my mentors had taught me that if I wanted to catch someone on a larger wrongdoing, I should always give them an out for a minor infraction.

Simon groaned, and I recognized his Sunday-morning sleep-in slur. "Sara? How the hell did you lose your phone? That was bloody near new."

No concern for my welfare, straight to the expense. Amazing how mean he could be with money, considering how much he liked to flaunt our wealth. "I dropped it in the sea."

Rick stiffened where he stood staring out of the large plate-glass window at the panorama of ocean and mountain laid before him. Damn, I hadn't meant to let him know about the phone; I didn't want him to feel responsible.

Simon groaned again, and I could hear him thrust the covers aside and his bare feet smack the hand-milled oak floorboards. I tried not to picture the nubile young body alongside him in the bed. Instead I reminded myself that I *wanted* him to be in bed with someone. That way, I also had a leave pass. And it might as well be Emma as one of the many other bits of skirt my husband chased.

I'd wallowed for a week or two in the Solomons, trying to hate the perky child-woman, but Simon was big enough and handsome enough to shoulder the blame himself. His looks had swept me off my own feet when I was a teenager, and the last twelve years had only improved him, his cynical, slightly dissipated mien presenting very nicely in his two-thousand-dollar business suits. Only a rare woman could resist his aura of money, power, and outright self-confidence. Bastard.

A rasp came through the speaker as though he passed a hand over his face. "Well, what is it, Sara?"

His coldness firmed my resolve. "The money, Simon. I told you I need to transfer it this weekend."

Shuffling noises now, as he moved across the room. Every sound so familiar, I could picture each movement. Twenty steps from the king-sized bed to Simon's walk-in closet, where his suits and business shirts lined one wall, and shelves with casual clothes filled the other. A rotating shoe rack near the entry into his en suite, each pair of custom-made leather loafers polished to a mirror-finish and held in shape by a hand-carved shoe tree. Opposite, the motorized tie rack holding his vast selection of imported silk ties.

With my eyes closed, I heard him reach for the monogrammed robe that hung from a set of solid brass hooks on the door. A creak of leather as he sat in the wingback chair alongside the dressing room. "Sara?"

"I'm here." Where the hell else did he think I'd be? Stranded with no money. This needed to be sorted, and sorted now.

Simon's tone softened, as though he spoke close to the phone. "Do you remember being in love?"

Shit. I'd not expected this. Instead, I'd persuaded

myself Emma would be there, that he would give me his blessing to even the score before we tried to repair our marriage.

Obviously, I should say yes. That'd be the polite response. The correct response. The female response. But truth was I didn't remember love. I'd been nineteen and in my first year of law. At twenty-eight and about to join his father's law firm, Simon had seemed far older, a powerful man. I had, literally, been swept off my feet, and I'd believed my friends when they told me how lucky I was.

Still, it was nice that he'd try for a trip down memory lane. Instead of answering, I deflected. "Do you remember?"

He chuckled, low and soft. "Of course."

Okay, I might not remember love, but I remembered the inherent sexual command of that tone, how I'd be wet in an instant. I smiled, moving the mouthpiece closer. "That's good."

He purred in my ear. "That's why I want to rush this through, Sara. I love Emma. Totally. Desperately. I don't see that we should be punished for your behavior."

I snatched the phone from my ear and glared at it like I held a cobra by the neck.

Love? I realized now why the concept had seemed so foreign. He had never even used the word before. He no more knew what it meant than I did. "What the hell are you talking about, Simon? Rush what through? And what behavior?"

He sighed heavily, his habitual cue for a pedantic dissertation. "Just because you choose to roam the world behaving as though you're a single woman, there's no reason I should be condemned to being alone."

"Alone?" I could barely squeak the word out. Simon's infidelity had never been a secret; he'd always taken great trouble to…not apologize, but to buy what he seemed to consider to be retrospective permission. For every affair I'd discovered, there'd been a new piece of jewelry, a new set of promises. "Since when have you ever been alone? And what the hell are you talking about? You know *I've* never been unfaithful."

Rick's shoulders tensed, though he kept his gaze on the window.

I angled slightly away from him, hissing into the mouthpiece. "Jesus, Simon, you know I've never had sex with anyone but you." I cringed as Rick fumbled the glass he nursed, then set it carefully on the side table, keeping his back to me.

Great, he probably thought I'd knocked him back because I was frigid, not because I was outraged at his proposition. Well, I needed to sort Simon before I could deal with Rick. I focused on our conversation. "And that's a damn sight more than we can say for you, isn't it? Anyway, what do you mean, 'rush this through'? Rush what, where?"

Simon didn't apologize or retract, but I hadn't expected him to. Twelve years had taught me something, at least.

As always, he kept his tone measured, cultured, and calm. "The divorce, Sara. I intend to marry Emma as soon as the decree nisi becomes absolute."

I hunched forward, gripping my stomach with the arm still in a sling. "What the hell, Simon? We said we'd take a break and talk about a divorce. We haven't discussed a damn thing."

"It was your suggestion; you made your stance quite

clear. And in light of the fact that you deserted me many months ago, I've already logged the requisite paperwork with the courts."

I was going to be sick. My eyes closed, I tried to make sense of what Simon—*my husband*—was saying. Cool air washed over me, and I heard Rick open the door and murmur to someone. He closed it with a soft rasp of the latch and crossed the room behind me, avoiding eye contact as he discreetly made his way back to his window-gazing position.

I unclenched my jaw. "Simon, you know that for a no-fault divorce we have to have been separated for twelve months."

His tone was icy now, no longer hidden from the woman sharing his bedroom. Bed. "Who said anything about no-fault? You deserted me when I was handling an extremely stressful case. Fortunately for my mental well-being, Emma was able to support me both professionally and personally. Everything you should've been doing, instead of holidaying around the world."

The breath exploded from me in a rush, and I stood quickly, hoping the action would somehow drag oxygen into my starved lungs. "Holidaying? You know I had placements in the Solomons, and I've been working over here. Simon, you said to take time out. I thought you meant we'd have a break, both work out what we wanted from this marriage."

"Oh, I have calculated precisely what I want. I want out. We'll have a no-contest divorce."

The bastard. The fucking bastard. Not so much for divorcing me, I wasn't even sure how I felt about that. Not unhappy. But I was furious he'd played me for a fool. I knew Simon. He had to have a reason why he'd fabricate a formal separation and rush his marriage to Emma. For love?

That thought stabbed deeper than any other. Why should he get to know love when I never had?

I pulled my arm from the sling and passed my hand over my eyes, as though I could wipe the confusion from my mind. "Okay. Whatever. Just unlock the account so I can make the transfer to the orphanage. I'll pick up a new phone and call you to discuss the d-divorce details later." Damn, why had my tongue stuttered on the word when, already, a spark of hope burned inside me? I'd be free. I could keep exploring the world or return to work in the Solomons.

My gaze slid to Rick's broad back, silhouetted by the mid-afternoon sunshine streaming through the picture windows and framed by the blue-green ocean.

I could do anything I wanted.

Or anyone I wanted.

No more rules.

Excitement tingled in my chest, the same sense of freedom and potential that the sight of the Na Pali coast stirred within me. Adventure, a foray into the unknown. If kissing Rick had driven me wild, what would the touch of his mouth on my naked flesh do?

"Sara?" Simon's cultured tone jerked me back to reality. Barely in time, as my hand had already found my nipple, caressing it as my breaths became short and I willed Rick to turn toward me.

"The bank accounts remain as they are until the divorce settlement."

"You can't freeze our assets, Simon. I need access to funds."

"They're not *our* assets."

I frowned at the phone. "What do you mean? All the accounts are in joint names."

"You've never worked the hours I have. Your income has never matched mine. I think you've received more than your fair share of my largesse."

An outright lie. Until the last year, I'd worked far longer hours than he had. Sure, not working for Daddy, like he did, I didn't get the mega pay packet. But nor did I spend money as Simon had.

"We agreed years ago that our finances were joint." I'd even transferred the house my gran had left me to Simon so he could benefit from negatively gearing a loan to avoid paying tax. A loan that provided money he used for frivolous purchases, cars, and clothes. A loan I'd then worked to discharge, even though I'd already owned the property. Everything we owned was in joint names. Wasn't it? Except for his garage full of imported cars which, in truth, I knew little about. But what else?

"That was before you took off on a year's holiday."

"It's not a holiday. My pay is still going into that account. I literally do not have money for food or accommodation or any other damn thing until you unlock the account."

He sighed heavily, his tone soothing an irate child. "Look, I'll tell you what. Open a new account over there, and I'll transfer you living expenses."

I couldn't open a new account, the banks were shut, and I'd be aboard *The Spirit of Ohana* on Monday.

Except, I wouldn't be. I had to return to Australia to sort this out.

The phone trembled in my hand. Shit, I couldn't return; I didn't have the cash for a ticket. Simon had effectively stranded me.

Okay, so I needed a counterproposal. I willed my voice calm, pretending I was negotiating a business contract. "Simon, I can't open an account over here. Listen to me. Minimize the balance of the joint account and unlock it so I have access to funds." I bit my tongue, hating to offer him such an advantage. But it was only temporary. I'd finish my job, earn enough cash to head back to Australia next month, and sort this mess out.

His stubble rasped as though he scratched his jaw. "Okay. How much do you need?"

I swallowed a sigh of relief. He could be damn awkward when it came to money, and for a moment I'd not been able to see a way out. "Well, most importantly, I need the twenty thousand for the orphanage. After that—"

"You're being ridiculous, Sara. By the way, I couldn't have the divorce papers served, as you're itinerant. Declaration of decree nisi is next week. Goodbye."

Chapter Twelve

Rick

I'd tried not to listen to the conversation. Well, not to be caught listening, anyway. But it didn't escape my attention that Sara hung up the phone without saying goodbye, nor that she replaced the receiver in the cradle softly, not with the slamming anger of someone deliberately disconnecting a call. Which meant she'd been hung up on.

I turned from the window, took in her countenance, and strode across the room to slide my arms around her. Pale as ivory, she sagged against me.

Great, the one time Marty wasn't hanging around like a bad smell. "Uh, can I get you anything?" So bloody wrong that the feel of her soft curves molded against my body stirred my cock right now. Didn't help that my hands rested just above the plump curve of her arse. I should move them.

I didn't.

She pulled away from me. Drew herself up straight, though confusion still clouded her eyes. "No, I—" She touched fingertips to her forehead.

"Are you okay?"

She nodded and shrugged at the same time. "Yeah. Apparently, I'm practically divorced. Did you have any luck with the aspirin?"

Divorced? That didn't play into my plan. I'd already bent my self-imposed rules from *no women* to *married women only*. Not that I'd actually gone there, but I was more than happy for Sara to be my first. I dug in my pocket for the packet room service had delivered. "Only these. Not particularly strong, but I've arranged for a doctor to come by and check you out. I'll have him prescribe something more effective then."

Sara had moved away, her fingers pressing white against the desk as she steadied herself. When she reached for the packet, her hand trembled.

"Sit down, first," I directed. "I'll get you a drink to take them with."

She held up one finger. "I've just got to pinch your internet again. Two minutes more, okay?"

"Whatever you need." I crossed swiftly to the kitchen. Aspirin wasn't going to cut it. Whatever she had heard on the other end of the phone, not all of which I'd been able to decipher, she'd damn near fainted. I'd seen that happen enough times to recognize the sudden pallor and cold skin, though Mother seemed to have a knack for deploying the malady at will.

I poured a slug of scotch into a cut-crystal glass. Filled another with water so Sara could make her own decision.

As I returned to the desk, she unwound a khaki-green money belt from around her middle. Red scored her flesh where the canvas had dug in. I could soothe that. Rub lotion into the abraded skin. Maybe kiss it better. My nostrils flared, and I forced my eyes away as she dropped her shirt back into place and rummaged in the money belt. She withdrew a credit card and a slip of paper. Chewing on her lip, she glanced between the screen and the card as she transferred information into the computer. Still standing, she drummed her fingers on the desk for a second, nodded decisively, and hit the enter key. Eyes shut, she blew out a short breath, then closed the screen and flipped down the cover of the laptop.

As she turned toward me, she flicked her ringlets over one shoulder and held out her hand for the tablets. Popped a couple in her mouth, eyed the glasses I'd placed on the desk, and picked up the scotch. She tossed the shot back in one smooth pro movement, her neck arched like a swan's. Then squinted up at me, her eyes watering as she coughed and spluttered, the knuckles of the hand holding the glass pressed to her mouth.

I hid my grin and took the scotch from her, nudging the water glass forward. "Not a big drinker, I take it?"

She waved me off. "Never had straight spirits in my life. Do they all taste so vile?"

I angled my chin toward the scotch bottle on the granite bench. The bar fridge suddenly hummed as though trying to draw attention. "Well, I'm not about to offer to try what is evidently poison, but I can assure you a nice single malt slides down far more easily than that appeared to."

Sara blew out a long breath between pursed lips, openly assessing me. The tip of her tongue appeared for an instant, chasing the alcohol. I swallowed hard, unable to look away from the tiny pink pyramid. Thinking of the other one that would match.

Her tongue seemed to take an unnecessarily long time tracing the perfect Cupid's bow of her lips before she spoke. "I do prefer something that goes down easily."

I should've had a drink to cover up my own urge to splutter. My interest flared. In my groin, to be precise, not that I'd managed to damp it down for long. This girl certainly liked to use her mouth. And if she wanted to play, damn, so did I. "I find it's best to find the perfect balance of rough and smooth. A certain edge adds a piquancy, makes the experience far more enjoyable." I closed the space between us, only our clothes separating us.

The green blaze in her left eye shot fireworks as a teasing grin lifted her lips. "It sounds like you're drawing on experience?"

I stroked a finger across her lips as though she'd missed a drop of scotch, then transferred it to my mouth. Her breath fanned across my chest, her pupils enlarging, though she didn't drop her gaze as I spoke. "Some things are worth taking a little time to perfect."

As I shifted my hand back to her face, the tip of her tongue crept out, brushing across my finger. *Fuck.* My dick actually hurt, straining against the confines of my chinos—straining to get to her. This unholy hell of tormenting banter was like nothing I'd ever experienced. Yet much as I wanted to pick Sara up, toss her on the huge bed, and thoroughly ravish her, I didn't want her to stop talking. Not unless her mouth was full of me, anyway.

She turned her head and mouthed my palm, her lips soft and firm, both promise and invitation. "So in your vast experience, do you find it better to go straight to the hard stuff or work up to it slowly?"

Oh, I was worked up all right, and well ready to give her the hard stuff. I pretended to consider her question, sliding my hands around to the small of her back, above the delicious curve of her arse. "My recommendation would depend on whether you've built a tolerance. While I'll happily go straight to the hard stuff, you're new to this, so I'd ease you into it." I indicated her empty glass. "Given that you're almost a virgin."

A shadow crossed her features, and I tightened my grip, afraid I'd overstepped the mark.

Her mouth twisted wryly. "Apparently. But when the rules are erased, it's never too late to learn, I guess. I planned to add different experiences to my résumé this year."

Rules? And different? How different did she want? I didn't want to bore her, but I also didn't want to come across as some sex-starved pervert. Though nothing I did with her would be perverted.

I slid my hands lower, cupping the full cheeks of her bottom. Damn, I needed to see that naked. My fingers stroked down the crease of her arse, and I pressed my lips experimentally to hers.

She responded instantly, leaning into me, her lips opening eagerly. Her tongue matched mine stroke for stroke, and I slid one hand into her hair, holding her close as I looted the sweetness and scotch she offered.

Her fingers worked under the hoodie I still wore, and I pulled back, ripped the sweatshirt over my head, and gave her hands full range. She slid them up over my abs and found my nipples. Pinched them as she studied my face, her lips parted and eyes dark with desire.

My chest heaved beneath her roaming hands. Christ, no woman had ever touched me like this, with this mixture of exploration and demand. Instead, they tended to be more focused on artfully arranging themselves across a bed, carefully displaying their underfed, overexercised figures to full advantage.

She had to stop while I still retained a modicum of self-control.

"Sara—"

She leaned forward and slashed her hot tongue across my erect nipple.

"Jesus!"

She jerked back, suddenly uncertain. "Sorry."

"No." I shook my head vehemently, unable to string words in a coherent sentence. "Good... But you need to stop." At least, until I had her naked.

I'd spoiled the moment, though, and she stepped away, neatly avoiding my questing hands. She fiddled with the untucked edge of her blouse. "Actually, I do have another favor to ask."

My gut sank. I'd known this was too good to be true; here came the sting. A twenty-thousand-dollar sting, to be precise.

She flipped open the top button of her blouse.

I swallowed hard.

Her lips quirked. Another button.

Oxygen was in short supply in the suddenly overheated room. Twenty grand wasn't really much in the scheme of things, was it?

She toyed with the next button. "Would it be okay if I used your shower? Looks like it'll be a few hours before I can get a room sorted, and work was kind of hectic this morning..." She wrinkled her nose adorably.

She didn't want my money? The unfamiliarity of the notion silenced me for a moment. Lord, she didn't need to shower; I'd happily lick the sweat from every inch of her sweet body.

Instead of offering to do so, I took the more

gentlemanly option and gallantly waved a hand toward the bathroom. "Sure. Help yourself."

She offered a small smile and headed toward the bathroom, tight butt wiggling alluringly beneath her black work pants. The pants she'd be out of, within seconds.

As the door closed behind her, I turned to the desk and picked up the phone. "Marty. Do something for me?"

"Live for it, lad."

Despite the bodyguard's heavy sarcasm, I knew the sentiment held true. "Happy to make you happy, then, Marty. Use the card and go pick me up a new phone, would you?"

"Same SIM?"

"No, new number."

"Don't you think that's taking avoiding your mother to extremes, then, lad?"

I turned a pen end over end, trying to balance it on the desk on each flip. Determined not to focus on the sound of running water, or visualize Sara naked beneath the cascade. "Not for me. Sara's lost hers."

"Sara, huh? Let me see, which one was she? Oh, the *married* mermaid, right? The one we just spent half a day ferrying around instead of checking into a backpackers? The same Sara you had me arrange a room here for? Oddly enough, I seem to be dangling the key for that room between my fat sausages, laddie. No one's come to claim it. Have ye lost her, then?"

"No, she's in the shower." I winced. That'd come back to bite me. I sure as heck wouldn't mention the divorce, then. "Make the cell phone top of the range, Marty. Get a nice case for it, too, okay?"

"Your word is, as ever, my command. Will I be canceling the extra room, then?"

My gaze on the bathroom door, I shook my head. No? Yes? "No. Just slip me the key when you bring the phone." That way I could pretend not to have it if things panned out the way I hoped.

The drumming of water in the adjacent room stilled. Amazing I could tell that over the increased pounding of my heart. I took a step toward the door. Should I knock and hopefully prevent Sara from getting dressed? But what if she didn't plan to go any further? What if she'd been toying with me—again?

The door opened before I'd made up my mind.

Sara wasn't toying with me. Or if she was, she played a damn-fine game. She hadn't dressed but wore a hotel-supplied fluffy robe, belted loosely at her waist. The front spread open in a deep V, framing the swell of her full breasts, the slightest hint of pale blush-colored areola peeking around the edge of the soft toweling. Her wet hair cascaded thick and dark, framing her slightly flushed face.

It'd be my greatest pleasure to turn that freshly scrubbed look into freshly fucked.

Chapter Thirteen

Sara

My nipples peaked hard against the soft toweling as Rick's gaze swept my body. God, I hadn't felt like this since…well, since forever. I'd been swept off my feet by my husband's—nearly ex-husband's—forceful attention more than a decade ago, but there had never been this animal attraction. Even with Jay, the one guy with whom I'd almost seriously have considered doing the dirty, the lust had never been this intense. Maybe because I'd always had rules to control me.

Well, not anymore.

I wanted Rick. And maybe I deserved him. I'd been a disciplined, altruistic wife-lawyer and was trying hard to be an all-round good person. Yet I'd almost died, and now my husband was ripping me off. Maybe Rick could be my reward, my gift to me.

I fought the impulse to pull my robe closed. I'd spent ages arranging the fabric in the bathroom's massive mirror, and my strategy certainly had the desired effect. Rick's gaze slammed to a halt on my breasts, the sculpted muscles of his chest quickly rising and falling. I stood still. If he wanted this, he'd have to cover the few feet between us. I'd been as forward as I dared. Anything beyond flirting didn't come naturally to me. Hell, it didn't even come practiced. Much as I enjoyed sex,

Simon had always orchestrated and demanded; I'd simply complied.

Simon.

Damn, I didn't need to be thinking about him right now. I'd maxed out my credit card and transferred the emergency fund I kept on my traveler's card. Though Simon was co-signatory on the cards, he'd overlooked them in his locking of the bank accounts. That left me only four grand short of the money I'd promised the orphanage, though I'd have absolutely nothing to live on for the next couple of days. But I couldn't do anything until Simon had time to gather himself and renegotiate. I knew him. Slamming down the phone didn't signify the end of the discussion; it was his signature move when he played for time to work an angle. If he wanted the divorce to go through quickly, he'd have to get back to me. The question was, would it be in time for the orphanage?

But that wasn't the question Rick's green eyes were asking as he slowly crossed the room toward me, one side of his mouth curving up to crease a deep furrow from the corner of his lips to the outside edge of his eye. He left almost eight inches between us. Enough room that he could watch as his forefinger traced slowly down the edge of my robe, never touching my skin. Down to the belt tied loosely around my waist and then back up to my neck again, as I arched toward him, willing him to brush my flesh.

He slipped his thumb beneath the robe and peeled it back to expose my shoulder. "I'm sorry." Warm breath whispered across my skin as he leaned in and pressed his lips gently to the lilac-and-sunset bruise that marred my shoulder. I flickered my eyes closed for a moment, the contact so soft I needed to close off my sight to enhance my sense of touch, to fully appreciate his caress.

His lips moved across the top of my shoulder and up the side of my neck, finding the frantically pounding pulse below my ear. Then his teeth closed on my earlobe, tugging gently on the gold hoops I rarely changed. His breath hot in my ear now, delicious tremors rippled through my body.

One of his hands found my waist, easing me closer. Just as well, because I needed something solid to lean on. And he was solid. Hard, in fact, despite the constraining fabric of his trousers. His erection was rigid and hot against my hip. I could feel his need, his desire, and it heightened my own.

I turned my head, seeking his mouth, and Rick obliged instantly. His lips teased and retreated until I slid a hand up over the defined mound of his pecs, across his hardened shoulders, and grabbed the back of his neck. I held him still as I plunged my tongue into his mouth, greedily stealing his taste.

His hand wound into my hair as though he'd not let me escape, and his tongue tangled with mine in the erotic rhythm that brought me so close to the edge.

Too close. I gasped and stepped back, but only a little. Enough that his hand could stroke down the robe again, the air between us charged with electricity, waiting for the contact of skin on skin to ignite the sparks.

He slid his fingers beneath the robe, stroking along my collarbone and then down, sliding over the curve of my breast. His lips curled into a smile as he found my nipple, large and hot enough to attract a volcanologist.

"Yes." The word hissed from him, a cheer, not a

question. "I need to see you."

I nodded but closed my eyes. The air was cool against my skin as he took the lapels of the robe, sliding it over my shoulders and down my back so it draped like a Grecian gown from my forearms, held in place by the belt.

Unable to bear the silence, I flicked my eyes open. Rick stood back a little, his lips parted, nostrils flared as though he struggled for breath.

He glanced up and caught my gaze on him. "You're...magnificent. Even better than I imagined. And I assure you I'd put quite a bit of time and effort into that imagining." The sardonic grin tip-tilted his lips again. "I was horribly afraid I'd be reduced to fantasizing like a teenager and never know the reality. But this..." His gaze was on my breasts again, and he seemed unable to look and talk at the same time. He extended a hand, almost tentatively, his fingers hot on my flesh as he traced the swell of my breast. Slid his hand beneath the pendulous curve and lifted the heaviness in his palm. "Good Lord." He cupped my other breast with his free hand and hefted the weight. His thumbs brushed across both nipples simultaneously, and the tight buds doubled in size. He groaned. "That is so bloody sexy."

Painful. That's what it was. If I didn't get Rick's mouth on my breast soon, I was pretty sure my nipples would explode.

But he had other ideas. His mouth captured mine, chest hard against my breasts. The contact of sensitive nipples against his honed muscles was unbearable ecstasy, and I moaned into his mouth and pressed harder against him. His hands stole up my back, then cupped my shoulder blades to pull me closer. His leg slid between my knees.

I ground against the ridged muscle of his thigh, my hand snaking up and around the back of his neck to support myself.

Rick bent his knee, thrust his thigh higher, and drew me down upon it, his hands closing over my butt to guide my rhythm.

"Enough," I managed to gasp, though my hips swayed in betrayal, every grind of my pussy against the firmness of his leg bringing me closer to orgasm. "I don't want to just dry hump you."

He pulled his head away a few inches, his eyes sparkling with laughter. "Did you seriously say dry hump?"

I nodded, then found my tongue. Unfortunately, briefly out of his mouth. "Uh-huh. Though dry isn't technically the right word."

"Lord, I think I love you." His hands tightened on my butt.

Okay, I could excuse him that oral slip. Heat of the moment and all that stuff. And it sure as hell was hot in here.

He pulled away from me as though the temperature was getting to him, too. "Bedroom?" He jerked his head toward the other room.

"Bedroom," I affirmed, though I wasn't too sure how I'd get there, my legs like over-chewed gum. Or was that under-chewed? I'd never gotten into the very American habit of gum-chewing. Oh, God, why was I thinking about gum now?

Rick took my hand and drew me toward the bedroom.

I flicked one finger up. "Hang on." I poured another

slug of whiskey into my glass. The stuff tasted vile, but along with the tablets, it seemed to make my headache recede. Not so much the pain in my shoulder, though. I held the glass out to him in offering.

A frown flickered across his face. "No. I don't need it."

He thought I did? No, I needed ice, something to cool me down so this wouldn't be all over too quickly.

He led me into the bedroom and guided me to the bed. As he wrapped his arms around me again, I flinched, his hard abs brushing my bruised ribs.

He pulled away. "That hurts, huh?"

"No, no. It's fine." Because, dammit, it had to be. I wanted this. The odd broken bone wasn't going to stand in my way now. Ha, no bone would come between me and Rick's boner. I snorted with amusement, then quickly sucked the snort back in. Shit, was I drunk?

My knees certainly seemed to think so. Either that or they just felt that the quicker I arrived on his bed, the better. The quicker I came on his bed, the better, too. I sniggered again.

Somehow, I was lying back on the bed, Rick alongside me, tracing his fingers down the parted front of my robe. He stopped at the belt, though. I needed him to go lower.

Braced on one arm, he leaned over me. He still smelled so good. I closed my eyes to breathe in the fragrance. Forcing them open again seemed to take a long time.

His lips found mine, and he kissed me deeply. His hand moved to my thigh, teasing at the edge of my robe. I allowed my thighs to part. Flat on my back, I'd look thinner, right? Or would everything spread out sideways? Dammit, my boobs had probably wandered off opposite sides of the bed.

No, at least the left one hadn't. I knew because Rick's lips were on my nipple, and I arched my back and thrust the fiery nub into his mouth. At the same moment, his questing hand found my core, tracing through my slippery folds and expertly locating my clitoris. The guy must be a gynecologist; he knew my body better than I did. Come to think of it, this was another nice hotel room. What exactly did Rick Winchester do for a living?

His thumb massaged my clitoris as his middle finger stroked my swollen cleft, and I moaned with need. Who the hell cared what he did for a living?

Tiny lines feathered out from his eyes. "Like this?"

I should think of something funny to say, keep the interaction light, but my entire focus was on the pounding, pulsing need between my legs.

He stroked the finger a little deeper, teasing but not quite entering. Brushed his lips across my temple, then murmured in my ear. "I want to taste you. Is that all right?"

How British could he be? Was he going to ask permission to make every move? And how in the hell was that such a turn-on that I'd completely lost the ability of rational speech?

He stroked my folds again and then brought the finger up to his mouth, slowly licking at my sticky musk.

I could barely breathe. "Oh, fuck." Yeah, six years of law school and that's the best I could manage.

He grinned. "I'll take that as a request."

The mattress shifted as he moved to his knees, bending over me to trail kisses between my breasts. He pushed aside my robe and swirled his tongue across my stomach, then peppered the inside of my thighs with tiny nips.

Heart pounding, I shoved up onto my elbows to watch his dark head disappear between my splayed thighs. But as I moved, pain speared from my shoulder to my ribs, stealing my breath and locking my body rigid.

In a flash, Rick moved back up the bed. "You're in pain?"

I tried to shake my head, but tears starred my vision as I grabbed at my injured shoulder. "No, it's okay." But it wasn't. The pain grew, as though I'd suddenly woken it.

His face loomed above me, a line etched between his eyes. "Sara? Are you okay?"

Yes, of course. I was practically naked in bed with a gorgeous man. And I was practically divorced. And practically drunk. But, damn, now the pain in my ribs was screaming as well, and I needed to drown it out, needed to dull it so I could focus on this. Only, what was this? Everything seemed to be slipping, and I couldn't afford to let it. I couldn't let go of the threads I was trying to hold together. The orphans needed to eat. I had to pray that I could work out how to get my life back together. And love, well, I'd love to have sex with this hot guy with the sexy accent, who loomed over me. Only, now he didn't loom. Now he'd rolled off the bed and picked up the phone on the nightstand. Spoke quietly into it, then turned back to me. He tugged a sheet from one side of the bed and gently covered me with it. Eased the edge of the linen down and bent to kiss my breast, a look of regret on his face.

Then he slipped away, fading as the room faded.

Chapter Fourteen

Rick

I slammed open the door at the first, faint sound of a scratch. "Jesus, Marty."

My bodyguard nodded. "Happy to answer to either name, lad."

I glanced frantically up and down the hall. Pointless, as Marty wouldn't let anyone follow him. Damn. I ushered him in. "You didn't see a doctor in the foyer? An ambulance?"

Concern clarified in his rheumy eyes. "What's wrong, lad? Are you okay? Is your head playing up?"

"Fine, I'm fine." I slumped into a leather tub chair, rubbing distractedly at my face. "It's not me. Sara. She's passed out."

He went straight into protective mode. "Where is she? Did she speak to anyone? Does anyone know she's here?"

"Fuck all that, Marty. She passed out. I don't know what's wrong with her. Reception is sending an emergency doctor."

"We need to get her to her own room, then." He dug a key card from his pocket, scattering a handful of the throat lozenges he habitually sucked on. "Where is she?"

"No, you're not moving her." I thrust to my feet, barring his access.

He held up placating hands. "Okay, lad, take it easy. I know you're upset. But this isn't going to add anything good to the publicity, is it? We'll just get her to her room and keep our noses clean, then there'll be no problem. No reason the lass shouldn't be staying in the same hotel as you. Pure freakish coincidence. But we've got to limit the adverse exposure."

"Christ, Marty! It's not all about appearances. We were…messing around." Fantastic, this took me right back to when I was seventeen and caught in the back of the four-wheel drive with Emmelina What's-her-face. "And she just went into some kind of spasm, then passed out."

"A spasm?" Now true concern pumped blood into Marty's ruddy face. "Hell, lad, I thought you meant too-much-champagne passed out. Does she have an alert bracelet of some kind? Is she breathing?"

I guiltily realized that I hadn't actually checked. One moment Sara had been totally into what I was doing, so incredibly sweet on my tongue, then she'd moaned, clutched at her ribs, and, turning whiter by the second, had slipped into unconsciousness.

Marty brushed past me, crossed the room, then dropped to his knees alongside the bed. He flicked back the cover to take Sara's wrist, to his credit only briefly glancing up at me as her luscious curves were exposed. "Her pulse is fine. Far as I can tell." He patted at her cheeks. "Lass, can ye hear me?"

She stirred slightly, shuddering as she moaned.

An authoritative knock on the outer door jerked my head around.

Marty was in front of me instantly. "Lock yerself in the bathroom, lad. Leave this to me. You don't need any more drama attached."

"No—"

"Trust me. Your mother rang. She's on her way over here. Private charter this time, not the broomstick, I believe."

Shit. This had gone to hell in a handbasket. Mother was precisely the complication I didn't need. Well, not that I needed this one, either. I rubbed hard at my jaw. It'd be wrong to desert Sara, but what the hell could I achieve by hanging around?

Marty gave me a shove, and I crossed to the bathroom as my handler made his way across the suite to let the doctor in.

My ear pressed to the door, I caught the doctor's low singsong cadence. "Has she taken any illicit substances?"

"Uh, no." Marty's uncertainty made it obvious he'd recognized the flaw in his plan.

"Prescription medication? Alcohol? How did she get these lacerations and contusions?"

As I pulled the bathroom door open, the doctor jerked upright from his bent position at the bedside as though he anticipated an attack.

I nodded at him. "She got the injuries saving me. From a boating accident."

Recognition lifted the doctor's eyebrows, and I groaned inwardly. Evidently, agreeing to host a press release had not managed to contain the news.

"Ah, yes, sir. Mr. Winchester, isn't it? I'd heard you are currently gracing our little corner of the world. It's something of a thrill to meet you in person."

The doctor seemed to have forgotten about Sara, and I gestured at the bed. "She had a finger of scotch, maybe a little more. And two aspirin. I don't know if she'd had anything aboard the ship this morning, though."

"Alcohol and aspirin?" The doctor made a small shrug, then ferreted in his brown bag. "Could you have someone call the boat, see if she was prescribed anything from there?"

"I'm on it." Marty stepped a few feet away from the bed, pulling out his cell phone.

"And do you know if she's eaten today?"

No, I bloody didn't. And obviously, it would have been a damn fine thing for me to suggest, instead of dragging her from one falsely booked-out backpacker's accommodation to another, then subjecting her to whatever it was that had gone down with her husband. I tried to block out what had happened after that phone call, because that just made me feel worse. "I'm not sure. She startled and grabbed her shoulder. Doc on the ship said it was dislocated."

The doctor turned down the bedsheet, and I averted my gaze, scowling at Marty as, still holding his phone to his ear, he failed to follow suit.

"Hmm, no, I don't think there's a dislocation. Definitely trauma, though, a sprain. Or it may have been dislocated and the doctor popped it back in? The bruising is extensive enough to point to that. But certainly nothing to worry about now."

Marty had scribbled something on a piece of paper, which he passed to the doctor as he shoved the phone back in his pocket. "The ship's medic has disembarked, but this is the information from her file."

The doctor glanced at the paper and bobbed his head happily. "Well, that pretty much explains it. No dislocation, but trauma and deep tissue bruising.

Extensive contusions to her ribs. Was the young lady exposed to the elements for very long? I think, sir, we'll find she's suffering from exhaustion, coupled with abuse of medication and alcohol. But she'll be just fine."

Exhaustion? It'd seemed far more intense than that. "Can you do anything more for the pain? Obviously, it's an issue." Actually, I was the issue. She'd been dealing fine until I shoved my way into her life. And then shoved her into my bed.

"Nothing to do for the shoulder, sir, except to keep it immobilized as much as possible. I'll ice the joint, and I can most certainly provide pain relief. Other than that, it's simply a matter of bed rest."

The word "bed" shouldn't be the one to leap out at me. I should focus on "rest." Which had absolutely nothing to do with what I desired to do in bed with her. "But you're sure she's okay?"

"I am, Mr. Winchester. Her pulse and respiration are entirely normal. If she is still in severe pain in a couple of days, I'd suggest she come in for an MRI and we'll check for further soft tissue damage, but I don't expect to find any. I could bring her round now, with a little ammonia, but it's better for her to sleep while she's able. An injured shoulder isn't the easiest thing to accommodate."

Yeah, and probably not made any easier by having a six-foot-four Neanderthal pawing at her. "Okay. Well, if you write scripts for whatever she needs, we'll get hold of it."

Marty grunted, doubtless knowing the job would fall to him. He closed the door behind the doctor and then turned back to me. "Right then, best we get you out of this room."

I picked up the empty scotch glass, only to shift it uselessly from one hand to the other. "What are you talking about?"

"Well, we can't move the girl, can we? So you take her room for now while we work out how best to clean up this mess. In any case, your mother will be here shortly. Probably best you distance yourself."

"Oh, believe me, I'd love to."

He rolled his eyes. "Distance yourself from Mrs. Grant, I mean." He stressed the title. "I don't suppose you happen to know how to contact her husband? As next of kin, I assume he should be notified of this change in circumstance."

"How the hell would I— Oh, wait. Yeah, I do know how." Redial. "But I think she's not on the best terms with him at the moment."

"Well, I doubt sharing that she's unconscious in your suite will improve that standing at all, but I'd say he has a right to know, don't you think?"

I thumped the glass on the table. "I'll call. You go get the meds."

The long-distance connection clunked and chirruped. Hopefully, Sara's husband wouldn't pick up.

Predictably, he did.

"Mr. Grant?"

"Prescott," a voice growled, exhibiting the usual degree of caution that accompanied answering unknown international numbers. Even I got those sometimes— though I quite enjoyed the chance to speak with someone who had no idea who I was, even if they did find it necessary to inform me my internet security had been compromised. Fat chance of that ever happening.

"Sorry, I'm looking for Sara Grant's husband."

"Speaking."

Great, not an auspicious start to the conversation. "Mr. Gr—Prescott, I'm a, ah, friend of your wife's. I'm calling to advise she's been involved in an accident."

Silence reigned for a moment as Prescott processed the information. No doubt working out how quickly he could reach his wife's side. "She has adequate travel insurance. The documents will be with her paperwork."

What the hell? "Mr. Prescott, your wife was quite seriously injured. I'll arrange for her care, but is there someone she'd like to be with her?" Anyone other than this arrogant twat. "I'm happy to pay the necessary fares."

"The fares?" A glimmer of either interest or suspicion crept into the bored voice on the other end of the phone. "Who did you say this was?"

"My name is Rick Winchester. I met your wife on the cruise ship she works on. Actually, she was injured assisting me."

"Then, Mr. Winchester, I'd suggest you are legally liable for all her costs."

I stared out of the window at the calming blue ocean, trying to maintain a level tone. "I'm not disputing that in any manner, Mr. Prescott. Simply apprising you of the situation."

I used my teeth to rip the heat shrink from the boxed phone Marty had left on the desk. "Your wife has a new cell. I'll give you the number, should you wish to contact her. But I assure you I'll make certain she has the best care available." I still didn't know what had gone down between Sara and this haughty bastard, but she'd said they were pretty much divorced. Five minutes of conversation with this git made it sound like she'd had a lucky escape.

Minutes after I replaced the desk phone in the cradle and still stood staring uselessly at it, Marty reentered the room with a chemist's sack. "Okay, got the works and I'm probably on every narc watch list in the country now." He unloaded the bag onto the table. "We need to shift your stuff and then hit that press conference. We're running a tad tight on time."

"We'll move rooms after the conference, then."

"No, I want this cleared up before your mother arrives. I tell you my job is not worth the money if she finds you in the same room as a naked, married Australian woman."

"Any of those facets particularly worse than the other?" I rubbed at my forehead, eyeing the medication. Something there would help with the pounding behind my eyes. "It's a seventeen-hour flight; Mother can't get here until tomorrow. Let's leave off worrying about that for another day."

His hand hovering above the bottles and packages, Marty selected one, plucked it up, and tossed it my way. "Try this. And I hate to burst your bubble, but your mother was already on her way here before you decided to pull that little stunt with the yacht. She called from LAX several hours ago. That's LA, six hours away. You're out of time, son. As it is, we'll be lucky to get the media release in before she shows up to tell us how to handle it."

I eyeballed him, hoping to find a glimmer of humor. "You are joking, right?"

"Despite my almost pathological desire to spend my twilight years playing pranks on you, lad, I'm not. You're in it up to your neck this time."

"Mother loathes the tropics. Why on earth is she headed over here?"

"Couldn't tell you. I use my erstwhile charms to get all the information I can, but even I'm not magic. I can only think it's probably not likely to bode well for you. Or your plan. Come on, we'd best clean up that noggin of yours first. Why the hell did you agree to a press conference anyway? You could have let the team handle it."

"Quid pro quo. I needed information from the captain."

"You didn't think I could find out what you wanted?"

Yeah, well, I hadn't been thinking with my brain.

Sara moaned, and I turned toward her room, but Marty forestalled me.

"Leave her be. I'll dose her up if she wakes. You go and shower while I pack up your room. Come on, you promised the devil his due; we'd best get a move on."

"It's not that devil who bothers me." I cast a glance at the mountain of paperwork on my desk, then shook my head. Problems enough to deal with right now.

I strode into the bathroom.

Wet again, with no one to rescue me this time.

****

As I exited the lift, I immediately noted Captain Raynalds, decked out in impressive white-and-gold regalia, pacing the lush leaf-patterned carpet outside the conference center. Predictably, the large room was filled with media types.

"You pulled this together fast, Marty." I tried to tone down the begrudging note in my voice.

"Hoping fast might be better. Managed to keep

numbers down to around fifty. We get it over and done with, keep it as quiet as possible. Mother's the word."

I snorted. "Yeah, hilarious. I'll pay that one."

The captain strode toward us, his hand outstretched. "Mr. Winchester. Again, thank you for agreeing to this little promotion. Unfortunately, I'm afraid we have a problem. Ms. Grant seems to be uncontactable. Apparently, she didn't check in to her usual onshore accommodation, and her cell phone is nonresponsive."

"Oh, she—" I broke off at the pressure from Marty's elbow in my midriff.

Marty extended his hand. "Pleased to meet you, Captain. Martin Griggs, head of security for Mr. Winchester. So what is the issue? You're unable to produce your party for this press release?" He sucked on his teeth as though Sara's absence was a major problem. "Well, that puts us in something of an awkward position, doesn't it? I suggest we keep the conference short. Mr. Winchester will express his gratitude, and we'll wrap up as quickly as possible before there are any questions about why your key staff are not in attendance."

Nodding at the captain as if he'd agreed, Marty shepherded me toward the podium at the front of the room, set below a white screen sporting a full-color picture of *The Spirit of Ohana*. A lifebuoy with the vessel's name decorated each side of the table, along with a phalanx of uniformed crew. As I surveyed the sea of reporters and crew, I recognized the entertainment director, Jay.

Catching my eye, he broke ranks as the journalists muttered and mumbled their way to their seats. He moved quickly toward me, and Marty tensed instantly. I signaled him down with a discreet wave of my hand.

"Mr. Winchester. Rick. I don't suppose you know where Sara is?" Jay spoke low, the concern evident in both his tone and the accusatory set of his shoulders.

I turned away from the crowd. I'd been caught out by lip readers before. "She's safe. Just not feeling up to a press conference at the moment."

Jay stared hard at me as though assessing my honesty. "Her phone's not working."

"Yeah, I think she lost it when she went into the drink after me. She has a new one. I'll get the number to you straight after the conference, okay?"

His nostrils flared, his jaw hard. "Maybe give it to me right now, huh?"

I could have the heavyset man removed from the room with a word. Marty would make short work of him, despite his impressive size. But none of this cock-up was Jay's fault, and venting my frustration, my irritation at being forced to go public, on him was pointless. I slid my own phone from my pocket. "Passcode's 4116. Her new number is under her name. You can call her from my cell, but she's asleep at the moment, so I'd appreciate it if you waited a while."

Jay faced off with me for a long moment before he nodded, but he didn't take the phone. "I'll follow it up with you after the conference. She's okay, though?"

"Yeah." At least, I hoped so. I glanced at my watch. Though Marty had moved my clothing to the smaller suite, I didn't want to leave Sara alone for too long. No telling when she'd come round. Or what she'd think I'd done to her. This time.

The room full, I turned to face the barrage of press. Stepped up to the podium. From the corner of my eye, I caught Marty frowning at his phone. Unusual, his attention would normally be keenly focused on the crowd, although I really didn't need protection.

My hand covering the central microphone, I leaned toward the handler. "Trouble?"

He nodded lugubriously. "The worst kind."

My heart thumped, sharp and hard, sudden concern tensing my gut. "Sara?"

The quizzical look he flicked me was pretty telling, and I hid my automatic cringe.

"You seem to think everything revolves around her, lad. No, your mother's landed."

Bloody wonderful.

"And she's on her way over. So I suggest we stop dragging our sorry arses and move this along."

Chapter Fifteen

Sara

The insistent tapping infringed on my consciousness. My eyes dragged reluctantly open, then closed.

I frowned.

Nothing had looked familiar. It was neither my shared cabin with Melanie nor my room at the backpackers. And the noise was all wrong. Backpackers would be loud with a dozen simultaneous conversations conducted in different languages, sounds of holiday happiness. The ship would throb with a deep white-noise thrum from the engines, close to the staff cabins.

But this was a repetitive sharp tap. It should have been rhythmic and soothing, but like Chinese water torture, it burrowed into my brain, refusing to allow me to slide back into the sleep my body desperately craved.

I forced my eyes open again, pushing myself up in the voluminous folds of luxurious bedding. My shoulder ached, and my ribs screamed. I gasped and snatched the sheets against my chest.

I wasn't alone.

Silver hair arranged like a steel helmet, a woman sat in a straight-backed chair placed at right angles to the bed. Where she'd even found such a spartan chair among the fine appointments of the room was a mystery. No more of a mystery than who the woman was and what she was doing here, though.

I rubbed my eyes, quickly compiling the sequence of events in my mind. Ship, backpackers, here. *Ugh.* That conversation with Simon. Then the decision that I was free, that I could have sex with the undeniably fine Rick Winchester. Rick. Where was he? Oh. Shit. He'd been going down on me, and I'd…pretty well passed out. Right after my overloud protest to Simon that I'd never had sex with anyone but him. Which probably made it look as though I'd fainted from sheer fear. Or pleasure. From what I could recall, it'd far more likely be pleasure.

With analytical precision, my brain slotted the pieces together but stumbled on the answers to where Rick was now and who the austere, silent—except for those annoying fingers, the nails tapping against a broad white-gold bracelet on her wrist—woman was. But more pressing than anything else, I needed to know how long I'd been passed out and what time it was. I had to chase Simon down and work out a deal that would get the rest of the money to the orphanage.

The woman folded long, narrow hands in her lap and pursed her lips. Like a cat's bum. "Just how much money were you hoping to extort from my son?"

Elbow clutching the sheet to my chest, I shoved a hand through my hair, trying to push the tangle back. "Your son? Who the hell are you?" My training kicked into gear. With my robe scrunched beneath me and the cotton sheet molded to my obviously naked legs, I was at a disadvantage, yet I wasn't about to divulge information in response to what was clearly an accusation.

The cat's bum tightened. No mean feat, considering

the woman was speaking. "I'm quite certain you've done your research, but for the sake of ending this unpleasant business as quickly as possible, my name is Elizabeth Winchester. Mrs. Winchester," she clarified haughtily. "I had every intention of thanking you for saving my son's life, such is the spin the media seem to have put on whatever actually happened, but then I discovered this." She snapped her finger and thumb near her ear, and a woman in a beige skirt and cream blouse, her hair caged in a tight bun, stepped forward and placed an envelope in the older woman's hand. Without moving any closer to me, Mrs. Winchester displayed the envelope, her face twisted in a sneer of disgust.

I made out my name written across the envelope. Copperplate script. The embossed logo of *The Spirit of Ohana*. The envelope the captain had handed me, which I'd pulled from my sling earlier and tossed aside with my clothes in the bathroom as I carefully arranged my robe. "I believe that is addressed to me. Please hand it over."

Mrs. Winchester's eyebrows lifted. Yeah, well, screw her—though I'd rather be screwing her son. But I needed to appraise all the evidence in this…whatever it was. And work out what I was being accused of.

Mrs. Winchester tossed the envelope onto the counterpane, and I winced as I leaned forward to retrieve it. With the stationery sliced open, unfolded notes peeped from within. Money. What the heck? A piece of paper wrapped them, and I unfolded it, revealing the neat script.

Sara, I am beyond words apologetic for our misunderstanding last night. I only ever meant to reimburse you, not insult you. This is all the cash I have on me at the moment. Please accept it with my apologies for the inconvenience and expense I have undoubtedly caused.

Best, Rick Winchester.

I scowled at the note. Two things were immediately apparent. Rick hadn't intended to see me again, far less engage in…what we'd almost engaged in a little earlier. And he still had a yen to purchase my services, whether that was pulling him out of the sea or blowing him dry. Entitled prick. I just did not get it. I'd jumped into the ocean to save him as a pure—probably misguided—reflex. Money didn't enter into the equation, either as payment or reward. What was with men and thinking everything revolved around money?

Shit. My fingers tightened on the envelope. They were right; it did. I still needed to find the money for the orphanage.

Ignoring Mrs. Winchester's harrumph of disgust, I slid the money from the envelope and thumbed through it. Just shy of sixteen hundred rather damp dollars. Rick sure carried a lot of cash. I did the conversion quickly in my head. Even if I took the money, I'd still be two thousand short. I had no option but to call Simon, see if he'd had time to calm down. He could have a damn divorce if that's what he wanted, but I wasn't stupid enough to let him control me. Those days were over.

"Is there a problem?" Mrs. Winchester couldn't have sounded more uncaring.

"Not at all." In fact, I kind of wanted to boast about how quickly I'd mentally sorted everything out, despite the dull pain pounding at the back of my head. First, I'd head back to *The Spirit of Ohana* where I had free board. That'd put a crimp in Simon's manipulations. I'd call him and demand he hand over the shortfall. He'd blindsided me earlier by locking the account, but he wouldn't argue over a couple of grand, mere lunch money to him, once I mentioned the risk of adverse exposure. We had mutual friends and professional acquaintances.

Tomorrow, I could get my account access reinstated, Sunday being Monday in Australia. And I'd let him know I'd be on the first flight back after my contract finished. Although he was playing the bastard right now, brave in the face of my isolation, once I got back to Australia, Simon would be desperate to keep things civil.

I smoothed a hand over the bedsheet, relaxing as the pieces of my plan fell seamlessly into place. Then my hand clenched the fine linen, screwing it into a ball in my fist; to organize anything at all, I'd need a phone. And of course, I wouldn't have the money for one until next payday.

Unless I used Rick's cash.

Which would mean he'd succeeded in purchasing me. I rubbed a hand across my eyes, weary though I'd only just woken. Why was it that, despite my certainty that life both could and should be simpler and not revolve around money, everything still came back to that one issue?

"Did my son not pay you enough?" Mrs. Winchester's voice splintered the air like a shattering iceberg. "I'm certain he wouldn't be aware of the—what shall we say? Going rate?—for a consort." Her gaze raked disgustedly down my sheet-shrouded torso, then averted, as though she'd risk contamination if she maintained the contact. "Especially one who has put so much apparent effort into achieving her target. However, I have the wherewithal to investigate the subject, and I assure you, the more quickly we can come to an agreement, the more quickly you'll get what you want. Now is not the moment to play coy. Name your figure."

Why would the crazy old woman think I was trying to extort Rick? "What are you on about? I don't want any money from Rick."

She nudged her chin toward the envelope. "Both your actions and that message seem to infer somewhat differently."

"My *actions*? I dove into the sea to help some random stranger. What the hell do you mean?"

"I mean your actions in immediately counting the payment my son left for you."

I caught my breath. Okay, that would have looked bad. "That's not why I was— Oh, look, never mind. What business is this of yours anyway? I don't want your son's money. I've already made that quite clear to him." Yeah, if I'd made it a tad less clear, I could have been having lustful, wanton sex with him, not facing off with this rigid old battleax, her legion of assistants hovering in the doorway as though they'd leap forward to protect her. Come to think of it, where was Rick? Had he sent his mother in to "deal" with me?

Mrs. Winchester snorted, yet managed to keep the sound refined, a tiny intimation of derision from the recesses of her autocratic Roman nose. "You don't want his money? Your husband seems to feel quite differently."

"My... You spoke with Simon? Why? How?"

Again, she snapped her fingers, and with creepy speed and prescience, the secretary stepped forward, cell phone already in her outstretched hand.

"Mr. Prescott rang on this cell. I admit it did throw

me a little that you have different surnames. I assume you've taken up with that fad of keeping your maiden name? No matter. In any case, Mr. Prescott said he was trying to contact my son, via you. And he found it expeditious to be quite transparent about the monetary issue, including the fact that Richard needed to fund your husband's immediate flight here to be by your side."

Simon was on his way? What for? He'd been clear that he planned to cut me from his life and rush the divorce through, so why would he now drop everything to charge over here? I'd been dangerously ill with influenza while in the Solomon Islands, but he'd done no more than suggest I drag myself to a pharmacy to get a script, and complain that he had a stinking cold which was, apparently, comparable. "But that's not my phone. How did he get the number?"

"I'm sure I have no idea, nor is that any of my concern. I've contacted my attorney, and my suggestion is we settle this before your husband arrives."

"Settle? Settle what? I told you I don't want any money." Except that which I guiltily clutched in my hand. Now my head was definitely splitting in two. Simon, the phone, this weird woman. "Look, just give me a little privacy. I need to shower, and then I'll leave." Back at *The Spirit of Ohana*, I could try to untangle some of this crazy. My plan was still valid, maybe even more so now, because Simon would come to me instead of me chasing him—and using Rick's money to do so. In fact, now I didn't need the envelope full of cash; I could persuade Simon to hand over the entire four thousand. I thrust the stash at Mrs. Winchester. "Here, take it back. Give it to Rick." *Or stuff it up your arse, whatever.*

"Oh no. Do you think I'm not wise to that ploy?"

The woman drew herself up, rearing back from the envelope as though she wouldn't touch anything as tawdry as paper money. "You disappear now, only to resurface later and make accusations of poor treatment by my family?"

Maybe I should tell Eccentric Elizabeth that, unless lack of an orgasm counted as poor treatment, I had no accusations to make. And sure, though I'd be feeling a darn sight better if I'd consummated the act with Rick, I wasn't about to go public with that fact. The whole extortion theme was utter madness, though. Considering his mum's high-level crazy, maybe Rick had been a fortunate near-miss. Shame, because just the thought of him made my heart do little flips of excitement.

Mrs. Winchester raised her right hand, and the PA leaped forward to take the phone, then scooted around the back of the woman's chair to lean awkwardly across and nudge it onto the bedside table. Mrs. Winchester didn't blink an eye as the phone reappeared on the table two inches from her left elbow. Apparently, that was precisely the service she expected. "I've scheduled a press conference in ninety minutes. The attendance of the captain of your ship, *your employer*, has already been confirmed by the owners of the vessel. It only remains to settle the sum you wish to extort from my son, and we can put this unfortunate business behind us."

"*Elizabeth*," I said very deliberately, "I don't understand a tenth of what you're going on about, but I suggest you tread very carefully with your accusations and insinuations. I'm sure your attorney would give you the same advice." Clearly, the woman was hankering for a fight. If I could just get my head around what it was about, I'd have some chance. "I have no intention of either attending a press conference or accepting—or, as you say, extorting—money from Rick. I tried to rescue your son from a storm. End of story. Now, if you'd leave, I'd like to dress and do the same thing."

"End of story?" Mrs. Winchester's eyes blazed triumphantly. "End of story, you say, yet you lie here naked in my son's suite, surrounded by evidence of alcohol and copious quantities of drugs? And your husband says he has no idea where you've been for months and that he's been frantic with concern about you? Seems there's far more to this story than you'll own. And don't pretend you don't want money. You'd counted the cash in that envelope before you'd even drawn a breath. Now. Just tell me how much to make this all go away. It will be your compensation for your appearance, preferably in complete silence, at the press release."

"I need four thousand dollars. No. Twenty-one hundred and this." I waved the envelope. If taking the money would make this weird witch disappear, whatever. I couldn't rely on Simon to make the accounts available as soon as he arrived, but this way I could at least tick the orphanage off my list of immediate problems.

"Settled. I'll have my attorney email through a release of liability agreement. I don't suppose you have an attorney able to look it over for you?"

"That won't be necessary." Much as my head hurt, I was still capable of handling a legal transaction.

Mrs. Winchester struggled to her feet, the personal assistant dashing forward with a cane. I winced in automatic sympathy as I noticed the older woman's arthritic grimace.

"Wait." I licked dry lips, suddenly aware of the effects of the alcohol and medication. My mouth tasted like the scrapings from a cocky-cage floor. I needed to clean my teeth before I saw Rick again. Well, not that I'd be doing anything but nodding farewell at the entitled tosser. If him leaving money wasn't bad enough, the presence of his mother flashed all kinds of neon warning signals.

I folded the envelope in half and reached for the complimentary pen on the bedside table. Scrawled on the side that didn't have my name etched across it. "Take this cash back and make the four thousand dollars payable to this organization, please. Have your attorney contact me on this email, and I'll forward them the organization's financial institution details."

Mrs. Winchester took the note reluctantly, like I handed her a poisoned apple. She scanned it, confusion playing clearly across her narrow features. "This is an orphanage? What is your relationship with them?"

Suddenly exhausted, I closed my eyes and slumped back in the bed. Maybe the woman would disappear, like a bad dream. "No relationship." With them, or anyone else. "Just a financial contribution."

"You do realize that if we make this payment in your name, the transaction still negates any further claim you may try to make against my family?"

"I'm not making any claim, further or otherwise. As you said, the remuneration is simply an appearance fee for this press gathering, for whatever reason you feel a need to have it. Just have your attorney email me the disclaimer."

"My people will be back to escort you to the function in thirty minutes. I'm sure your captain would appreciate it if you were somewhat more presentable."

The air pressure in the room changed, and I tried not to heave a sigh of relief. I felt like I'd fallen down a rabbit hole, but perhaps that was a side effect of the medication, a vast array of which I could see spread across the nightstand as I slit my eyes to check that I was truly alone. No, I wasn't. The mousy PA still hovered against the far wall.

I shoved upright, drawing the soft robe around me.

The secretary stepped forward timidly. "Goodness, that's an awful bruise. Did you do that rescuing Richard?"

Surrounded by very correct British accents, I fought back an almost overwhelming urge to imitate the plummy tones. Funny how Rick's inflection could sound so damn sexy when the others made me want to snigger like I was watching a British sitcom. "Um, yeah. It's nothing. Looks worse than it is." Why did I always feel the need to downplay? Truth was, if the assistant hadn't been in the room, I'd down two of each of the tablets on the table.

Probably not a good idea, if I had to face Elizabeth Winchester again.

The assistant's phone pinged, and she pulled it from a pocket in her A-line skirt. "Oh, here's the agreement from Mrs. Winchester's legal counsel. Would you like me to explain it to you?"

I swallowed a grin. "No. I should be able to make sense of it. Just forward it to my email, and I'll sign. Oh no, wait. I don't have a phone. Crap. I'll have to boot up my laptop."

The secretary crossed the room on silent feet and retrieved the cell Elizabeth Winchester had so exultantly displayed. "This was on the bedside table when housekeeping let us in." She glanced over her shoulder warily and then drew a slip of hotel stationery from her pocket. "Along with this."

I took the note.

Sara, it seems I'm rather fated to write you apology notes. I have to step out briefly. This room has been transferred to you for your convenience. Please make yourself comfortable...or as comfortable as you are able in the circumstances. The doctor has prescribed the medications on the nightstand for you. Personally, I'd be quite happy if you stuck to the whiskey. That seemed to be working rather well for us.

I've replaced your cell...well, more specifically, and as he will no doubt be at pains to point out, Marty has. I was otherwise, and exceedingly pleasurably, occupied at the time.

Your new number is inside the case, and I've taken the liberty of inserting my number in the memory.

I look forward to inserting more.

R x

Well, at least he hadn't ridiculously said he loved me this time. But a kiss? And why did the note bring a stupid grin to my face?

The PA hovered over me, her plain face lit by a shared secret. "Mrs. W—that is, Mrs. Winchester— didn't see the note. I only noticed the phone when your husband called, and I picked it up."

I rolled my eyes, warming to my new companion. Or guard. "Probably just as well. Seems I'm in enough trouble as it is, though I can't for the life of me work out what I'm supposed to have done wrong."

"Well." The assistant plopped unceremoniously

onto the side of the bed. "Mrs. W is exceedingly protective of her son. Not that he needs any protection. I mean, seriously, have you seen—oh!" She broke off, covering her mouth with one hand, color rising in her cheeks. "Sorry. Obviously, you have."

I snorted, liking the woman more by the second. "You wouldn't believe me if I told you. By the way, I'm Sara."

"Chrissy. And please feel free to tell me anything. I mean, seriously." She fake-swooned, the back of her hand to her brow. "I could talk about that man all day long."

"Then I'm sure you know him far better than I do."

She glanced around the suite, her eyebrows almost in her hairline. "Uh-huh."

"Looks can be deceiving." Sadly, too true. Both Simon and Rick looked good on the surface.

I thumbed into the phone, logged into email, and scanned the waiver. Basic form. No red flags. Done.

I thrust aside the covers and dropped my legs from the bed, hoping Chrissy couldn't smell sex as strongly as I could.

"Your clothes are hung in the bathroom." She stood as well. "Don't be late, or Mrs. W will throw a fit. The limo will be waiting to take us to the convention center."

"Convention center. Here? Waikiki? You realize that's only a few hundred meters away, right?"

She tidied the bed. "And you expect Mrs. W to walk there?"

No. But the woman probably had a broomstick stashed somewhere.

Chapter Sixteen

Rick

The questions came fast but were predictable. What was I doing in Hawaii, and was I here alone? Who was the woman who'd rescued me, and did I intend to see her again? Was I scouting for real estate investments in the Hawaiian Islands, and would I consider moving here on a permanent basis? If I did move, would I be alone?

I responded to each as patiently as I could, well aware the printed "facts" would bear little semblance to my carefully stated truths. But I'd promised Captain Raynalds the promotion, and as Marty had always taught, I needed to honor my promises. Even when talking incessantly of the woman who had saved me prevented me from being with the woman who had saved me.

Marty nudged me, and I refocused. Dammit, I only had to give a second's thought to the feisty Aussie, and I completely lost track. The non-consummation of our relationship was to blame. The sooner I could take care of that, the better. Though that would now be complicated by the suspicions of the entertainment director, who seemed far less affable than he had the previous day. Still, I'd wind this up, then take Jay back to the suite so he could see for himself Sara hadn't been abducted or worse.

Then I'd—what? I could think of plenty of things I wanted to do, but the matter seemed to be getting more complex by the minute. The odd discussion with Sara's husband, the intrigue with her divorce, the fact that she appeared to be temporarily penniless. Not to mention my mother's imminent arrival. Obviously, the most logical move would be to wrap up the conference and distance myself from all of them.

The door at the back of the room opened, and Sara slipped in. I stiffened. As in, all of me. Damn. Absolutely no distancing would be going on.

My mother and her entourage followed Sara, schooling around her like piranhas. Well, at least the sight of Mother took the instant rigidity out of my cock, and I didn't need to hide behind the podium. But what the hell was she doing here? And why with Sara? How had she met Sara? And why did the thought of that event sit like lead in my gut?

"Well, this is going to get interesting, lad," Marty murmured alongside me.

Unable to tear my gaze from Sara, I was aware of the susurration of interest, of the journalists turning to follow my focus. Sara wore her uniform, though her hair was loose, curling down around her shoulders. Covering her breasts. The breasts I now knew intimately. Damn. I couldn't move toward her, not for a moment. Or two. If I was any closer, I'd be able to smell her. My mouth salivated. Christ, I could taste her again, and the surge of instant desire was almost uncontrollable.

Captain Raynalds stepped up to the microphone, taking advantage of my discomposure. "Ah, I'm glad to see Miss Grant has, after all, been able to join us. Ladies and gentlemen of the press, may I introduce Miss Sara

Grant, prized employee of *The Spirit of Ohana*."

Sara looked like she wanted to run. No doubt she was unaccustomed to being the focus of attention, and I'd brought this down on her.

I made to step forward, but Marty stayed me with a hand on my sleeve. "Let it be for a moment, lad."

With a glance at my mother, Sara walked purposefully down the center aisle, her stride resolute, her gaze directly on me. My mother's minions skittered behind her. I should be trotting out some trite yet intelligent greeting, welcoming Sara to the conference, but all I could do was stare at the mesmeric roll of her hips, focus on the apex of her thighs, knowing what a prize the snug black pants hid.

She mounted the two steps to the podium and offered me a brief flash of a smile before facing the crowd. I palmed her back, ostensibly to draw her closer to the microphone. No doubt she'd need the support if she was to address the gathering. This would be absolutely nerve-wracking for her. Mother must have forced her here, but why? And how?

My hand brushed across Sara's back. No bra. Lord, how could I stand alongside her knowing that only her arm, held across her chest by a sling, separated me from those magnificent breasts roaming free beneath the white fabric of her blouse?

Marty stepped from the podium, assisting Mother to a seat nearby. I hadn't seen Mother for some time, and I was startled to notice her carriage wasn't as rigidly upright as normal. Instead, she stooped, leaning on the cane she'd always carried as an affectation, its true purpose being to keep the hordes at bay by *accidentally* rapping ankles. She patted at Marty's hand as she settled in her seat, and he bent low, speaking to her.

A line appeared between her brows, her gleaming silver hair not daring to move as she stared piercingly at my forehead. I'd forgotten the piratical stitches and guiltily swept a hand across my face, as though I could hide them.

Mother's press secretary, James, insinuated himself on the podium, shooting his cuffs as he addressed the gathering. "Ladies and gentlemen of the press. Representatives of Mr. Winchester and Ms. Grant have established an exclusive coverage negotiation with HBO and Sky News UK. As such, they'll be taking no further questions this afternoon. We are, however, happy to provide a photographic opportunity to wrap up this session."

The cameras were clicking before James had finished speaking, and I tried to angle to protect Sara from the worst of the barrage. Not hard to do when she was so tiny alongside me. And turning her to face the correct camera meant I could conveniently pull her in a little closer and feel those luscious curves melt against the hardness of my hip. Never before had I actually enjoyed having my photograph taken.

Eventually, Marty threw open the double doors at the rear of the room, his message clear. The journalists packed up their equipment, no doubt frustrated at their curtailed interview.

Ignoring Mother's unblinking laser vision slicing us apart, I stooped to Sara's ear. Pretended not to be breathing in her rich, honeyed scent, imagining her personal musk into the fragrance. "Are you okay?"

She nodded, smiling for a last, lingering photographer. "Somewhat confused, but fine."

The dark shadowing beneath her eyes belied the words, the green bloom from the center of her pupil seeming duller than before. "Somehow, I've fallen afoul of your mother, though I'm buggered if I know what my crime is supposed to be. Whatever it is, I'm pretty sure I've been tried and found guilty. Does she maybe have a very healthy insurance policy on your life?"

I covered my chuckle with a cough. "I'm willing to wager she now wishes she did. My mother's simply a very private woman. She doesn't appreciate me dragging the family through the muck like this."

"Private?" She swiveled to face me, her folded arm nudging my stomach, but I kept my hand in the small of her back, not willing to let her go. "I'm not sure how an exclusive television interview rates as private."

I tried to restrain the urge to sway closer to her. Wasn't entirely successful. But, hell, the slash on my forehead could be blamed for affecting my balance. "Oh, trust me, for Mother, that *is* private. None of the uninvited hoi polloi, you see. No muckraking, like this lot would have eventually devolved to. It'll be in a setting she can control, with a journalist quite likely already indebted to her in some manner. That, my love, is British privacy."

She didn't recoil at my flippant use of the endearment, but perhaps I shouldn't be surprised, considering how intimate my fingers had already been with her. Or how much more intimate various parts of my anatomy were increasingly desperate to become.

I looked over her head as Mother's entourage approached. "Come on, I'll introduce you properly."

For the first time, Sara looked wary. "I don't think that's necessary. Your mother and I became quite well acquainted over the last hour or so."

"That long? You mean she bailed you up? I thought you'd run into one another at the door. Hell, I'm sorry, Sara." Damn, why had I assumed Mother would come looking for me first? I shot a glare at Marty, who'd moved alongside. He should have known my mother's intentions; he usually had his finger infallibly on the pulse.

He shrugged, though he looked rather happier than I'd seen him for some time. Well, as happy as a bloodhound was able to look.

A wave of expensive fragrance announced Mother's proximity. "Richard."

"Mother." Seemed the introductions would happen whether Sara liked it or not. "I take it you've met Ms. Grant?"

"Mrs. Grant and I have become acquainted." Mother stressed the title, and I fought the instinctive clench of my gut.

So much more explaining to do now. Explaining stuff I hadn't even gotten my own head around.

"Are you all right, Richard? That wound looks nasty. We'll get you into Kensington Park to have it re-sutured."

"I'm fine, Mother, and there's no need for further surgery. Though you may well have been conducting a funeral had Sara not dived into the midst of a hurricane to save me."

"Hmm." Mother had an uncanny ability to impart a clear message without so much as parting her lips. "It seems Mrs. Grant may have a knack for being centered in tempestuous conditions."

I didn't bother hiding my grin. Yeah, Hurricane

Sara. That fit her perfectly.

Mother turned stiffly. "The limousine is waiting outside to convey us to the convention center for the conference. We should have time for a glass of sherry beforehand."

"She'll be right. I'll walk there." Sara eased away from me, her face closed.

My arm falling from her waist, I denied the sudden proprietorial urge to press her against my side again.

"She'll be right?" Mother repeated slowly, as though the words were in a foreign tongue. "What on earth can you mean?"

To her credit, Sara swallowed the sigh I felt willow through her. Though feeling it meant I was still standing somewhat closer than societal niceties allowed.

"I'm sorry, that's an Australian term. Thank you for your kind offer of transport, but I shall make my own way to the meeting."

Good Lord, I wanted to applaud the woman. She seemed not in the least cowed by Mother's demeanor, a feat that only Marty had ever previously managed.

"Ridiculous," Mother said. "You're already in a certain amount of...deshabille. I hardly think hiking through the streets will improve upon that."

"I said I'll walk." Sara's voice held steel now.

I glanced at Marty, looking for corroboration that I didn't imagine her tone or sheer nerve. He inched one shoulder up but seemed content to watch how the scene would play out.

"Actually, I could do with a walk myself," I said as Mother drew herself upright. I'd inherited my height from her, and I didn't want her using that loftiness to diminish Sara. Not that Sara seemed the least intimidated. "Sara, do you know how to find the convention center?"

"It's barely around the corner."

The green in Sara's eye blazed defiance, and I had to tear my gaze away. "Good. Mother, we'll meet you there shortly. Feel free to order me a beer." She hated when I drank like a "commoner." I gestured toward the door. "Shall we?"

A momentary standoff ensued as Sara and Mother eyed each other, almost as though they sized one another up, deciding who should take precedence in passing through the doorway, despite it being wide enough for four men abreast.

Sara's lips curved. "After you, Mrs. Winchester."

"Thank you, Mrs. Grant."

The gauntlet had been thrown. Or slapped across someone's face. Thing was I wasn't entirely sure which of the women had done the slapping.

As my mother's entourage swept toward the limousine pulled up at the main entry, I held Sara back a little. "Are you really okay?"

For a moment she appeared still tense and annoyed, her forehead furrowed and eyes narrowed on my mother's back. Certainly not the first time I'd seen that expression on a woman's face, but it was most definitely the first time I'd seen a woman unafraid to do it *to* my mother's face.

Then Sara grinned. "Yeah, I'm just *hangry*. You know, angry and hungry. But it kind of seemed like the wrong thing to say in front of your mum. I need to grab a shake before I go anywhere."

"Good call. You're quite right; Mother wouldn't understand. She's far more disposed to sucking the blood from lifeless corpses."

"Oh, so that's something we do have in common, then."

I frowned questioningly as I moved to block her from a lagging paparazzi, and she clarified sweetly.

"A love of sucking on things."

My heart juddered to a standstill like a knotted rope snagging in a sail pulley. This woman had me twisted around her little finger. Or around that agile tongue, which she now used to trace her upper lip. Dammit, I had to taste her again; my hunger for her was ludicrous, ridiculous. And undeniable. "Come up to the suite. I'll order room service."

Sara shot a glance toward the lift, and I wanted to think she looked tempted. "Uh-uh. Nope. We'd best not keep your mum waiting. There's a coffee shop over there. I'll just grab a drink."

She reached for the money belt she wore beneath her shirt, but I stopped her. Didn't bother pretending my hand lingered on her bare waist accidentally. I stroked my fingers across her flesh. "Let me get it."

She hiked an eyebrow. "I won't stop you."

Yes. That was most definitely an invitation. Beneath her shirt, I slid my hand across her smooth skin into the hollow of her back. Pulled her in close, careful not to crush her shoulder or ribs. This time I'd get it right. *Do* her right. Her lips curved only inches below mine, her pupils dilated with a hunger that maybe could match my own.

The distinctive noise of an SLR camera intruded, the flash tearing my hand from her waist.

"Damn." I'd grown up with the media, so I knew the ways to avoid—or at least limit—their intrusion. Making out in a public place was not on that list. "Sorry. Let's get you that drink."

"Sara."

The deep voice cut through my offer, and I glanced up in annoyance. Jealousy prickled through me as Sara flashed a bright smile at the cruise ship's entertainment director.

"Hey, Jay."

Jay's stern features seemed to instantly soften at Sara's greeting. Damn, it was like she had power over all men. Definitely a siren. "Your phone's not working."

"Nope. I sent it for a deep-rinse cycle. Apparently, I have a new one, though." Her tipped lips created a tiny dimple in her cheek as she lowered her voice. "Thanks, Rick."

It was the first time she'd used my name, and for no good reason, it thrilled me. Like I was some ridiculously infatuated school kid, longing for a glance, a word, a stolen touch.

Jay had closed in on us, and I was struck again by Sara's diminutive size.

"Are we still on for tonight? Give me your number, and I'll call."

Her dark ringlets brushed my hand as she shook her head. "You can have my number, but I'll be back onboard tonight."

My fingers clenched. "Monday," I corrected hopefully.

Jay flashed a knowing look at us.

Color rushed to her cheeks, and she nibbled at her lip for a moment, the first sign of uncertainty I'd seen. The reaction twisted my gut. Despite her teasing, she still wasn't sure about us.

Then her lips twitched, and I realized she'd been hiding a giggle. "Uh, yeah, tomorrow. I may be a little busy. I'll call you, okay?"

Jay directed a long, hard look at me. Hell, was the guy taking on the big-brother role or that of a jilted lover? Either way, his unspoken message was clear; hurt Sara, and I'd have a fight on my hands. Not that the challenge worried me, I could take him. But I didn't want to hurt her.

The entertainment director gave a quick nod. "Yeah. Okay. Tell you what, Sara, call me tonight, anyway. To give me your number and let me know you're all right." Evidently, he'd resigned himself to the role of her protector. But as far as I was concerned, he'd had his chance there, too. The role was mine now.

Apparently, though, Sara was more than capable of taking care of herself. She snorted with sudden laughter. "Really, Dad? Based on previous shore-leave, you'll be far too busy to take my calls. You go have fun. Keep it legal, and I'll see you back onboard for the next circuit."

Jay scowled but then nodded. "Yeah, right. Well, give me your phone, and I'll put my number in. If you need me, I'll pick up your calls. Anytime." He stressed the penultimate syllable.

She passed him her phone, and he thumbed at the digits, then pressed send so he'd have her number. With one more long, searching look at each of us, he strode off.

Sara shook her curls forward, hiding her from the journalists who'd been eagerly cataloging the encounter, and I guided her to a tiny shop in the foyer, which advertised the best coffee in Hawaii. I ordered, tapping my fingers on the counter as I tried to distract my attention from her nearness.

Handed her the milkshake.

"Thanks. I don't like to be too dry."

I tried to tear my gaze away as she took a drink. "I don't suppose you could manage that without a straw, could you?"

Her eyes danced as she used her tongue to reposition the straw. Hell, she used her tongue to caress the damn thing.

Okay, I definitely could look away, because I absolutely had to. Also had to stuff my hands in my pockets. "Well, lead on. Which way to the convention center?"

"Is it safe for me to lead?" She stepped in front of me and shot a coquettish glance over her shoulder.

Christ, she'd clearly said on the phone that she'd never had sex with anyone but her husband. How the hell could she be this saucy? I cleared my throat. "I'm not bragging, but if you don't move about eight inches farther away, you won't, technically, be in front of me."

She swiveled, dropping her gaze to the front of my dark suit pants. "Promise? Or threat?"

"Whichever way you like it."

A frown flickered across her face, and she pressed her lips together, chewing at them for a moment. Then she turned to lead the way out of the foyer and down the street, the air soft with the late afternoon glow. She didn't speak until we'd threaded between several groups of tourists who wandered the street in a potent haze of perfume and coconut sunscreen.

As we neared the beach, her voice was low. Almost apologetic. "Rick, you need to know that I took your money."

"Pardon?"

She stopped to look up at me, her forehead clearly furrowed now, a blush mounting her cheeks. "Your money. The envelope. Well, the money I berated you for trying to give me. I took it."

Unaccountably, my heart plummeted. She was making it clear our relationship, such as it was, was fiscal. Well, that was fair. And honest. I should be relieved. At least one of us was setting boundaries. "Ah. Fine."

She held up one hand to stop my words. "It's a short-term loan. I needed to make good on a financial obligation. I told you about it earlier today? Well, sort of told you anyway. I just have to sort out access to my funds, then I can repay you. I will repay you."

"But didn't you say you needed twenty grand?" Yeah, that didn't sound like I was offering to tuck dollar bills into her thong. Much. Damn, I shouldn't have thought about her thong.

"No. I sorted most of it already. Well, with your mum's help."

"Mother?"

"Yeah. Don't worry, it's complicated. Just trust me, okay?"

Were any less trustworthy words ever uttered between a man and a woman? Why then, realizing that, was it that I couldn't give a fiddler's toss? I'd hand her my credit cards on a silver platter if she'd take them. "Don't bother about it."

She shook her head as she adjusted the sling around her neck. "We all work hard for our money, yeah? I'll get it back to you in a few days. I'm good for it, I promise."

I wanted to make a joke about her being *good for it*, but she seemed so earnest. And the inference that she'd still be in contact in a few days sent a surge of anticipation through me. Maybe I could get her to consider a longer-term loan. "Actually, I want to know more about this orphanage. Is it the only one in the Solomons?"

"No, far from it. They all have a commonality, though; they're operating on a shoestring. Or the last thread of a shoestring."

"So you promised your hard-earned cash to them?"

"It's the least I could do. I loved working there, loved the kids, but money is what they really need."

"What exactly did you do there?" I was torn between genuine curiosity in her reply and being entranced by the animation in her face and the movement of her hands as she sketched a verbal picture of the orphanage.

Her eyes narrowed as though she tried to assess my true interest. "I don't know how much you know about the Solomon's, but as I said, the last earthquake knocked out masses of infrastructure. They went from being a struggling community to really floundering. Not all of the kids are orphans in the true sense of the word; some have been surrendered because their parents simply don't have the wherewithal to provide for them."

We strolled toward the oceanfront, carefully not touching, mindful of the paparazzi a few feet behind. Not that Sara would be accustomed to dealing with any degree of fame—or infamy—but she seemed to easily fake the required amount of indifference to their presence as she continued speaking. "I'm not qualified, but I helped around the orphanage with basic chores. And spent ages with the kids, reading and teaching. Just talking, showing them some love. They're almost as hungry for that as they are for food. There was one girl…" Her words trailed off, and her footsteps slowed as she gazed over the ocean.

The gentle wash of the waves would have been soporific had I not been so focused on every word she uttered. "One girl?" I prompted.

Sadness tugged at the corners of her mouth, and I grunted, shoving a palm against the jab in my chest.

Her gaze was far away. "One little girl I connected with more than the others. I considered adopting her."

"Oh, you can't have kids?" I winced at my crass question. Why had I assumed she didn't have any kids anyway? Actually, most everything I knew about her was based on assumption. Which should be just fine, I didn't *need* to know anything.

But I certainly wanted to.

She lifted one shoulder. "Far as I know, I can. But it seems to me there are plenty of children already looking for love."

It'd probably be better if she stopped talking, because every word she spoke was reeling me closer. "I agree. The desire to have kids generally seems a purely narcissistic perpetuation of self." Though Sara would make beautiful babies. "But you've decided against adopting?"

"Seems I no longer have a stable homelife to offer." She gestured to the path in front of us, ending the conversation. "We'd better leg it." The setting sun on our left burnished her hair with red and gold highlights as she flipped it over her shoulder to speak to me. "It's a good fifteen-minute walk. Especially as I'm taking you the long way around—we need to head inland, but the scenery this way is beautiful." She tipped her chin toward the ocean where shades of blue feathered out to meet the candied pink and yellow stripes of the horizon.

"It certainly is." Suddenly, desperately, I wanted this to be nothing but a romantic stroll along the esplanade with this intriguing woman.

Absurd.

I knew nothing concrete about her beyond the fact that she was Australian, broke, nearly divorced, had volunteered at an orphanage, and worked as a steward.

Sara slowed her pace as she looked out over the white sand. "It's funny, no matter where you are in the world, the ocean remains a constant. I mean, different oceans, different seas, but somewhere, it all combines and exchanges. No matter where I am in the world, the ocean gives me a sense of continuity."

"I guess the Solomon Islands, Australia, and here have a lot of inherent similarities?"

Her eyes flashed green and blue as she glanced up at me. "Some similarities in climate, I guess. But the oceans remain a constant across all the continents, regardless. Africa. Asia, Europe. Turn here. We have to head back onto Kalakaua Avenue."

"You've backpacked to all those places? Or volunteered there?" That shouldn't surprise me. Low-cost travel seemed to be a popular thing among a certain set. She was probably working her way around the world.

Annoyance flickered across her features. "Neither. But I have traveled them."

Something about the inflection sounded funny, but I couldn't place it. Mainly because I couldn't focus on much beyond the magnificent view I had of her cleavage.

Best perk of being tall. And yeah, shallow of me. But still.

She raised the milkshake toward me, and I shook my head.

"Not a fan." Disconcertingly, I wondered how the drink would taste secondhand. Licked off, say, her soft stomach. Or breasts. Or thighs.

"Creamy drinks not your thing, then?" She kept a straight face as she flipped the cup into a trash can.

"No. But I'm quite happy to provide for you."

A grin teased the corners of her lips. She pointed ahead of us to an arrangement of glass sheets that reflected the sun from the hexagonal surfaces. "Convention center."

I surveyed it gloomily. "I guess it was pointless hoping for something a little more circumspect." Pulled out my phone. "Marty said he'd text the precise location. Yeah, here we are. A courtyard on level three."

Sara's face became serious again, and I wondered what had sparked the change.

She tugged at her sling. "Your mum was probably right. Now I'm hot and sweaty as well as—what was it she said? Disheveled?"

"I believe she rather incorrectly used the word *déshabillé*. Which, for some reason, brings to my mind pictures of a tumbled bed and beautiful, sex-mussed hair."

"Well, maybe not so much incorrectly. She did find me mostly naked and in your bed."

"Half her luck," I murmured. Our footsteps had slowed again, and I reluctantly gestured at the glass porte cochere. "Let's get this over with so we can return to where we were before all the interruptions, shall we?"

She made a beeline for the reception desk in the main lobby, displaying none of the timidity I'd expect from a woman truly out of her comfort zone. "Aloha. We have a meeting in the courtyard on level three."

The receptionist consulted her screen. "Party for Winchester, Pa Kalihi Courtyard? Take the escalator up to level three, then turn left as you step off. You'll find Pa Kalihi at the end of the concourse."

"Thanks." Sara started to turn away, but I leaned over the desk.

"Is there an elevator?"

"Certainly, sir. Directly over there. Mahalo."

"Mahalo." If I spent more time here, maybe I'd study the melodic language. Add it to the Spanish, Italian, French, and German that I spoke like a native.

"You don't like escalators?"

The booming vastness of the hall swallowed Sara's words. "It's not that. I'm hoping like hell they're not glass elevators." I put out a hand to prevent the door from closing and ushered her into the lift. "Good. They're not." I selected the rooftop button from the lit panel.

She pointed at the directory. "No, it's level three."

"I know. Scenic tour." I punched the button to close the doors, quickly repeating the action and ignoring the raised hand of a man approaching the steel doors at a fast clip.

Sara looked questioningly at me.

"We need a nanosecond of privacy." Did I sound too demanding? Was it possible to have an unreasonable expectation, to be too forward with a woman after my fingers had been damn close to inside her? Hell, I didn't have any expectations, only desire. I'd take whatever she was willing to give; she held the reins.

And I really wanted her holding other things.

"Ah. I like your thinking." In a quick rustle of fabric, she pressed up against me, her arm snaking around my neck to drag my head down toward hers.

"Your ribs. Be careful," I managed to caution.

"Screw my ribs." Her breath was hot and urgent.

"Well, maybe not your ribs, but I do intend to work you over very thoroughly."

My lips crashed against hers unintentionally hard as gravity deserted us for a moment with the elevator liftoff. She giggled but opened instantly beneath me, more demanding than I would have believed possible. I backed her into a corner, praying the elevator didn't have CCTV. Damn, I should have thought to check first. Too late now, because no way in hell was I going to stop a second before I had to.

My hand slid beneath her shirt, and she lifted the sling-holstered arm from her chest, granting me access to her stunning breasts. How could she not walk around caressing them all day? The hot, pendulous weight cupped in my hand turned me on more than I could recall anything ever having done. Not that my brain was truly on point at the moment.

The elevator dinged, and I slammed blindly at the door close button with one hand. Groaned as I heard it slowly slide open behind me anyway. My hand still under Sara's shirt, I tore my lips unwillingly from hers and glanced over my shoulder and out onto the rooftop courtyard. People everywhere. No hope of a private moment there.

Sara reached under my arm to jab at the lobby button. "Round trip." As the door closed again, she ground her hips against me, not hiding her desire.

"Damn, you are the hottest, wildest woman," I mumbled against her neck, longing to bite and mark her. She teased, yet she wasn't into coy games and pretense. She was truly all woman.

She arched back, offering her throat to me. The elevator slowed and pinged again. The door slid open to reveal the same, somewhat irate-looking man in the foyer.

I eased my hand from beneath Sara's shirt, stepping forward slightly to shield her as she rearranged her clothing. "Dashed lift seems to be playing up." I made a show of holding the doors open. "We're just trying to get to the third."

"Base," Sara muttered behind me, and I rubbed a hand across my chin to hide my smirk.

"Fourth for me." The guy peered at us suspiciously as he retired to the opposite corner of the small elevator. Definitely not far enough that I could get away with touching Sara up a bit more, though.

I smoothed my hands across my hair and adjusted my suit. Then I moved to lean against the back wall, slipping my arm around her waist. My eyes straight ahead, on the elevator door, my hand crept down to cup her buttock, gently squeezing the luscious mound. I'd release her the moment she shrank back.

She looked up at me, all wide-eyed and innocent. And then deliberately shifted so my fingers slid into the crease of her plump, round arse.

Chapter Seventeen

Sara

I'd do whatever Elizabeth Winchester wanted, say whatever she desired, and sign anything that was put in front of me. As long as I could get Rick back to the hotel room—or a dark alley or an elevator or pretty much anywhere—but quickly. I'd explode if we kept up this foreplay much longer. I'd promised myself that we were through, that his mother's intervention was the final straw in what was an unfathomable, senseless fling. But then what place did sense have in a fling?

One glance at him, as he stood in command of the podium, had fanned my desire again.

A fling. Nothing else. I'd be in charge.

As in charge as I could be when the guy was driving me crazy.

I'd felt a brief flash of guilt at Jay's concern after the press conference. After all, we'd both been playing the flirting game pretty hard—but neither of us truly expected it to go anywhere. In any case, pulling my attention from Rick had been nearly impossible. Maybe it wasn't my fault; maybe the suave Englishman's pheromones called out to my...girl pheromones? Well, whatever hormone of mine it was that responded to *very* male pheromones anyway. Considering how his accent made my stomach do weird little flip-flops, perhaps my reaction was linked to the whole British dominance of Australia thing, some race memory? Whatever, the reason didn't matter; I was practically divorced, didn't work with him, and fully intended to screw his brains out before I had to reboard the ship.

Well, before my husband turned up—purportedly to check on my welfare, but no doubt maximizing the opportunity of the gratis airfare to finalize our divorce. My flare of excitement fizzled like a spent firework. I still had that whole mess to sort out. And Sulky Simon, separated from his girlfriend of the moment—correction, from the woman he was *totally, desperately* in love with—would not be easy to handle.

Rick's partner, Marty, waited for us toward the end of the short corridor. His legs-akimbo stance, coupled with thick arms crossed over his burly chest, made him appear more of a guard than an associate. Then again, several of Elizabeth's acolytes had the same demeanor. Either that or abject servitude. Odd.

Marty smirked at Rick. Or scowled. His beaten, weathered face made it a little hard to discern the expression. "Long walk, was it, then?"

Resisting the urge to straighten my clothes, I met his knowing gaze, refusing to back down. My professional persona was easy enough to summon; I'd not be cowed by a bully.

Rick lifted his chin toward the courtyard that lay behind the older man. "Are we ready to roll?"

Marty nodded.

"Press been briefed as to content and form?"

I frowned. Assertive and businesslike, Rick seemed familiar with fronting interviews. And that reminded me I didn't know what he did for a living. But the fact that I intended to get down and dirty with him made that kind of conversation inappropriate. If we'd been an item, it would have been acceptable, as it would if we were mere acquaintances. But our hands and lips had put us in a weird territory of uncharted awkwardness where asking questions could be misconstrued.

Marty straightened Rick's tie and then assessed him up and down. "Usual package. But Americans, you know. I'm not sure we have much control over them."

Usual?

"Any idea what Mother's promised them?"

"Captain Raynalds has ten minutes to tout his wares and set the scene, then they've ten minutes with you, for your side of the story, all while Ms. Grant is in makeup. Then five minutes as a trio."

"Ah." Rick's voice lifted questioningly. He seemed surprised but pleased. "She's decided to keep it tight, then?"

Marty made a phlegmy noise in the back of his throat that might have been a chuckle. "I've heard that's to be desired. Damage control, I believe it's called, lad. Your mother's not entirely sure she can trust you to maintain the correct façade."

An expression, almost a flash of regret, passed across Rick's face. "She may have just cause. What about you, Marty? Do you trust me?"

"With my pension plan, lad, remember? Which you know is worth more to me than life itself. Shall we?"

As we entered the atrium, I was quickly ushered to a small anteroom. To my relief, I recognized Chrissy among the people who busied themselves seating me, tucking a large white paper napkin around my neck, and then fussing with my hair. As though they had any hope of controlling it, after nearly a year of no hairdresser. Still, feeling groomed once again was pleasant. A flashback to my previous life.

"Oh, my word, I can't believe you did that!" Chrissy hissed.

"What?" My stomach lurched. Had our bit of fun in the lift been outed?

"I can't believe you stood up to Mrs. W like that. Honest, I thought she'd throw a fit. Lucky Marty was around to talk her down."

"Stood up to her? What the heck did I do this time?" I'd signed what I was told to and agreed to respond only to the questions posed. I had zero interest in this fiasco beyond wanting to retain my job, which necessitated keeping the stakeholders of *The Spirit of Ohana* on side. As Elizabeth Winchester had made it patently clear Captain Raynalds expected the interview of me, I had little choice in the affair.

Chrissy clucked her tongue. "You know. Refusing to ride here with her."

"Well, I didn't so much refuse as chose to take a walk." Hell, these Brits were uptight. Some of them. I bit my lips together to trap the grin that threatened to spread across my face. Because some of them were downright lascivious.

"Chose? We don't get a choice! And Richard went with you!"

"Well, he's a big boy. I'm sure he's quite accustomed to doing whatever he pleases." And in about an hour, I planned for our pleasures to coincide. I screwed my eyes shut as a makeup artist powdered at my face.

"Well, yes. But that's not to say that his mother

approves."

I popped one eye open. "Do you think he cares what his mother thinks?"

Chrissy giggled. "If he did, I'm quite sure he wouldn't be in Hawaii. He's left half of England pining for him, and his mother's desperate to get him married off. Though, from what I overheard of her conversation with Marty, it seems she can't quite decide whether she's relieved or furious that you're married."

"Me? What do I have to do with anything? And in any case, I'm separated." The word felt odd rolling off my tongue, though not at all unpleasant. But the revelation Rick was a playboy hadn't escaped me. Maybe I should tread a little more carefully.

Chrissy did a double-take. "Separated? Funny, your husband made no mention of it. Anyway, Marty's been trying to persuade Mrs. W that your marital status puts you beyond reproach."

"Reproach for what?" I'd thought Simon obnoxious with his pretensions, but Rick's mother carried on like having a bit of cash to her name meant she was royalty.

Fortunately, Rick didn't seem cut from the same cloth.

Marty stuck his head around the doorframe. "Five minutes. Are you ready, Ms. Grant?"

I cocked a brow at him. "Sara."

He scrubbed a meaty fist across his chin. "You Aussies don't stand much on ceremony, do you?"

"Pfft. We don't even stand for our national anthem."

He nodded slowly, sizing me up. His eyes gleamed with sudden humor. "Interesting. This should prove very, very interesting. Come on, then."

The interviewers occupied wing-backed chairs, with

Rick and Captain Raynalds seated at either end of a cream-colored couch absurdly set among the greenery of the courtyard. Two interviewers. Not so bad. I'd had to face more cameras and respond to more reporters than that in my career. A brief stint in litigation had been enough to give me a healthy dislike of the media but also leave me blasé about facing them. Besides, I probably only had about thirty seconds worth of grabs for them, and it'd be all over.

The female interviewer looked up. "We're just going to take a quick break, and when the program resumes, Ms. Grant will join us." She smiled directly into the camera for a heartbeat, then dropped the look and reached for a glass of water on the floor alongside her chair.

A producer nudged me forward, clipping a microphone to my sling. "Okay, ma'am, in there, take a seat between Mr. Winchester and the captain. Don't bother about looking at the cameras, just focus on the interviewers."

I nodded to Captain Raynalds and sat carefully, leaving a decent space between Rick's thigh and my own. Well, somewhat less of a space by the time my thigh had spread a little farther than I anticipated.

As Rick greeted me with a wink, the interviewer bent toward us. "Hi, I'm Angela. Sorry we didn't have a chance to chat before. We've been put on a very restrictive time limit." She flashed daggers somewhere beyond me. Presumably to where Elizabeth Winchester hovered. "Rick"—the reporter favored him with a lingering smile—"has given us all the background. So if you just jump in and answer any questions Neil or I address to you, we'll be done in a flash. Oh, here we go."

Angela straightened, squaring her shoulders as she faced the camera. Without the sling, I'd have copied her stance; it shaved off a good five pounds and ironed out any hint of a double chin.

"And we're back and very excited to welcome the heroine of this tale, Ms. Sara Grant. Ms. Grant—may I call you Sara?"

"Of course." Back home, no one would think to call me anything else.

"Sara, then, did you have any inkling, any kind of premonition, this wouldn't be a normal work day for you?"

Seriously? The questions were going to be that level of inane? I bit back an urge to claim a sixth sense, lead the story along a bit. But I had to play by the rules—Elizabeth Winchester's rules. Short, polite answers, no extra details. "No, not at all. The rest of the cruise had shaped up to be very standard. Beds to make, toilets to clean."

Angela nodded understandingly as though she knew what it was to clean toilets for a living. "I imagine you've seen many interesting things on your journeys, though perhaps nothing of this magnitude. Tell us a little about yourself, Sara. A steward on a cruise liner is an interesting career choice. Is this the type of employment you've always been engaged in?"

"Not exactly." My profession was none of their business, though. "I also worked with an orphanage in the Solomon Islands. Actually, an orphanage that could do with some financial assistance, if anyone out there is looking for a cause to support." My friends had dug deep but now turned a deaf ear to my pleas on behalf of the orphanage, but this was an opportunity to tap a larger audience, garner more support. Maybe Captain Raynalds could persuade the owners of the cruise liner to offer sponsorship, given that they were benefitting from this publicity stunt?

The other interviewer, Neil, leaned forward, forearms on his knees, legs spread in an attitude of male dominance. I deflected by turning my legs neatly to one side, ankles crossed, knees pressed together. Just happened that the position shifted my leg against Rick's. Sun-kissed lines creased the corner of his eye.

Neil's hands dangled, unwittingly drawing attention to his crotch. "It'd seem that funding could be taken up with Mr. Winchester, don't you think?"

I frowned. They knew about the four thousand? Then did they also know Simon had temporarily frozen my funds? Surely Rick wouldn't tell them about that—which meant…shit. His mother had gotten her two cents worth in first. What had she said?

Rick's deep tone smoothed across the stilted silence. "I'm very interested in Sara's philanthropic work. It's most certainly something we will make time to discuss."

Wait, he was telling the world we'd spend time together? Suddenly, I was tongue-tied. What was it I'd read about a woman's sexual prime being at forty? If I had another ten years of heating up like this, I'd internally combust.

I fidgeted, uncrossing my ankles and shifting from one buttock to the other. Not because my damp panties were decidedly uncomfortable. And most definitely not because the slippery friction was about two breaths away from getting me off. Nope. Not that at all.

Rick cut his eyes sideways at me, a slight grin tugging the corners of his mouth. Like he knew what I was doing. What I was imagining him doing.

Angela smiled encouragingly as though she fully understood our wordless interaction and knew where my mind was at. Given the sexual tension in the air and Rick's debonair charisma, her mind was probably in the same place. "I imagine you'll be offering to reward Sara, Richard?"

Between our thighs, hidden from the cameras, Rick's finger stroked my upper leg. "I've already tried to compensate Ms. Grant, but she had little interest in what I offered. I may have to renegotiate and improve on my proposition."

Neil broke in. "Speaking of financial compensation, let's go back to this orphanage in the Solomon Islands, Sara. It must have come as a surprise to discover you and Lord Tertanth share similar passions."

"Who?"

Angela jerked forward. Held one finger up to pause the conversation, which had, in any case, fallen ominously silent. Then she slowly pointed the immaculately manicured digit toward Rick. "The Lord of Tertanth. The man you, ah, rescued."

My head whipped toward Rick.

He massaged the bridge of his nose, not meeting my gaze.

Oh. Shit. I'd known he looked vaguely familiar but thought it was because of his resemblance to an actor, like I'd told Melanie. Or maybe because my hormones had been raring to get it on with him. But the sense of déjà vu, of already knowing him, was because I'd *seen him on the damn TV.*

Rick. Lord Richard Winchester of Tertanth. I racked my brains, trying to recall what I knew of the public figure. British playboy. A peer of the realm or something equally wanky. Most certainly a tosser by any name or title. Holy crap, no wonder he tried to fob me off with money at every turn. And there I was, faffing on about how I'd repay his measly four thousand, like it meant a darn thing to him. He probably paid that much for a decent cup of tea.

Angela moved to the edge of her seat. "Sara, you didn't realize who it was that you saved from certain death?"

"Well, I wouldn't say certain death…" I hedged, still trying to put the pieces together.

Rick grinned. "You wouldn't. You're an Aussie. You guys call a hurricane a bit of a blow, don't you? A poisonous snake a legless lizard? I can tell you, from where I was lying in the bottom of the yacht, it very much felt like certain death. Until you, ah, joined me."

Captain Raynalds interjected, "I'm positive Ms. Grant would have made the same decision regardless of the identity of the victim."

Neil seemed suddenly invested in the interview. "So, Lord Tertanth"—he drew out the title—"Ms. Grant's reaction makes it apparent you've not chosen to share your identity with her. Why the reservations?"

Yeah, Rick, why exactly was that?

Rick leaned back in the seat, his smile slipping. "It's actually Richard, Lord of Tertanth. But please, call me Rick. And I can't say I had any such reservations. Sara and I have been afforded very little time together. I'm certain there are things I've yet to discover about her, as she has—had—about me."

"Really? I believe you have rather intimate knowledge of me." Anger licked inside me, hot and vicious. He knew all about my temporary cash-flow problems and that my husband was divorcing me. He even knew about my sexual inexperience and was the only person I'd ever told of my longing to adopt Sophia. Hell, he knew everything, had somehow insidiously discovered my secrets, yet he'd deliberately shared nothing of his own life. Why hadn't I trusted my instinct?

I raked my hand through my hair, too angry to speak. Clearly, he'd avoided telling me who he was for fear I'd hit him up for money. Though he'd been happy enough to splash the cash for the right service, buying himself a bit of low-class holiday fun, he'd probably become paranoid the moment I divulged my accounts had been frozen. Just like Simon, he was rich—and mean with it.

Neil read my thoughts. "Your position would require you maintain a level of discretion in your relationships, wouldn't it, Richard? There'd be a concern that any prospective partner's interest may be predicated on your title and standing?"

"Of course—"

I thrust my ring finger up at the interviewer, wishing I had an excuse to use my middle one instead. "I'm not a prospective partner. I'm married. And I'm not the least interested in Rick, wealth notwithstanding. For the record, and strangely enough, I didn't know who he was before I jumped into the ocean. At the time, it seemed the right thing to do."

Angela smirked like a dog who'd snuck into the kitty-litter tray. "At the time? You're saying, had you realized who was in the capsized yacht, you may have chosen not to rescue Richard?"

Blood pounded in my ears. I snatched at the

microphone pinned to my blouse. "Of course I'm not saying that. And the yacht was not capsized, and Richard Winchester was not near death. What I am saying, however, is that this interview is over." I stood and flung the tiny microphone at the table, though it hooked on my finger and made the gesture a lot less final than I'd have liked.

"Sara, wait—" Rick half stood, but Neil reached an arm across him, speaking directly into the camera.

I strode off the set, almost colliding with Marty lurking in the gloom.

"I'll run you back to the hotel, Sara," he said.

I scowled, though he'd not see me in the dark. "I'm not going back there."

He touched my shoulder gently as though I needed reminding of the ache that spread from shoulder blade to chest. "Just to pick up your pain meds, okay, lass? Then I'll take you anywhere you want to go."

"Fine." I pretended not to see as he waved Rick back down into his seat. Or maybe I pretended not to see that Rick chose to sit back down. Clearly, he had nothing to say, no excuse for his…well, not dishonesty, but certainly, lack of honesty.

Marty guided me to one of the cabs parked beneath the palms on the boulevard, and opened the rear door. I slid in and stared out of my window as I tried to get my head around what had happened. Replaying my interactions with Rick over the last twenty-four hours.

Eventually, I rounded on Marty but recoiled a little as I found him silently observing me. "So you're a bodyguard, right?" My tone came out harsher than I intended. Not harsher than he deserved, though.

"In a manner of speaking, lass. Among other

things."

I wasn't sure what I'd expected him to reply or what I tried to prove. Anger seemed to have stolen my rational thought process. Hell, it'd probably stolen my job, too. Furious in the face of yet another man's lies to me, I'd not even given a thought to Raynalds as I stormed out.

We pulled up before the hotel, and I let myself out of the cab before either Marty or the doorman could assist me. Threw the cabbie a handful of the few precious notes I still had in my money belt, pretty much just to prove that I *could.*

Marty came up behind me at the elevator. "You've nowhere else to go tonight, right?"

Great, everyone knew of my penniless state. I scowled and punched the button for the top floor harder than I needed. Could I even go back to *The Spirit of Ohana* for the night? Or was dismissal instantaneous? Maybe Jay would know.

The illuminated buttons lit one by one as I refused to think about the last elevator ride I'd taken, how different it had been. Except that was precisely what I was thinking about; the recollection of Rick's lips on mine, his hand chasing up inside my blouse, jumbled my thoughts like a cocktail blender. When the hell had I become so invested in him?

"Sara?" Marty prompted.

"I'll sort something," I snapped. Rick had done wrong. Hidden who he was. Deliberately. Unnecessarily. I wanted nothing from him. Well, nothing that came from his title or wealth anyway. He could put any spin he liked on it, but basically, he'd treated me like I was a commodity to be purchased. Must be some hooker fantasy he got off on, because a guy like him would be able to get a woman wherever, whenever he wanted. Even if he hadn't been one of the wealthiest men in Britain.

I didn't realize I'd paused, lost in thought in front of the penthouse, until Marty took the key card from my hand and swiped it. He pushed open the door and stood back for me to enter.

Following me in, he picked up a brown paper sack from the table. He dropped in the prescriptions that lay on the coffee table, then headed to the bedroom. I frowned. A ridiculous amount of medication was spread throughout the apartment. Though maybe some of it was Rick's. The line of ragged stitches across his forehead sure looked like it'd be the cause of more than a minor headache.

Served him right.

Marty picked up a bottle from the bedside table. "Are you due another dose?"

What was he, a nanny? "They're not all mine. Some must be for—" I wanted to spit *The Lord of Tertanth* to underline my disdain. But the title didn't seem to fit the man I knew. Or didn't know.

The pills rattled as Marty shook the bottle. "The lad didn't send me to get anything for him. Told the doc to provide a buffet of whatever might help you."

"Very noble, I'm sure."

He didn't react to my snark, and I kind of hated myself as the waspish words left my lips. Plus, he was right. My ribs were aching, a dull burn made worse when I heaved a sigh.

"Yeah. Probably due a dose."

The guard passed me the bottle and moved into the kitchen. He returned with a glass of water. No doubt he'd heard all about how the whiskey/drug mix affected me.

He handed me the glass. "Listen, Sara. There's no point you rushing off anywhere tonight. Rick will steer clear. You'll have the place to yourself if that's what you want. You've had a pretty eventful day, and I daresay a little sleep wouldn't go amiss."

The bed, remade in the couple of hours of my absence, certainly did look far more inviting than the narrow bunk that awaited me on *The Spirit of Ohana*. Or maybe didn't await me. I drifted farther into the bedroom. "I don't know. Last time I woke in here, I found I wasn't exactly alone. Nor with the company I expected."

The thick curtains swished as Marty pulled them across the vast expanse of window, making the room dim and restful. Like I needed it to be more tempting. The bed could only call louder if Rick sprawled naked across it.

No. No Rick, naked or otherwise. My hormones obviously weren't up to speed with my brain yet.

"Ah, yes. Mrs. Winchester paid you a visit, I understand."

I scowled at him. "Can you imagine waking to that?"

His twisted face screwed into something approaching a conciliatory smile. He took the empty glass from my unresisting fingers. "Actually, yes."

"Well, it was a new experience for me." Though I was close to Simon's father, his mother had passed long before, and I'd never had the joy—or otherwise—of a mother-in-law. "About the last thing I expected was to wake up in a strange hotel room with some guy's mother."

"I admit I was surprised that Elizabeth—Mrs. Winchester—chose that course of action."

I didn't bother to hide my snort. "You mean she doesn't generally butt in on her son's bedfellows?" Well, not that I'd been much of a bedfellow. That whole plan had gone south pretty quickly. Shame, when what I'd really wanted was for Rick to go south.

Marty indicated the chair near the door as though he needed permission to sit. I nodded.

"I assume she was unusually concerned with her son's welfare. When the storm blew up, it did seem perhaps the lad had taken his recklessness a little too far this time."

Recklessness? What was it about that word that sounded so damn sexy? Maybe that it painted a portrait of a man so different from my husband—soon-to-be ex-husband—and yet embraced the new life I'd created for myself over the last few months. *Recklessness*. It invoked a sense of freedom. Of potential, of excitement.

But the word was all wrong for a mummy's boy. "Seems an odd descriptor to attach to some blue blood raised in a rarefied atmosphere."

Pulling back his sleeve to check his watch, Marty didn't look up at me. "Know much about him, do you, love?"

"Rather more now than I did half an hour ago."

"Ah, you mean you've now discovered the *important* details? You were already aware of his hands-on aid work? His partnership with the Angolan landmine clearing team, his work for Engineers Without Borders?"

My cheeks flamed, and I glanced at my knuckles to see if the verbal rap had left a mark. Who the hell was Rick Winchester? How had I not heard of those endeavors? "Well, no. But then I have no interest in following the exploits of public figures."

"You won't find any of that information on your social media or tabloid platforms anyway. The lad keeps himself to himself. Even his mother doesn't twig the half of his philanthropic ventures." He grunted, pushing his hands on his knees to stand. "Well, more like not even a tenth, but the less said about that, the better. She'll learn soon enough."

"Is that—" Ugh, why was I intrigued by the backstory of a guy who'd lied to me? "Is that what the interviewer meant by Rick and I sharing a passion?"

"Well, lass, given that I don't know much about you, I'm not really in a position to judge that, am I?"

Ouch. I fired back. "I guess you have to defend him. It's what you're paid to do." Much like my job.

"Defend him? Regarding what?"

"His dishonesty."

"I doubt he was dishonest, lass."

"Well, he wasn't exactly forthcoming."

"Ah. That's another matter entirely. Tell me, what did you think when he offered to compensate you for your time the other night?"

"That he was a rich manipulator who figured either I was for sale or that I required payment for an altruistic act."

"So that impression would have been vastly improved if he'd said 'I'm Richard, Lord of Tertanth. I'm exceedingly wealthy. Here, take my money. It has no value to me'?"

Crap. I had no comeback, and not just because my head was spinning and my chest and shoulder aching abominably. Marty was correct; if Rick had divulged his identity, I would have assumed that he tried to impress me—buy me—with his wealth. Instead, he'd offhandedly offered to compensate me for lost wages.

Still, did that make his evasion acceptable?

Marty took hold of the door handle. "Now, if it'll make you feel better, I'll take up a station in the outside room. I promise no one will bother you. You can get a good night's rest and see how all this looks in the morning."

I groaned and dropped to the bed, letting my anger slide. Not necessarily a great idea, because disappointment would quickly replace it. I knew that much from experience. "There's no need for you to stay, Marty. I'm sure you have duties to attend, and I'm quite capable of latching a door." A grin of reminiscence lifted my mouth. "Actually, a lockable door is something of a luxury. I've been sharing a cabin for months, and we were in tents in the Solomons for a good whack."

"Is that so? When you were with the orphanage, you mean?"

The drugs were working their magic but making my lids heavy and my processing slow. "Yes. No. When I was working with the Public Solicitor's Office. Outreach services for the Family Protection Unit."

"Outreach? You mean, as a lawyer? Well, lass, seems Rick's not the only one with a few secrets, huh?"

I tried to focus, as much as I was able with the soft mattress swallowing me. "Hey, no one ever asked me about my profession." Had they? "It's not my fault if you—he—made assumptions. Assumptions which, might I point out, seem to have made your boss feel it appropriate to offer me cash incentives."

"Indeed. Assumptions can be a terrible thing. I'll be

outside the door if you need me."

Why did his words make me feel chastised? Though the admonishment was softened by the fog in my brain. "No, no, that's not necessary. Don't bother." My head found the pillow, my words slurring. A breeze caressed me as Marty crossed the room, tugged a folded blanket from the bottom of the bed, and dropped it lightly over me.

"It's no bother, lass. I'm grateful to ye."

I quirked an eyebrow, or at least I thought I did.

"For saving the lad. In truth, he's like my own. Right royal pain in the arse, but he has a manner of working his way under the skin."

"Like a splinter?" I giggled, envisioning Rick *inside* my skin rather than under it. As in, inside me.

No, I couldn't think about that anymore.

He was a liar.

Just like Simon.

Or…just like me?

Chapter Eighteen

Rick

How had I not foreseen the journalist's revelation? I wasn't an idiot. Not a complete one anyway. I knew the media interest related both to my wealth and to the unfathomable American obsession with British titles. But why had Sara reacted so angrily to the disclosure? And maybe more importantly, why was it that a tiny part—actually, a well above average-sized part—of me was totally turned on by her fiery response?

As Mother sat in her corner of the limo, hands and lips folded in unusually silent disapproval and the rest of her entourage relegated to a cab, I mulled it over. Actually, the reason was twofold and clear. I was stirred by Sara's passion. She was not a woman who would tolerate being fooled or manipulated and wasn't intimidated into silence by the unfamiliar surrounds of a television interview. But the second reason for my intrigue was, perhaps, more telling. Sara had flirted with me, played an intense oral and physical game that had me continually hot for her—yet it had been done with no artifice. She hadn't known "who" I was.

I flicked a finger repeatedly against the leather armrest. Bloody hell. She'd wanted me because she wanted me, nothing more. And that knowledge rated as the biggest turn on in the history of British peerage titles.

"Really, Richard…"

I reluctantly dragged my mind out of my pants. Sara's pants. Silence was not only golden but entirely ephemeral where Mother was concerned. "Yes, Mother?"

"A married woman, Richard?"

"A married woman…what, Mother? Did you want me to vet anyone who leaped into the ocean, verify whether they were a suitable candidate to effect my rescue?"

"It's not your rescue I'm talking about, as you well know. It's more about the fact that I found a married woman in your bed in that mundane suite you took."

I rubbed my chin. The scrape of bristles, auditory proof of my unforgivably bohemian ways, would annoy Mother. "I'm quite sure Marty made it clear to you I'd vacated the suite."

"He did. But I'm not certain the media will see that as quite so cut and dried. What, precisely, do you even know about this woman?"

"Very little, Mother." Far too little. She tasted like honey. She was thoroughly wicked. And the briefest thought of her had me as hard as a polo mallet. And that other, completely intriguing facet—she was thoroughly invested in helping the orphans of the Solomon Islands. "I didn't feel I was in a position to conduct an interview when we met, and opportunity has been scarce since then." Any opportunity I had with her, I didn't want to waste on talking. Except, inexplicably, maybe I kind of did, because I wanted to know more about her. But it'd be a far more efficient use of time if I uncovered her story while she was naked.

"Dare I ask where you are now staying, then?"

Mother's tone could frost the tinted windows of the limo, and I grinned. The reply would probably infuriate her rather more than the not-very-shocking discovery of Sara in my bed. She wasn't under any illusion as to my interest in the opposite sex, nor unaccustomed to my dalliances. But she did like to orchestrate and approve suitability.

"A regular room. On the lower floors."

To my surprise, Mother simply nodded. She looked a little defeated. Tired. "And your head, Richard. Does it hurt? It looks rather nasty, but Martin assures me that it is, at least, the most serious of your injuries."

"Well, my pride was also somewhat bruised." Marty must have done quite a lot of chatting. "But I'm fine. I was in the hull of the yacht, so relatively protected. Sara fared far worse, flinging herself into a mountainous ocean with only a life preserver. She has severe bruising and trauma to her ribs and shoulder."

Why did I keep bringing her up like I was an infatuated adolescent? Although I had the woman on my mind—not precisely where I wanted her—succumbing to a constant desire to include her in the conversation wasn't acceptable. Especially when talking about her injuries instantly took my mind to the location of said bruising. The satin-smooth touch of the slightly swollen flesh beneath my fingertips. The purple bruise shading to blue, pink, then the soft cream of her full breasts.

Mother shot me a sideways glance, which I ignored and moved my hands to loosely cover my groin. Her clipped tone generally acted like a cold shower. I only needed to hide the evidence of the betrayal of my memory for a second or two.

"I cannot say that I noticed any significant injury,

but perhaps you investigated rather more thoroughly than I, Richard? I will allow Mrs. Grant does seem quite a remarkable young woman. Shame about that temper. And the husband."

That final word did the trick. Softer than a Victoria sponge. I let my hands fall from my thighs. "*Shame* about the husband?"

"Yes. I had a conversation with him. I cannot say I was particularly impressed. He seemed very focused on…financial compensation." Mother rarely used the word "money."

"Wait, *you* spoke with him, Mother?"

"He telephoned some time ago, while I was in your—Mrs. Grant's—suite. He claims you had initially made contact and foolishly supplied him with your name. Of course, foolish wasn't his choice of word."

No, really?

"He was at great pains to accurately establish your identity. I rather suspect he'd… What is it that your generation does? Scrambled you?"

"Googled, Mother."

She wasn't ancient, but she did like to disavow all knowledge of technology. As she'd never even learned to operate a television remote control unit, the affectation generally proved credible.

"Precisely. In any case, he'll be here in the morning. I assume to escort Sara home."

Why were my hands bunched into fists? "I doubt he'll be taking Sara anywhere. As I understand the matter, they're practically divorced." Or did I understand wrong? What if the argument I'd witnessed had been nothing more than a tiff, Sara's reaction a moment of pure anger with her husband? I'd already discovered she was fiery as all hell and likely to arc up.

And she hadn't put out. Three opportunities and I'd not managed more than a brief caress of her soft flesh, a tantalizing taste of her essence. Was that coincidence, or was her flirting nothing more than a knee-jerk reaction to an argument with her husband?

I raked my hands through my hair in sudden frustration. Had she played me? Or had she been prepared to go further than adolescent making out and use me as a revenge fuck?

It no longer mattered. With Simon flying in, I'd lose my window of opportunity.

I pounded the door handle softly. Truth was I was losing so much more than that. When Sara left with Simon, she'd take that smart little mouth, the fiery wit, the hot innuendo, the sumptuous curves, the whole of that perfect package, back to Australia. The woman was wild, unpredictable, and unsettling. She stirred me to my core, like the pent-up kinetic energy in a hurricane.

And I wasn't ready to have her blow on by.

Still, she was just another thing I had to get sorted. "Mother, why are you here? I didn't think the tropics were at all to your liking."

Her face softened a little. "I find I rather like the climate. What little I have experienced of it, in any case. Perhaps I see why you wanted to come here. One of the reasons, anyway."

That almost sounded as if she understood. Impossible. "But you're here because…"

"Because Martin was concerned about you."

What the hell, Marty had sold me out? "No reason to be. I just made a mistake in taking out a craft I wasn't experienced in handling and failed to check the weather forecast. No harm done."

"While I'm exceedingly grateful, possibly more than you'll ever realize, for the lack of harm, it wasn't this incident that caused Martin's concern. Well, not initially, anyway. Though I'm certain his underwear got in quite a bunch once he realized he'd misplaced you." A glimmer of a smile ghosted Mother's lips, and I did a double-take. But then she continued. "Tell me, what do you make of Mrs. Grant's display in the interview?"

"What's to make of it? She was angry I'd not been open with her."

"Was there any reason you should have been?"

"What, beyond the basic requirement for human decency, do you mean? Or is that not something you ascribe to?" I was being unfair, taking my frustration out on her. For all her faults, she was honest. Usually scathingly so.

She pinned me with a steely gaze. "I mean, would she have any reason to expect you to divulge personal information? Because the truth is I'm confused. I pride myself on being able to read a character, but Mrs. Grant vexes me."

"How so?" Interesting that she would nail the same issue I had. Though I'd rather employ Braille to read Sara than adopt Mother's interrogative style.

"Do you believe her interest in the orphanage is real or a ploy to entice you?"

"I'm sure it doesn't matter what I believe, Mother, because, if I know you, you've already ordered an investigation into her association with the institution."

She dipped her chin but didn't look the least chastened. "And you don't consider that advisable? I'd like to think you've had Martin initiate the same search."

I frowned, turning to stare out of the window at the palm trees flashing by. "No. No, I haven't, and I don't think I will."

"Why not?"

"Why would I? Why shouldn't I simply believe what she tells me? What does she have to gain by lying?" I recognized my mistake the moment the words left my mouth.

"You'd already offered her cash, though I'm sure I don't want a detailed accounting of precisely what for. Cash that she accepted. A young, uneducated, Australian tourist engaged in menial employment at minimum wage. I would say she has more to gain than she could ever imagine, wouldn't you?"

"Cash she accepted and turned over to the orphanage! How can you continually adjust the facts to suit your own argument, Mother? Sara's not like that. She's… Well, I'm not going into details with you. But as you saw, she had no idea who I am. And she's genuinely angry about it. I'll be bloody lucky if she even speaks to me after that debacle. Which was, might I add, your doing."

"Perhaps she has superlative acting skills and we've only just scratched the surface. After all, what do you truly know about her? But in any case, her surprise—or otherwise—at your identity is not why she vexes me."

"Really? Because you did a damn fine job of making it sound like that was the case."

"Richard, there is no reason to curse."

Yes, there was. Every bloody reason. Because, deep down, a part of me that I didn't want to acknowledge registered the truth in Mother's words. My money had fucked everything up.

Mother held her torso as rigid as her voice. "I do believe her reaction in the interview to be completely honest. She was blindsided and, to be frank, appalled to learn who you are. Yet that reaction simply does not gel with the way her husband spoke to me. He was very clear about having done his research and having a pecuniary interest in you. Is it not just too convenient for her to be sweet and surprised and for him to swoop in looking for a reward? Surely Mrs. Grant must know the manner of the man to whom she is married. And there's something else I noticed about her." She frowned, though as usual, she kept the movement restrained, not allowing permanent lines to mar the smooth skin of her face. "She's not entirely...who she seems. Her persona changes. I saw flashes of someone else when I spoke to her."

Enough, already. Why the hell wasn't Marty here? He seemed far more inclined to tolerate Mother's pronouncements than I felt. Patience must come with the pay packet. "How can you see 'flashes of someone else' when you don't even know her?"

"You're quite correct, Richard. I phrased that poorly. What I meant was Mrs. Grant neither spoke nor acted in the manner I would expect, given her employment."

"Really, Mother? You think it's reasonable to have expectations of the way people should act based on their employment?"

"Yes, of course I do, Richard. As does the rest of the world. As do you. There are expectations placed on you and me; we're expected to act in a manner that may not be true to our nature. But I play that part far better than you. It is the same for everyone; societal mores are closely tied to social strata. You do yourself a disservice by pretending you believe any differently."

She was right. Sara's confidence and deportment had both struck me as odd, but I hadn't wanted to admit my prejudice, the fact that those attributes seemed abnormal solely because I had a different expectation of how she *should* act.

But I was at least *trying* to be different, to kick the ingrained habit of assessing people based on what they owned and who they were. "Can't you see how wrong that attitude is, Mother? That we claim, by the mere fact of our birth—or marriage—that we are inherently better than other people."

"You misheard, Richard. I didn't say I believe I'm any *better* than anyone else. I'm merely acknowledging the existence of different sociodemographics, not judging them. Pretending such a division doesn't exist won't create this utopia you envision. Acceptance of that must come before change. And change is the only way to create the world that you want."

I rubbed hard at the leg of my suit as though removing an invisible stain. What did she know of the world I wanted? Of my desire to negate the inequality between the haves and have-nots? Yet maybe I didn't know Mother as well as I assumed. I'd certainly never expected her to give the issue any thought, much less to arrive at a seemingly rational conclusion. "Mother, would you do me a favor?"

"That seems a rather crass manner in which to ask, but of course."

"Would you give Sara a chance? You say that you assess people rather than judge them? Well, don't assess her based on her husband's actions. From what I understand, they're about to finalize their divorce. I cannot comprehend why he's rushing over here now, as he wasn't the least interested when I contacted him to advise of Sara's injuries. But to be quite frank, I hope you're right."

"Right about what?"

"I hope he has scented money and is out for what he can get."

"You hope that *is* the case?" Mother's voice, usually well-modulated, rose an octave.

I nodded. Remaining silent would be wiser. I'd already given her far more information—ammunition—than she required. But I was unable to hold the fear within myself. "Yes. I hope he's after money. Not coming for Sara."

Fortunately, the ride to the hotel was short. I needed to get out of the limo before Mother exploded.

Yet she remained uncommonly quiet. Reluctantly, I turned to face her. I refused to plead my case or to promise to return to the Priscillas and Drusillas of Mother's matchmaking machinations, but still, I had no desire to upset or disappoint her. Lord knew I had a big enough shock in store for her in a few days' time.

She toyed with the locket she'd worn for years, a filigree flower. It had always intrigued me, neither ostentatious nor obviously expensive like her custom-made pieces, but tiny and delicate. Understated. Everything that she wasn't, yet she never removed it.

The pendant slid up and down the chain as a tiny frown marked her brow. "Richard, I handed control of the estate to you because I trust your instinct. Not so much your fiduciary skills, but your instinct to do what is morally correct."

Never before had she intimated any such thing, and the information stole the wind from my sails far more effectively than the eye of the storm had managed. Which meant there would be worse to come.

The far side of the storm hit with Mother's next words. "So you think Mrs.—Sara—is someone special?"

"I wouldn't know. You may recall we only met yesterday. I barely know her." Sod it, I sounded as though I was pumped full of porridge, all stodge and no drive. No desire. Which couldn't be farther from the truth, the rush of unfamiliar emotions had me more churned up than the hurricane-stirred seas. But then why was I backtracking, trying to deny the spiraling rush of hope and desire and longing and fear that twisted my gut and confused the hell out of me? It wasn't like I required Mother's approval for a fling.

Or for anything more than that, either.

My brain stalled on the thought, refusing to follow through, to process the unprecedented notion.

"You don't need to know someone well, Richard, to *know*." Mother's voice, unusually soft, interrupted the appalled silence that echoed between my ears.

"What on earth are you talking about?" Was she losing it? Surely not. Over the last twelve years, I'd watched Father slowly crumble from a stern patriarch to nothing more than a room ornament. Disease had stolen both his mind and movement. But Mother, she was made of steel. Unbending, uncompromising, and often unfair. She'd handed me the reins of the family empire when I was only twenty-three, forcing me to step up to the plate. Thrust into a world of high finance and avarice, I had to take on responsibility I didn't want, for an inheritance I'd rather disavow.

Four years ago, at thirty, my autonomy had become complete when Mother had supposedly taken a back seat in the affairs of the estate. Except, for Elizabeth Winchester, taking a back seat merely meant she needed to raise her voice a little for the driver to hear her. Or pass the directions, barely disguised as suggestions, through one of her minions to me. Or to my right-hand man, Marty.

Mother had grown up wealthy and entitled, proud of both her heritage and the peerage into which she'd married. What I intended to do now would devastate her, yet my plan relied on her backbone, her British stiff upper lip to carry her through. She'd never allow anyone to know she was disappointed with her son, and that need to save face would force her to comply with my scheme, to be seen to condone it so there could be no gossip among her peers.

I pulled at my shirt collar, which had grown unaccountably tight. To a huge extent, I was counting on Mother's prickly demeanor and unapproachable manner to absolve me of the guilt I felt at the thought of irrevocably changing the lifestyle she expected as her due.

She couldn't go soft now.

Proving that she wasn't, she imperiously indicated the driver, although he was separated from us by a wall of glass. She lowered her voice. "I'm simply saying, Richard, that love can strike when you least expect it. It can blindside you in an instant or grow so slowly over the years that you are only aware it exists when you're faced with the threat of its loss. It is the emotion that is important, not the duration of the birth pains. Ms. Grant intrigues me. I can only imagine what she does to you."

The driver had pulled in to the curb and moved quickly to open my door.

Appearing lost in rumination, Mother gave herself a visible shake and then smiled faintly as I stepped out. "Have a good evening, Richard. Let me know how you intend to deal with that rather odious-seeming husband. Oh, and when Martin is dismissed, would you send him to my suite, please?"

Chapter Nineteen

Sara

The room seemed gentle around me as I woke, a lamp in the far corner casting soft tones of gold across the sumptuous furnishings. Comforting. Until I attempted to roll on my side, forgetting about my bruised shoulder and ribs.

I groaned and forced myself upright. With no clock on the side table, I scrabbled for my phone. My new phone.

Juvenile excitement thrilled through me as I picked it up. He'd touched it. Bought it for me. Cared enough to do so.

Hot on the heels of that came the anger. Rick hadn't bought it; he'd sent a servant, Marty, to do it. Because he was a rich, entitled git who'd allowed me to make an idiot of myself on international TV.

I slumped back against the pillows. God, had I really stormed off the set? I didn't usually lose my cool. Not over anything. Witness, one philandering husband. Control was one of my best qualities; it's what made me a decent attorney. I didn't have the showmanship Simon exhibited, but I did have the ability to remain calm and collected, to bring a deal to closure no matter how venomous the proceedings.

Had the ability anyway. Until—how long had I

slept? I checked the phone. Until nine hours ago. Bloody hell, that scene would no doubt live forever on social media, severely affecting my professional credibility. Had I even spoken? Or had I just rushed out of the makeshift studio?

The phone flashed with two missed calls and a text from Jay. Three a.m. He'd likely still be up. I'd have to get back to him, it was unfair to ruin his night with concern for me—though the footage would have made it online by now, and he'd realize I was in hiding.

I sat and pulled my knees to my chest, then rested my forehead on them. The waistband of my work pants forced the money belt tight against my flesh. I reached beneath my crumpled blouse, tugged the strap free, then rubbed at the welts left on my skin. The fabric strip flopped onto the bed, mocking me with its emptiness.

Wait, if I'd been asleep for nine hours and Simon had already been on his way, he had to be darn close to landing in Honolulu.

I scrubbed both hands over my eyes. I hadn't seen him for the better part of a year, yet never had I wanted to see him less. At least that level of disinterest would make the divorce painless, though I still couldn't fathom why he suddenly found it necessary to come in person. He'd already organized the decree nisi; he didn't need my compliance. But I did need him to sort our financial affairs, and his presence would expedite that. Then I'd be completely free.

A faint noise from the adjoining room penetrated the drugged fog of my brain. Voices. Marty had stayed, despite my protestations, but who was he talking with?

The contrast of Marty's strident accent and the other speaker's cultured tones was inescapable. I'd recognize that deep throb of a voice anywhere. I thrust from the bed and headed slightly unsteadily for the en suite bathroom. Used the toilet, splashed my face with cold water, and then raked my fingers through my hair as I made for the adjoining room.

Marty glanced up from a deep armchair as I swung the door wide. "Ah, there you are. I wasn't sure how long those painkillers would keep you knocked out."

I ignored him, directing my anger at Rick. "What are you doing here? I understood you'd taken a different suite."

Rick placed a cut crystal tumbler on the table and rose, like a great cat uncurling. He still wore a suit, though he'd discarded his tie, and his shirt was unbuttoned to halfway down his chest. How had I forgotten how tall he was? He dominated the room.

"I have. Just thought Marty could use the company."

Well, that made me feel like shit. Not helped by the fact my knees turned to water at the sight of him, and I had to clutch the doorframe. And, hell, my knees weren't the only bit of me to instantly go to liquid.

No! I was angry at him; I had to maintain my fury.

I rounded on the older man. "Why are you still here? I told you there was no need to stay, didn't I?" Actually, I wasn't too sure what I'd told him. The drugs proved great at giving pain a fuzzy edge, but unfortunately, they also did the same thing to my brain.

Marty stood far more slowly than Rick had. "Promised you I wouldn't let anyone into your room, love, and I didn't. But as you're awake now, I have things to do."

Rick strode across the room to open the door into the corridor. "You're going to see Mother? At this hour?

You seem to have something of a death wish lately."

The handler grunted. "You're a fine one to talk about death wishes, considering what's brought us all here. Your mother will be fine. You worry too much, lad. About pretty much everything. Anyway, I'll leave you two to it." He clapped Rick heavily on the shoulder and trundled out of the door.

I didn't wait for him to leave. I could faintly smell the fresh soap and pepper fragrance of Rick's cologne—or perhaps it was a memory from the elevator, when I'd been so close and we'd—no! I had to keep my head straight and needed to put some distance between us. But he stood in front of the only escape route.

Right, then, he could start making his case. Because he damn sure had a lot of explaining to do. "You didn't see any need to tell me your family's pretty much royalty?"

He lifted one shoulder as though that made a defense. "Hardly royalty."

I snorted. "Okay, let's say the British version of the Kennedys, then. You'd better not expect me to curtsey."

His eyes caught the reflection of the lamps and glinted wickedly as he prowled toward me. "I'm not even going to pretend I don't like the idea of you bobbing down in front of me, but I feel that I should be the one to…go down. On my knees. In light of the fact that you rescued me, I mean."

We were back to this. And I was doomed. I could feel it in my knees, in my bones, in the throbbing apex of my thighs. Dammit, even my uterus ached at the nearness of the sexy Brit, his accent lending a thrilling edge to his teasing. What was it Jay had said about a Chinese proverb binding me to Rick? If only that were true.

I forced my shoulders back. One of them, anyway. "Time we moved past that—though not necessarily the going down bit." *Seriously, what the hell?* Was this how I now conducted a takedown of the opposition? I couldn't keep either my mind or my mouth clean when this guy was around.

I cleared my throat, dug my nails into the doorframe, and started again, trying not to focus on the sardonic tilt of Rick's lips. "I mean, move past the rescue and explain why you chose not to inform me who you are. Why you were willing to allow me to look like a complete idiot." With the memory of my embarrassment, the anger flooded back. "What's with all the press releases anyway? I get it, you thrive on the publicity, but hey, if you've got a boat to row—though I'd suggest, given past experience, you should probably avoid water—that's fine; just leave me the hell off it."

I flinched as he took my arm. Not because I didn't want him to touch me, but because any contact would make it that much harder to remember my fury.

"Come and sit down, Sara. Please?"

He guided me to the lounge. Waited until I sat before he started pacing the plush carpet on the opposite side of the low occasional table. "I'm sorry. And I'm also sorry that I seem to be spending so much of our time together saying sorry." He shot me a rueful grin, but I refused to return it. "You're right. Maybe I should have told you, but to be honest, it's not something I like to think on. It's not anything I earned."

"What, famous, wealthy, and adored, but you're going to complain it's for the wrong reasons?" Why did that notion intrigue me so much? Perhaps because it seemed to indicate that Rick might shun the trappings of wealth that came with his inheritance.

No, that was ridiculous. I was hoping for too much.

Yet I was so vested in his reply I was almost breathless as he squared up to me.

"Precisely. Above all, I want one thing. To be no one, not to be recognized. It's just a name, a title, and I didn't think it relevant. Or more truthfully, I didn't want to think it would have any relevance."

I frowned, trying to discern the meaning behind his words. "The issue isn't the title; it's the deception. The fact that you didn't tell me. Or more insultingly, that you felt you couldn't. Were you afraid I'd try and fleece you?" To be fair, from a legal standpoint, he would have been inviting potential extortion. But I didn't feel like being the least bit fair. I felt confused and hurt and...belittled.

He paused, rubbing at his chin, the uncertain action at odds with his usual confident demeanor. "Not that at all. It was more that...I didn't want to risk messing up what was happening between us. Or given our false starts, what I hoped could happen between us."

"Honesty is usually an issue in your relationships, then?" I was being harsh, but ten years of Simon's lies weighed heavily. I couldn't afford to misjudge another man. "I don't understand why you'd feel it necessary to keep your identity a secret."

As I spoke the words, I recognized their fallacy—because Rick was right. If I'd known who he was, I'd have run a mile. Wary of comparisons to his undoubtedly gorgeous socialite lovers, I'd never have gotten naked in front of him. But more importantly, I'd have nixed anything between us from the outset, afraid of being drawn back into a world of consumerism and avarice.

But those were my issues, not his—and because of his choice, we'd already sidestepped them. What right did I have to maintain my anger when, as Marty pointed out, I hadn't been entirely open with Rick myself?

I held up a hand in surrender. "Okay, I'm sorry. That was out of line. I guess I can understand your motivation, and I get that it's not an honesty thing."

"Not entirely, anyway. But then I've never been in this position before. I've never dated anyone who wasn't already completely aware of my circumstances."

I stood to navigate the coffee table between us, my heart beating far faster than could be healthy. "I wasn't aware we were planning to *date*. It's certainly not what I had in mind." I seemed to be making a new habit of partial dishonesty as my words weren't entirely true. A date would be an opportunity to learn more about this man, maybe hear about the charity work Marty had alluded to—and right now, even more urgent than my physical desire, was a longing to know Rick. But admitting that would reveal far more vulnerability than I could permit.

"Oh." He looked disappointed, and the familiar high of closing a winning case surged through me.

I pressed my advantage, ignoring my inner voice. I wasn't about to let another Simon make a fool of me.

Though was this man truly like Simon?

It didn't matter, I couldn't risk finding out. I had to keep this light. Fun. Acquaintances with benefits. Nothing more. "I have no intention of wasting our time wining and dining. I'm due back aboard *The Ohana* early hours tomorrow morning." If I still had a job, that was.

Rick's smile lifted, and he took a swift step toward

me. "I think perhaps you should eat."

I grinned. "Oh. Yeah. Sure. I just bet you do. I thought we'd negotiated on that point, though."

His hand ran down the side of my cheek, and I quivered at the contact. His callused fingers, the hands of a fisherman despite his aura of wealth, now made sense. Marty had said he worked with humanitarian enterprises. Evidently, he literally meant hands-on.

His breath fanned across my face, rich with the hint of whatever he'd been drinking with his security guard. "No, I mean, really. You didn't have anything yesterday, and I don't want you fainting."

"Uh-huh." I leaned closer, tipping my face up to his, longing for a kiss. "Okay. Fine. I'll grab a shower, and you grab something out of the fridge. Deal? We're on countdown."

His fingers reached my chin, tilting it up so his lips could brush mine.

I staggered, the contact surging desire through me, tingling in my fingertips. And other places.

He spoke against my lips. "I'll ring through for room service. But you needn't think I'm going to let you shower alone. We don't have time to waste."

If I lost my job, would it be so bad? I shook the errant thought out of my head—mainly by tugging Rick's dress shirt free of his pants and running my hands up beneath it, over the hard ridges of his abs. Yes, of course it would be bad. I needed to keep my focus and had to earn a living. Pay the bills.

But right now, I cared about none of that. For the next few hours, I'd give myself over to desire. I pressed my lips to Rick's and then took a step back. "You order. I'll warm up the water."

He nodded, but then his pupils flared as I flipped open the first button on my blouse. "No. Wait. I want to do that."

I swallowed. Hard. I had no issue with him undressing me but wasn't sure my knees would hold up.

His fingers moved to my buttons. Deftly undid each. Leaving the blouse closed, he unclipped the hook on my pants. Damn. If they'd been looser, they'd have fallen, but it always took a bit of a wiggle to release them.

As his hand worked into the back of my hair, Rick pulled me close. My blouse fell open, and my breasts pressed against the fine linen of his shirt.

"Your shirt." I gasped. "I want it off." Man, did I want it off.

He obliged instantly, expertly flipping his cufflinks free and tugging the buttoned shirt over his head.

I had to be standing in a puddle. That ripped, sinewy body. I wanted to run my tongue all over it.

"Fair turnabout." He stepped back, away from my questing hands, and reached for my pants again. Unzipped them and hooked his thumbs in the waistband.

I shimmied my hips, hoping it looked sexy rather than desperate. Though, right now, I'd happily rip my own clothes off, uncaring of the inelegance, just to be naked against him.

Finally freed of my hips, the pants slid to the floor, and I kicked them aside. Rick had his hands back on my blouse.

"You're cheating. It's your turn to strip."

"No. I want to see you. All of you. Now." The command in his tone was unmistakable.

It should annoy me; I should arc up in feminine outrage. But the simple fact was the quicker I got my clothes off, the quicker I could get Rick's mouth on me. My mouth on Rick.

Rick inside me.

Eleven months had been too long. I couldn't wait.

He lifted one eyebrow and, at my nod, slipped the blouse from my shoulders and down my arms, then dropped it to the floor with my pants.

Which panties had I worn? Hopefully, something skimpy.

It didn't matter, anyway. His gaze had stalled on my breasts. A low growl of desire rumbled up from his chest. "How can they be more magnificent every time I look? It's not like I haven't tried to memorize them. But still..." His chest rose and fell rapidly, and he dragged his gaze back to mine. "Do you really want to shower? Because I want you. Now."

"Hmm." I pretended to think about it, though I was having trouble catching my breath. "You mean if I take the time to shower, you might lose the urge?"

"Hell, no." He reached one hand to cup my breast. "If I have to let you go tomorrow, I'm trying to calculate how many times I'm good for it in one night, and plan around that."

"If I recall correctly, even exhausted and half-drowned, you put on a fairly impressive display." I slid my hand to the front of his pants, palming the hard, thick length. He wasn't lying. He was totally ready for me. Yet after waiting so long, I had an urge to draw this out. I hadn't waited only eleven months—it had been years. Years since I'd felt this mix of desire and interest and intrigue. No, scratch that. There'd never been the intrigue with Simon. I'd known exactly who he was and what he expected, right down to having a last-minute prenup drawn up to protect his wealthy family and stipulating I couldn't take his name in marriage—which had worked out just fine because it meant I'd never lost my own identity.

Rick, though. Rick was different. He exuded a sexy, unknown quality. Maybe it was sheer animal magnetism. Or maybe something else. Something more.

I only knew that I wanted to fuck him.

"This bit's always kind of awkward." He ducked his chin, ran a hand through his short hair. "There's no way to make it sexy, but—"

"But dying of an STD is even less sexy," I finished for him. "Tested clear, done every six months. Implant birth control." I tapped my left upper arm. "You?"

His shoulders sagged with relief. "Same. Except the birth control, obviously. But—every six months? You're married. Or you were."

"And sometimes my husband seemed to forget that fact."

"Then the man is mad." Rick bent to take my nipple in his mouth.

"Woman make pretty. Man get food," I directed, scooting out of his reach. "And you'd better order quick; I'm fast in the shower."

"Surely, you're not trying to tell me you don't stay wet for long?" He managed to brush a breast as I retreated.

"I'm a firm believer in the hygienic principles of air drying. So the length of time I remain…damp…is dependent upon the incipient humidity. Among other factors." I turned away, aware of his gaze on my backside, and dashed for the temporary safety of the bathroom.

The mirror revealed my flushed face, and I splashed it with cold water, then took a cursory swipe at my errant curls. Gripping the edge of the basin, I took a few deep breaths, eyeing myself in the mirror. *Come on, calm down.* A few more breaths. I'd done this before. Just not for an incredibly long time. And I'd forgotten what it was like to *want* it so desperately that it felt I might explode at any second.

A light tap sounded at the door. Seriously, already? Okay, so I was really going to do this. "It's open." I backed up against the basin, bending my elbows so I could grip the counter, as though that'd help me retain a grasp on normality. "No way you could have ordered room service that quickly."

A grin quirked Rick's lip. "In the spirit of our new accord, I'll be completely honest. I just rang through and had them send the first four things on whichever menu they chose to work from. I didn't even glance at it. Remember, we're short of time."

"Uh-huh." That was all I could manage because he strode across the large room and came to a halt, his hands resting on the countertop either side of my hips, his thumbs stroking across my flesh. Momentarily, I wished the bruise marring my shoulder and upper chest gone, but at least it would distract from any other flaws and imperfections on my body. Not that Rick seemed inclined to notice them.

"No shower." He muttered the directive against my neck as his lips trailed from my throat to my ear. His teeth tugged at my lobe.

My hand moved to the waist of his trousers. "No shower," I agreed. "And no pants."

His lips not leaving my skin, he undid his trousers,

dropped them, and kicked them aside, the buckle of his belt clicking and skittering across the tiles. One hand behind my neck, he bent to nip and lick at my throat, chasing the fluttering pulse as his other hand twisted the thin band of my plain black cotton underwear, as though he could tear through it.

Come on, I'd checked; they were grocery-store panties. Surely, he could rip them apart. *Please, God, let him rip them apart!*

I spread my fingers over the muscled rounding of his shoulders as his mouth worked down toward my breast. I couldn't get my hands on enough of him; I wanted to explore the sinewy, hard planes of his body. I needed to discover if he tasted like he smelled.

I hiked myself awkwardly up onto the counter, balanced on one butt cheek. That whole lack of upper-body strength thing again, coupled with short legs. I definitely needed to work out more.

Rick pulled back, his gaze traveling straight to the apex of my splayed thighs.

"Now," I said urgently. "I want you now." The full-length mirror to my left wasn't kind. How come the pose appeared effortlessly sexy in movies, yet reality found me half hanging off the cold marble, panties creeping up my ass, and desperately worried my thighs, pressed against the unforgiving stone, looked twice as wide as they actually were? Plus, I'd just worked out I couldn't get my underwear off while I was sitting. And the position made the rounding of my stomach more obvious. Total passion killer. Except...except Rick had moved between my knees and slid his hands around my waist, easing me toward his groin.

I instinctively wrapped my legs around his hips,

urging him closer and moaning as he thrust against me, hard and urgent even through our underwear. My fingers clawed into the corded muscles of his biceps as his lips found mine, his kisses more demanding now, his tongue thrusting into my mouth. I opened to him eagerly. The whiskey I'd not enjoyed drinking tasted so much better this way, mixed with Rick's heat and panting breath, hot in my mouth, urging me toward the edge.

His cock strained at the thin material of my panties with each grind of his hips. Any second now, he'd be inside me, fabric notwithstanding. And I couldn't wait.

I released his arms and flattened my hands on the counter, leaning back to ease his access. Damn, that hurt my right shoulder, but I couldn't move now, because he towered over me, lowering his mouth to my breast, suckling on my nipple. The sensation shot straight from my breast to my groin, and I whimpered. "Oh, God. Yes. Now. I need it right now, Rick. I can't wait; I'm going to come."

He lifted his head, grinning wolfishly. "Not yet. There are other things we should do first. I don't want to rush this, not a second of it."

"Who died and made you boss? *I* want it *now*."

He laughed, his teeth glinting in the overhead light. "I thought there was supposed to be a standard pattern to this kind of thing. You know, bases to reach."

"Bases? That's a bloody American thing, not Australian!"

His hand had moved from my breast to my panties, stroking up and down the soaking slit.

"Okay, that's at least fourth base right there. Warm-up done, dude. You know what, fuck the rules. Fuck *all* the rules."

Rick pressed his flattened hand firmly against my sensitive, swollen pussy lips, the pressure smoothing out the ragged edges of my desire. Then his fingers went to work again, ratcheting my craving up so fast I could barely snatch breath. He leaned forward and caught my bottom lip between his teeth, then tugged gently before releasing. "Oh, I intend to fuck everything, all right. But before I do, I want you screaming my name. I want you begging to have me inside you."

He had to be kidding. I was already begging.

Chapter Twenty

Rick

Could this woman get any more wanton? Ordering me to break all the rules, demanding I take her right now. And yet wild as she was, I still wanted more. I wanted her to beg. Not because I craved control or needed to dominate her, but because I wanted to know she desired me more than she'd ever wanted anyone else.

Because, right now, I'd be prepared to beg her.

Her panties were sodden, so wet I glanced down to make sure they were still there. The engorged lips of her sex swelled against the material, wisps of dark, curly hair peeking around the edges of the fabric. Holy hell, I'd never seen anything so erotic in my life.

I stroked my finger along the clearly delineated cleft. *Fuck.* I could barely control myself. Maybe that shower would have been a good idea, both to distract me and to cool down.

Tearing my gaze away, I traced my thumb across the perfect, pouty bow of her lips. She shifted her head, snaring my index finger with her mouth. Sucking it in deeply. Swirled her tongue around it. My cock twitched in time with the pulse of her tongue.

"I seem to recall we had an agreement about this?" My voice came out gravelly, my craving for her lending a harsh edge.

Her eyes sparkled wickedly, the green blaze shooting fireworks as she flicked my finger with the tip of her tongue, then released it. "It was something about showering and eating and I don't know what else, wasn't it? I'm having a hard time focusing. My mind is definitely elsewhere. And it seems my mouth wants to follow." She glanced meaningfully down at the bulge in my boxer shorts.

No. I couldn't let her go there; this was supposed to be about her. Gratitude and apology. And pure desire. I had to find the way to make her beg for me. I trailed my wet finger down the center of her chest, between her breasts, though it was hard to pass them by, and then gently grabbed a handful of her stomach, kneading the flesh. "You're so soft, so smooth."

"Saltwater immersion therapy, remember?" She was trying to joke, but the sensual hitch in her voice, the dilated pupils, gave her away.

"You are so perfect." Though I'd found her sexy the moment I laid eyes on her, the work uniform didn't do her justice, hiding the body of a Renaissance goddess. And I wanted to see all of it.

I hooked my thumbs in the sides of her black panties. "I need these off. I need to see you. To taste you." My words were thick with lust, but she understood, lifting her buttocks momentarily off the marble. What I wouldn't give to be that stone slab.

The underwear fell to the floor, and she was exposed before me. Two spots of high color painted her cheeks, but other than that and the bruised shoulder and ribs, she was porcelain white. Flawless, except for the injury I'd caused. Suddenly, I realized she'd been balancing her weight on her left arm the entire time, leaning awkwardly to avoid using the injured arm. Damn, she had to be hellishly uncomfortable.

I moved between her legs, letting my covered cock rub up against her. Not that I'd be able to stop it, seemed it had a mind of its own, aching and straining to escape. One arm around Sara's waist, I guided her feet to the small of my back and easily lifted her from the counter. "I'm taking you—"

"You're all promises." Her voice lilted with laughter.

"Taking you to the bed, I was saying. Because I want you spread before me like a banquet. I intend to worship every inch of you."

"And then you'll fuck me?" She said it as a joke, yet clearly she staked a claim.

"I promise." Yet as I said the words, doubt stabbed me. Would it honestly be just fucking? Animal rutting purely to relieve our physical desires? Or was I already, my body aching with lust, trying to work out how I could keep her here for longer, how I could discover more about her, how I could work my way into her life?

Which meant I was in way over my head. Obviously, I'd let my self-imposed abstinence run for too long, and now my mind played tricks. "More times than you can count," I added, trying to keep the mood light.

She twined her arms around my neck, her breasts crushed against me, her nipples hard nubs of promise against my chest. Her mouth close to my ear, her murmur was all sultry siren. "I'm very good with numbers."

"I plan on being very good at distracting you." I laid her on the bed, the covers still rumpled from her earlier sleep, and stretched alongside her, my cock eagerly nudging her hip. The sensation of my sensitive head straining against the fabric to brush her smooth skin was…everything. Pre-cum slicked her leg through my shorts. I was so damn desperate to have her I could get off just like this. "But I have a problem, Sara."

A tiny line formed between her brows, her tone suddenly wary. "What is it?"

"Well, I want to ravish you in the worst possible manner. But I'm afraid of hurting you. Hurting this." I ran my fingers across her ribs, noting her quiver, and pressed my lips to her bruised shoulder.

"You won't. I'm dosed up on a cocktail of drugs. Marty made sure of that."

I jerked back. She was joking, right? Because I wasn't taking her if she wasn't fully into it or if she'd later think she'd been manipulated.

My expression must have betrayed me because she laughed. "Don't worry, I haven't had anything since I woke. And it doesn't hurt that bad anyway. Nothing you can't take my mind off, I'm sure."

"Hmm. Well, as it happens, I do have a solution." Her hair stirred as I breathed against her neck. My fingers danced deliberately across her skin, teasing the hard mountains of her nipples, circling her navel, then exploring farther down.

As I stroked along her slit, so slick my fingers slipped between the pouting, begging lips, she quivered, her eyes almost closing. "Which is?" She gasped.

"Well, it seems to me that anything below about here"—I walked my fingers back up to her navel, noting the involuntary arch of her back as she tried to keep them between her legs—"is unharmed. So if I focus my attention right about here—" This time I stroked more firmly down her labia, allowing my fingers to penetrate the folds, just barely, enough that she could feel me. Enough to make her moan. Enough that I could feel her incredible heat. "I figure I can't do any damage."

"Your plan does have a certain plausibility." Her voice cracked, and she licked her lips.

Christ, it was all I could do not to head back up there, kiss her some more. I'd never be done kissing her.

"But there is a flaw."

"I find that unlikely." I stroked again, sliding my fingers deeper.

This time her eyes closed, and her hips lifted to meet my caress. She fisted the sheets as though she struggled for control. Eyes still shut, she panted the words out. "If you keep touching me like that, I'll come."

God, I wanted to see that so badly. Wanted to see her lose control under my touch. Another stroke. A faint sheen of sweat dewed her forehead, the linen trembling in her hands. I fought the urge to plunge my fingers deeper. I needed to taste her so badly. Needed to drive my tongue into her and lap at her essence. "Yet I still don't see the flaw in my plan."

"What if I'm a one-shot kind of girl? What if I roll over and go to sleep once I'm done?"

I was pretty sure she was teasing. In any case, I'd have a jolly good time finding out. "Then it seems the risk is all mine." It was true; there was a risk. Not that she'd reject me after one orgasm, but that I wouldn't want to let her go. I had to remember we had hours together, that was all. And I didn't need the complication of anything more than that.

I pushed from the mattress and moved to the foot of the bed. Took each of her ankles and drew her legs apart.

She kept her eyes closed now, but I couldn't tell whether it was from embarrassment or to better focus on the sensations. I hoped the latter. If it wasn't, it would be by the time I'd finished with her.

I kissed each ankle in turn, then kissed the inside of each knee. Encouraged her legs farther apart as I moved up the bed. I could smell her sex now, warm and musky, and hell, I had to employ every ounce of my self-control not to scramble up the bed, release my aching cock, and plunge it into the warm wetness. Instead, I inched higher, kissing the insides of her thighs. Familiar territory, we'd done this before. But now, now came the good part.

Her pink clitoris peeked from between swollen labia. I extended my tongue, just touching the tip.

Sara shuddered. "God, yes. Again. Again. No. Stop. Don't do it. It's too much."

Lord, she was verbal. I'd never known a woman to do more than moan or lie in long-suffering silence, no doubt reciting my peerage to get themselves through the ordeal until they came to a tight-jawed orgasm. If Sara was going to totally get into it, I definitely wouldn't be able to last.

With thumb and middle finger, I parted her labia, exposing her clitoris. Breathed against her, smiling as she quivered. "More?" I murmured, close enough that she'd feel the vibration.

"Yes, more!" She released the sheets she'd scrunched in her hand, found the back of my head, and forced me closer. "More, now."

That was all the encouragement or permission I needed. I drove my tongue deep, right into the core of her, while my thumb rubbed her clit in tiny, fast circles. Christ, she was sweet and salty and all I could ever want for a last meal.

"Oh, Jesus!" Her heels dug into the bed, and she thrust her hips toward my mouth. "Yes, now, Rick, now. I'm coming. Ohhh."

Despite her warning, she climaxed quicker than I'd expected, quicker than I could have imagined possible. Heat and sugar flooded my mouth, and I licked greedily, plunging deep with my tongue as she bucked against me.

She'd be sensitive now, and I should stop. I shifted to my knees on the mattress, intending to move away, to give her a moment to recover. But I couldn't.

Instead, I knelt alongside her. One hand on her breast, toying with the massively erect nipple, I slipped two fingers into her tight wetness, groaning as the last spasms of her orgasm seized me in a velvet fist.

She didn't slap me away or complain at my greed but arched her hips higher, impaling herself on my fingers, forcing me to follow her rhythm. "Yes. Fuck me like that, Rick. Fuck me with your fingers. Make me come again."

"Jesus." I let go of her breast and grabbed my cock, unsure whether to tug it or encase it in a steel grip so it wouldn't explode.

Sara's eyes flickered open and focused on my hand. "No." She stretched toward me and expertly released my cock from the confines of my shorts. Wrapped her fist around it, circling her thumb through the pre-cum on the tip. Her face flushed, words disjointed, she gazed up at me as she pumped my cock, my fingers still buried inside her. "Come with me, Rick. I want you to come with me, like this. Do it to me. Make me come, Rick!"

Focused on her filthy, gorgeous, wicked mouth, my fingers plunging furiously inside her, I was powerless to stop. My cock grew thicker, stiffer, the pressure swelling up from my balls. Sara fisted me tighter, faster, harder, as her pussy gripped my fingers and she ground herself up against my hand. My buttocks clenched, tightening even as my balls tightened.

"Fuck, now, Rick, now!"

I couldn't hold back another second. As she arched her pussy toward me and the wetness of her second orgasm gushed across my hand, I shot my load, thick jets of cum bubbling over her pumping fist and spraying across her stomach in hot white streams.

She milked me until I was dry, her eyes half-closed, though her mouth remained temptingly open as she gasped and trembled. Just the sight of that mouth was enough to make me semi-hard again.

This time, I slowed the pace of my fingers, allowing Sara to come down from the orgasm. Largely because I needed a minute myself. Or an hour.

Damn, that had been intense.

And loud.

Although I hadn't physically exerted myself, my heart thumped hard in my chest, the blood pounding in my ears.

No, wait, that was actual knocking on the door. I blew a long breath between pursed lips, trying to calm down so I could speak. Bent over and pressed a kiss against that beautiful pouty mouth. My cock twitched, protesting its noninvolvement. "Room service. Have you worked up an appetite?"

Her hand still wrapped around my cock, Sara smiled wickedly. "You have a menu suggestion?"

"You are heart attack material, woman." The knock sounded louder. "Just leave it at the door," I called over my shoulder. If Sara was offering, I was sure I could rise to the occasion, given a minute.

The knock came again, louder.

She grumbled as she released my cock. "Maybe you'd better get it before they wake the neighbors."

"Yeah, like they aren't already thoroughly roused. Or aroused. And jealous." I rolled from the bed, looking around for my pants. Ah, that was right; she'd had them off me in the bathroom.

As I returned, carefully zipping the fly over my still-bulging dick—seemed the damn thing was determined to remain ready for action as long as Sara was around—she passed me in the doorway. "This time I *am* going for that shower. To freshen up."

Innocent words, but as she spoke, she traced a finger through the long strings of cum glistening on her belly. Her tongue chased across her lips.

My heart drummed harder than a polo pony's hooves.

I'd never be able to get enough of her.

Chapter Twenty-One

Sara

If I took long enough in the shower, maybe Rick would join me. Because, despite my swollen, tender flesh, I hadn't had nearly enough of him.

I frowned, lathering thoroughly. He was an itch that I needed to scratch, induced by my celibate lifestyle. Nothing more than that. Even if I was looking forward to sitting down to a meal with him, the chance to chat, get to know a bit more about him. The social media stalking could wait for when I was back aboard *The Spirit of Ohana*.

Except, of course, our fling would be over by then, and there'd be no point stalking the guy.

But also, no harm either, right? In fact, maybe we could even stay in touch. I wasn't planning to write him sonnets and love letters, but he might be a useful contact for the orphanage, going by what Marty had said.

Yeah, I could definitely excuse my continued interest on that basis.

And we still had hours together before I needed to worry about that.

The knock at the door soft, I quickly sluiced the suds from my body, sucked in my stomach, and angled my hips provocatively. I hoped. The bathroom countertop sex pose hadn't worked too well, but maybe I'd get lucky this time. Not that getting lucky seemed to be an issue with Rick. Anticipation quivered through me. I was still on a promise. As soon as we'd had a little time to re-energize...

Rick stuck his head around the jamb, but a frown flickered across his face. He stepped inside, unhooked a fluffy robe from the back of the door, and handed it to me.

Clearly, I hadn't nailed the pose.

After leaving the shower, I shrugged into the robe but left it open and ran my hand over the taut ripples of his naked chest. He felt so good, his skin smooth but ridged with lean muscle. And his nipples... I'd never had an urge to bite at a man's nipples before, but I wanted to pay his just as much attention as he paid mine.

Rick flinched and took a half step away from me. He caught my wrist, stopping my hand. "Sara. That wasn't room service."

"Good, so we have time for round two—oh!" My hand flew to cover my mouth. "Noise complaint?" Rick, a prim and proper British gentleman—though not so much when he was between my thighs—would be mortified. And the suite was in his name. No wonder he looked a little distant. Shit, what if this leaked to the tabloids?

Still holding my wrist, he tugged me closer, and my nipples brushed his abs. His nostrils flared as he glanced down, but he firmed his jaw. "It wasn't a noise complaint. Not exactly, anyway. It was your husband."

I staggered back against the solidity of the counter as the blood drained from my face. "No. Here? Why? How did he find me?"

"Seems Mother saw fit to provide him with the

details."

"But *you* answered the door. We'll pretend I'm not here, that I went back to the ship."

A wry smile twisted Rick's lips, and despite being flustered, I wanted to stand on my tiptoes to kiss his concern away.

"Apparently, he was knocking for some time."

"So? It won't kill him to wait five min—oh." He'd been standing in the corridor for some time while we'd been…busy. Hell, what exactly had I yelled?

"He's waiting in the lobby. I'll go back to my room and give you some privacy. Just ring down and have the front desk send him up when you're ready."

I'd never be ready. Caught cheating on him, how could I face my husband?

"Unless you want me to stay?" Rick's frown deepened like he couldn't decide what he was supposed to do. "I'll do whatever you want me to."

If that was true, we'd find the back door and run away together.

No, that was ridiculous. I had no reason to run, not even any reason to feel guilty. I'd made an informed, adult decision to abandon the rules, which apparently only I lived by anyway. "No. It's fine. Simon's just here to settle the divorce. Though I don't know why he couldn't wait until a decent hour, like a normal human being."

"Sara—" Rick said hesitantly. "That's not what it sounded like. I don't know the guy, but he seemed pretty upset. He was throwing around a whole lot of accusations."

"Accusations? About what?"

"About our '*affair*.' And the fact that I'm trying to

break up your marriage."

Lucky the counter was behind me. "You're trying to do what, now? What the hell? He's already filed for divorce; decree nisi is next week. And he's in love with his PA."

"It didn't look much like that from where I was standing. He seemed genuinely upset." He ran a hand around the back of his neck.

"Oh, you don't know him. He's a damn fine actor. Goes with the job." I tugged the robe closed and tied the belt firmly. "Do you think the room smells like sex? I hope so. I'll have the desk send him up right now."

I strode toward the door, but Rick stopped me. He gazed down, but I couldn't interpret his expression.

"Sara. Do what's right for you, okay? You know this"—he waved a hand between our semi-clad bodies—"was just a fling, right? It doesn't need to be anything more. Don't let me mess up your life."

The floor seemed to tip beneath my feet, but I ignored the instinct that urged me to grab on to his hard body. "Yeah. Sure. You'd better go."

Of course I'd known it was a fling. I was the one who'd set the figurative timer, giving us until I reboarded the ship. So why did Rick finding it necessary to point that fact out sting so badly? And why, now, did I feel the need to dispel the smell of sex from the room, to drag my clothes on before I faced my husband?

"Do you mind if I wait?"

"What?" I'd pulled my pants on, sans underwear, and distractedly thrust an arm through the sleeve of my blouse, wincing as I twisted my shoulder to shrug it into place.

Rick crossed to me and, without a trace of desire on

his face, buttoned up my shirt. He stepped back and regarded me, nodding as though I passed muster.

Must be some weird Brit thing, probably taught by their nannies. *Tidy up when you're finished playing with your toys. There's a good boy.* "There's no need for you to stay."

"He was angry. I don't want to leave you alone with him."

Like he cared. He'd just carefully outlined the limitations of our fling. "It's fine. Simon's my *husband*." I stressed the word to see if he'd flinch.

He didn't, but his lips firmed into a thin line.

"Honestly, the situation will be worse if you're here."

"You know that for certain?"

Was he trying to catch me out, insinuating I made a habit of sleeping around, cheating on my husband? Fury blazed, and I snapped, "No, I don't know it for certain. I've never been in this position." Was that a flicker of relief that crossed his face? "But I do know Simon. Please, just leave."

Rick nodded slowly. "All right. But I'm calling Marty. He'll wait in the corridor. Just yell if you need him."

A mental image of the burly guard in the hall spiked my sense of humor. "Lucky he wasn't there fifteen minutes ago, then." I couldn't help myself. Yeah, I was mad at Rick for calling time on our fling, but he hadn't actually done anything wrong. We were both adults, had gone in with our eyes open, swearing to tell the truth after our earlier hiccup. And that's all he was doing, telling the truth. I couldn't deny he'd been fun, and I refused to be some petty, weak female, holding grudges simply because my time had been cut short and I wasn't quite finished with him yet. Probably wouldn't have been done anytime in the foreseeable future. But better to make a clean break.

"Fifteen— Ah." A grin tipped the corners of Rick's mouth, and he reached for me—but allowed his hand to drop without making contact. Instead, he leaned in to press a chaste farewell to my cheek, his breath musky with my scent, and then moved to the door.

As he stepped into the corridor, he spoke over his shoulder. "I'll ask reception to send your husband up. But whatever you decide, don't disappear on me."

What the hell? What did that mean? Hadn't he just said we were through? We'd conducted the most adult of breakup scenes ever.

I was still staring at the closed door when a knock sounded minutes later. I twisted the handle and stood back, nervously patting at my hair. Despite the hour and the climate, Simon wore neatly pressed slacks and an impeccable dress shirt. He always looked good—and constantly managed to make me feel inferior with a glance or a supposedly casually placed comment. Funny, I hadn't felt that way at all with Rick.

"Sara, I was so worried about you."

Room service had followed him up the corridor, but predictably Simon ignored the woman who wheeled a cart in behind him.

"Good morning, ma'am. Would you like these in the kitchen or the lounge?"

"Kitchen, please." Unable to meet Simon's scrutiny, I crossed to the bedroom to collect my money belt as the woman placidly unloaded the trays onto the kitchen counter as though delivering meals at four thirty in the morning was entirely normal.

"Mahalo," I said, slipping her a bill. One of the last. Though my stomach rumbled, I tried not to look at the food, the feast Rick had ordered for us and which I could practically inhale right now.

"Odd hour to eat," Simon observed, gray eyes raking me from head to foot. "Though it looks like you've been doing a bit of midnight feasting. Found your way into the good paddock, did you?"

Straight in with the knife, delivered with a side of sarcastic humor, Simon style. "Why are you here, Simon? I understood you'd arranged all the divorce documentation. In my absence. Without my agreement."

He ran a hand across his distinguished salt-and-pepper hair, which never needed coaxing into place. "The moment I heard you'd been injured, I realized my mistake. I'm so sorry, Sara. I had to rush here to make certain you were truly all right."

"Rush here—on the Winchester's money?"

He flinched, so I pressed my advantage.

"Yes, I am aware of that little fact. If you were so concerned about me, why didn't you come under your own steam? And you sure didn't seem too bothered when I called you."

"You caught me off guard—"

"With Emma, the love of your life, in your bed."

He didn't respond to my attack. He often ignored me, like I was a petulant child, not worth the trouble of admonishing. At least not until he'd thought of a worthy comeback, then he'd reopen the conversation. "Elizabeth Winchester insisted she should pay. Clearly, she felt it important I be here."

I crossed my arms over my chest. More to hide the

fact that I wasn't wearing a bra than to block my husband. I didn't need chastising for my sloppy attire. "That's somewhat odd as it's not the impression I received from her at all."

Simon sighed heavily and wrapped me in an awkward hug. He pressed a kiss to the crown of my head. "Anyway, how are you, Sara? How serious are your injuries? We should organize an independent medical assessment."

"No doctors required. I'm fine. Much as I have been for the last eleven months."

He released me and glanced about the room. "Winchester paid for this suite?" At my nod, he wandered across the room to finger the ornaments. "Good, good. Excellent, in fact."

"What are you talking about? And you still haven't told me why you're here." Or more importantly, why he'd interrupted the one bit of fun I'd had in years.

"Come on, Sara, we're a team, remember? *Sira*." Simon crossed back to me. Laid his hands heavily on my shoulders, talking down to me. Literally and figuratively. "You know how precedent works. Winchester pays for a room for you because he feels guilty about your injuries, meaning that he recognizes his culpability. He thereby establishes precedent, which gives us the basis for a case. Now we can encourage him to settle."

I shoved my husband away. "What are you on? This was Rick's room. He gave it to me because my regular accommodation was booked out. And because I needed to urgently use the internet to sort out my finances. Finances that *you* fucked over. So you can just stop with this bullshit about culpability. If you're here to sort out our money, fine. If not, you can bloody well leave."

His face darkened, the veneer of affability vanishing. "What the hell's gotten into you, Sara? Or should I say, who the hell?" he snarled. "You're smarter than this. This is a golden opportunity for us; we either settle with him out of court, or we make a name for ourselves." He sketched a banner headline in the air. *"Sira takes down the Lord of Tertanth."* He reached into his breast pocket and withdrew an envelope, then slapped it onto the desk. "And anyway, I brought the money you asked for."

I pressed a hand to my forehead. I hadn't hit the meds again, but I certainly felt light-headed. Lack of food, probably. Nothing he said made any sense. "What do you mean, 'take down'? Rick did nothing wrong."

Simon wagged a finger in my face. He'd always loved to lecture me. "Not true, Sara. He took a craft out when a dangerous weather alert had been issued, a vessel he was clearly incapable of handling. By doing so, he not only put himself in danger but also you because you felt compelled to try to rescue him. You realize if you'd died, I could've had him up for involuntary manslaughter." Avarice gleamed in his gray eyes.

He was joking, inviting me to join in his grim legal humor. Well, tough. I was hungry, tired, and still—incredibly—horny. It was time my husband left and time I sorted out Rick's dichotomy over where we stood. "How very unfortunate for you that I didn't die, then. Since when are you so hard up for a case anyway? I thought you had plenty to keep you busy. In fact, I'm surprised you found time to bring the documentation over here. I expected you to email everything through."

"What documentation?"

How did he have such a great professional

reputation when he seemed determined to be as thick as two short planks? "Statements of assets and finances. To settle the divorce. That is what you're here for, right?"

"The only document required for settlement would be the prenup, Sara, and that clearly states anything in my name is mine alone. Only the house is in joint names, and that's mortgaged—which you'd be aware of if you ever showed any interest in our life instead of flitting around the world."

"I know damn well it's mortgaged, Simon. Remember, my salary's been paying off the loan for years, too. But I'm also well aware of the equity in that mortgage."

Simon tugged at his earlobe, a tell I knew well. He was lying. Over the last decade, it was amazing he hadn't pulled his ear clean off. "You'll find the market's dropped since you've been gone."

"I'm willing to accept a drop. I'm not willing to be robbed. There's also the bank accounts and the share portfolios."

"Empty."

I gaped at him in disbelief. "You can't do that!"

"Me? Maybe they were exhausted financing your holiday lifestyle. I already told you you've had your share of the cash."

"The cars, then." I knew how much Simon loved money, how it filled some deep need within him, and I'd known he'd be awkward as all hell about dividing everything up. But I'd not expected him to be blatantly dishonest.

"They're in my name. And in any case, cars lose value the moment you drive them from the showroom."

Probably not the historic vehicles he collected, but I

was willing to cede the cars. "You can keep the bloody cars, Simon. All of them. Just give me my grandmother's house back."

"Your grandmother's house?" He let go of his ear, his forehead creasing.

"*My* house. The one my grandmother left to me freehold and I transferred to you so that you could negatively gear the repayments and benefit from the tax break. But I also worked to pay off that loan, remember? A loan for something I already fully owned."

He shook his head, reaching for his phone as "Ride of the Valkyries" exploded into the room.

"Simon! My bloody house. We agreed the sale was in name only, it'd always be mine, because Gran left it to me." Sure, it'd been a decade ago and such an inconsequential sum of money in Simon's eyes that he could have forgotten the deal. But that didn't mean he was getting away with it.

He glanced at his phone and held up a finger to stop me speaking. "Yes. What is it, sweetheart?"

Oh, hell no, it couldn't be—even he wouldn't— would he? I stared at the screen of the phone, not caring that I was being obvious. Yes, it was, and yes, he would. He was talking to baby-faced Emma right in fucking front of me. After he'd had the audacity to elbow his way in here, declaring his undying love and regret.

I snatched the phone from his manicured hand. "I'm sorry, Emma. My *husband* doesn't have time to speak with you right now." I clicked disconnect and flung the cell toward the lounge.

Sports had never been my thing. The phone fell about three feet short, skittering across the floor as we both watched in appalled silence.

"That was the latest model, Sara."

Of course it was. Damned if I was going to apologize, though. "And we were talking about my gran's old house, Simon. Your girlfriend was not invited to join the conversation."

"Don't be so callous. I left Emma alone to rush to you; do you have any idea how she feels?"

"Strangely enough, yes, I do. *Abandoned* comes to mind. But I'm sure you can tell me exactly how she *feels*." Not that my indignation was truly righteous anymore. Pot calling the kettle black.

He didn't get my sarcasm. "I don't recall you being so hard, Sara. Where's your empathy? Emma is having a hard time dealing with the fact that you and I are back together."

"Back together? Jesus, you're delusional, Simon! We were just discussing how to divide our assets."

"No, I was clarifying how you'd stand to lose from such an action and why I'm therefore unwilling to divide anything. So we stay married."

"No." I held my hand up, palm out. "Hell, no. That's not happening. You said the decree nisi is already organized and you're madly in love with Emma. Why would I stay married to you?"

He closed his eyes and smoothed his hair again, as though it'd become ruffled by the hot breath of my anger. "Because it would look rather bad for Mr. Winchester should the facts go public. The wealthy aristocrat seduces the loving wife of a hard-working attorney after she's risked her life to save him. With all the current scandals and media furor about men in positions of power coercing women into sexual acts, I wonder how the supporters of his absurd charities will feel about that little scenario?"

I crossed my arms, hoping Simon felt the weight of every ounce of the loathing I projected toward him. "You're overlooking one thing, Simon. I wasn't coerced; I wanted to have sex with Rick. In fact, in case you missed it, I begged him for it. Your blackmail attempt is pathetic. I'll just go public and tell everyone, and I mean *everyone*, that I chose to sleep with Rick."

"And how do you think that will look, Sara? The poor little cabin steward states in an interview that she didn't know who she'd rescued, but a few hours after discovering he's wealthy, she claims that she's always wanted to screw his brains out."

"I don't suppose anyone will care." Not beyond the tabloids, anyway. I winced at the thought of Rick's embarrassment and Elizabeth's scathing fury. "Let them say what they want. It makes no difference."

Simon's voice lowered, the deceptive calm that came over him when he knew he'd won a case and he was closing in for the kill. "You're not thinking this through, Sara. I promise you it'll make a difference to Richard. You see, on the recording I accidentally made while waiting in the corridor, you clearly ask Mr. Winchester to stop what he's doing. It's obvious that, although you were swept off your feet by his wealth, you changed your mind. But he, a man of power, refused to acknowledge that."

"Recording? You know that's illegal!"

"As is rape. And I was careful to stipulate that the recording was accidental. I was recording my thoughts, and you just happened to be louder than I was. As usual."

"Recording on your phone?"

"Of course." He looked nonplussed as I smiled

triumphantly.

I pointed to the shattered cell. "That phone?"

"Ah. I see your point." He shrugged. "It's fortunate that I'd forwarded the recording to my PA before you had your little tantrum, then, isn't it? You see, Sara, whichever way you try to spin this, you both lose. Either way, he's a rich bastard out to abuse women. The only thing you have any control over is whether or not you're portrayed as a tramp."

Shit. He was right. Tears thickened my voice. "But why, Simon? You have Emma. I said yes to the divorce. Why this?"

"Money, Sara. I wasn't prepared to lose anything in a divorce, not a cent. But now you've handed Rick Winchester to me on a platter. We stay together, *Sira,* just like we've always been, and allow Rick Winchester to make a magnificent gesture of gratitude toward you, and all these rumblings of his lack of integrity simply disappear."

A sudden glimmer of hope reignited my fight. Thank God for Elizabeth Winchester's prescience. The stern woman had been right on the money—probably sitting on a golden egg, actually, considering her slightly constipated mien. "There'll be no gestures, Simon. I signed a waiver."

"What do you mean?" He'd wandered off to examine the trappings of the room again, easily distracted by pretty things. Now he strode back to stand over me.

Maybe he was capable of causing me physical harm. I'd heard nothing to indicate Marty was in the hallway.

My breath quickened as Simon seized my upper arms, and I winced at the pain in my shoulder.

"You signed something?" he snapped. "Why would you do that, Sara? Why didn't you consult me first?"

"Consult you? You've not exactly been on my speed dial for the last year, Simon. And I'm perfectly capable of comprehending a legal document."

"What were the conditions? Show it to me." He appeared more flustered than I'd ever seen him. Part of his undeniable charm lay in his apparent nonchalance, the ease with which he achieved his objective, without seeming to strive for it. Uncertainty and insecurity did not sit well on his shoulders.

"I don't have it on me, Simon. And truly, it is none of your business. The Winchesters and I have settled. That's an end to the whole issue. Now we have only to sort the terms of our divorce."

He stroked at his chin, narrowing his eyes on me like he stalked prey. "If you've signed a waiver, you're worthless to me. And that changes the plan. But I can tell you the new terms right now; I'll give you that divorce you want, Sara, but I'm taking everything. If you argue, if you put one single anthill of a roadblock in my way, the facts about your tawdry little affair will come out and your boyfriend's reputation will be irreparably damaged." He jerked his chin at the side table. "And I'm taking that money with me."

As he reached for the envelope, I slammed my palm on it with such force the pain radiated through my wrist and up to my shoulder. "Like hell you are, Simon. You're not taking a damn thing."

Chapter Twenty-Two

Sara

I didn't need Marty's help to bundle Simon out of the room.

Envelope of cash in hand, I strode to the door and yanked it open.

The burly security guard leaned against the wall opposite. He lifted his great, leonine head, bloodshot eyes regarding me unblinkingly. "All right, love?"

"Fine, thanks, Marty. My husband is just leaving."

Simon started to protest, but then his gaze slid to the guard. "Okay, keep the money. That's nothing. But you understand me now, Sara? I'm going to catch a few hours' sleep, then I'll be back. The settlement process will be expedited if I have your signature, so we'll get those papers sorted out. Just as you wanted." He sneered the final words.

"I won't be here. I'm due back onboard in a few hours." My tone dull, I couldn't afford to let any emotion intrude into my words, or even my thoughts, not until I could work out what my husband had done to me.

"No, you're not."

He pecked my cheek as he passed, and I cringed. His gesture held no affection, simply patronizing ownership.

"I contacted the company and advised them, as your lawyer, that you wished to tender your resignation in light of the injuries you'd sustained whilst in their employ."

"Why would you do that? What do you care where I work?"

"Well, to be honest, I was afraid that after your televised outburst, they might dismiss you. And we wouldn't have wanted that tarnish on your character or affecting our case. But don't worry; I'm sure you can get a job cleaning toilets elsewhere." He swiveled back to face me, his voice dropping dangerously, his face thrust close. "And by the way, Sara, if you run telling tales to your boyfriend, I'll most definitely see that as an attempted roadblock. In fact, as I don't take kindly to being made to look a fool, it'll be in your best interest to remember that you're married until I tell you otherwise. After all, you wouldn't want to add to idle gossip, would you?" He strode down the corridor without waiting for a reply.

"What gossip is that?" Marty asked, scowling after Simon.

"At the moment, something of my own creation."

"Hmm. Well, gossip doesn't sit too well with Elizabeth, as you may have noticed."

"That's what Simon is banking on." That was the second time Marty had used Mrs. Winchester's first name.

"The lad said to let you know he's waiting for you to have breakfast. Something about you both having worked up an appetite, which I'm not happy about having to repeat, let alone think on. I'll tell him you're ready now."

I grabbed his sleeve. "No. Don't do that. I have to think some stuff through first."

"Oh?" He folded his arms across his barrel chest, swaying back on his heels. "Back to the husband, is it, then? Maybe Rick was right about married women."

I didn't have time to worry about what Rick might have said about married women. "No. Just…Simon pointed out some information that could turn out to be detrimental to Rick."

"He did what, now?" Suddenly, Marty was all business, his roguish, affable air evaporating quicker than dog pee on a cement sidewalk in summer. He took my elbow and guided me back into the room. "Take a seat, young lady. Tell me exactly what your husband said."

I bridled, hating to be told what to do. Remained standing. "I'll handle it."

"No. This is my job."

"Well, it's my business."

"The second you said Rick could be affected, it became my business. Either you tell me what your husband said, or I'll go find out for myself."

The last thing I needed was a bull-in-a-china-shop approach. I had to outwit Simon, not have the hired muscle terrify him. I couldn't let my almost ex-husband ruin Rick's reputation, but Marty wouldn't have the finesse to handle a slick lawyer. "Look, it was basically that if I embarrass Simon by being seen with Rick, he'll have no reservations about sharing certain knowledge with the media." Why, even now, did I need to cover up for Simon? Apparently, old habits died hard. I'd been conditioned by years of pretending I was okay with his affairs, that he hadn't cheated behind my back, that we had an open agreement, so his reputation wouldn't be tarnished among our associates.

I tried again. "I don't know what Rick told you." The heat climbed my cheeks faster than I could talk. I moved behind one of the leather lounge chairs, toying with the thick seam along the top cushion. "But Simon has some compromising information."

Marty snorted, crossing to the kitchen and drawing a glass of water. He handed it to me. Obviously thought I was about to self-combust. "The lad's too much of a gentleman to tell me anything, but given that he's pacing my room instead of sleeping and has been calling me every ten minutes asking if you're all right, I think I have a fair read of the situation. As he won't let me buy you flowers, seems you'd best go discuss this with him."

"Flowers?" I raised one eyebrow, too busy cycling through possibilities and outcomes to deal with cryptic puzzles. "No, that's just it. I can't see Rick again. If I do, I'll lose everything." And Rick's reputation would be compromised. I needed to wait until he'd moved on to do…whatever it was that Rick did. Hopefully with another woman, so any gossip my husband tried to stir would be irrelevant. Except the thought of Rick moving on, of him doing literally *anything* with another woman, shot a dart of jealousy into the center of my chest, into a part of me that I didn't even want to consider being involved in our brief affair. He had already moved on. Made it clear that we were nothing but a fling and he was done.

In any case, I had to be free to fight Simon. Take him to court, even if it ruined my career.

Because no way was he keeping my gran's house.

Marty's phone beeped, and he held it up so I could see the caller ID. Rick. "And by not seeing him, you win?"

I winced, trying to swallow past a sudden lump in my throat. "No. But Rick knows there are…boundaries." He'd imposed them himself. If he hadn't, maybe I'd have confided in him. Regardless, the problem was mine alone; I couldn't permit him to be dragged through Simon's filth with me. "But this way, at least Rick wins."

"And that matters to you, lass?"

"Of course."

"Even though you don't know him?"

"You don't have to know someone well to realize they're a decent person." A person I would have liked to know a lot better, under different circumstances.

Damn Simon.

"Okay." Marty heaved a sigh and trundled to the door, the daunting security guard replaced by a middle-aged man who might have been pudgy, rather than muscular, beneath his dark windbreaker. "I'll let the lad know to eat breakfast on his own, then."

I chewed my lip. It'd be easier this way. Easier to let Marty do it, to not say goodbye, to pretend that when Rick had walked out of the door an hour ago, I'd said all I wanted. But it would also be cowardly. "No. I'll text him." Yeah, right, because sending a message rather than a messenger was *so* much braver. "Do me a favor, though, Marty? Don't let him come down here till I've cleared out."

"I'll try."

"You said yesterday that you'd keep him out of my room if I wanted. I'm calling you on that promise now."

"Nicely handled." He touched a finger to his forehead in salute. "I'm sure I'll be seeing you."

Seriously, did nobody listen to what I said? As he left, I picked up my phone. Though I'd switched it to silent, several messages from Jay flashed up, along with two from an unknown number. That was the problem with a new SIM; the contacts all disappeared.

And three messages from Rick.

No doubt gentlemanly iterations of the "thanks for a great time, see you around" variety, but I was feeling too fragile to listen to more of that. Instead, I'd leave him my own blow-off text.

—Hey Rick, it was super fun…though don't think I didn't notice you broke your promise! Catch you on some other cruise.—

Crap. Even if he came looking for me—which of course I absolutely, definitely did not want—he wouldn't find me on *The Spirit of Ohana. Thanks, Simon.*

My finger hovered, deliberating over my sign-off. Screw it. If he could do it, so could I.

—Sara x—

I hit send before I could reconsider.

The phone rang as I crossed the room to put it on the bedside table while I dressed. Rick. I pressed a key to send whichever automatic reply came to the top of the screen and tugged open my backpack. Time to find some of my own clothes to wear, for the first time this weekend.

Pulling out jeans and a tee, I sat on the bed despondently. The phone blipped again.

—Please pick up. Marty says you've asked me to stay away from your rooms, and I respect that. But I need to speak with you. How long until you have to be back aboard? I have a promise to make good on. Rick xx—

Was he thinking of the same promise I'd meant? The promise to fuck me? So with my husband safely out of the way, he considered the fling still on?

Didn't matter.

I had work to do.

But did the extra kiss mean something?

Nope, didn't matter.

Anyway, I couldn't risk seeing him.

But maybe not only because of Simon.

I pulled my clothes on, ran a brush through my hair, and checked the time. Did the conversion. Six on a Sunday here made it far too early on a Monday morning in Australia. Not that it mattered overmuch, as my father-in-law would always take my call. But I could wait a while.

I flipped my laptop open and logged in. Opened a document and used the suite code to connect to the internet. My heart beat faster as the banking site accepted my passwords. Then my breath eked out. Simon had spoken honestly about one thing, at least; our accounts were empty—and now that he'd cleaned them out, he'd unblocked my access. Nice.

The first task of any case was always to record the facts. Adding pen and paper to my work area, I started on the primary account, trawling through the entries, databasing the withdrawals over the last twelve months, color coding whether they were made by me or Simon.

The phone lay face down on the desk and switched to silent, so I managed to ignore the faint flash each time a message came in. By the time I finished with my records, I'd missed—avoided—seven messages from Rick. I flicked past them and opened Jay's voicemail instead. The familiarity of his deep, rich voice chased away some of the tension coiled in my belly.

Until I remembered I'd have to say goodbye to him today. Whether Simon had tendered my resignation, or whether I'd lost my job after the interview, didn't matter. The end result was the same.

Jay's calls were to say he was checking in on me because I'd failed to get back to him as I'd promised. His final message said he'd contacted Rick, had my suite number, and would come by around ten.

I warily opened the messages from the unknown number, sagging in relief as I recognized Melanie's voice. Both calls were from the previous evening, the first saying she'd hit Jay up for my number and suggesting we all catch up for a drink. The second, straight to the point.

—*What on earth was with that interview? How could you not know who Rick freakin' Winchester is? Like, sure, on the ship you were kind of out of it. But by Saturday night? Girl, I have got to talk to you. Where you hiding?*—

I checked the time and sent a group message to both of my friends. A few months back I'd discovered a terrific Portuguese diner a block away. It looked pretty ordinary, with chipped laminate tables and mismatched chairs, the windows painted out with advertising. But they served an awesome all-day breakfast, incorporating American and Portuguese cuisine. And more importantly, really good, strong coffee. That'd be my sole complaint about Hawaii; the coffee was insipid compared to Australia.

I eyed the platters of food on the kitchen counter across the large room. So much for my new mantra. *Love* had taken a beating, and now even *Eat*, always my easiest accomplishment, wasn't working out too well; I hadn't touched the room service Rick had ordered us. *Pray* would be all I had left soon, and right now vengeance was featuring far too prominently for me to be racking up any points with that one.

The phone chimed with Jay's agreement to breakfast. As I waited for Melanie's response, I flicked through the database on my computer and found my father-in-law's phone number. I picked up the handpiece of the hotel's landline. While the dial tone clicked and whirred, connecting the miles, I blew out a heavy breath.

I hated to ask Derek for a favor. Unlike his son, my father-in-law hadn't been born to money; he'd worked his way up, establishing his legal practice in his early thirties. Even now, forty years later, he maintained a strong work ethic and a philanthropic bent. Had I asked, Derek would have given me the money I'd needed for the orphanage. But Simon would find a way to twist the loan to his advantage, to insinuate the money was his inheritance and I'd accessed it unfairly. Besides, I'd had money. I hadn't needed to beg charity. I'd only needed to be able to access that money.

"Hello?"

Derek sounded sleepy, and I guiltily double-checked the time. "Hi, Derek, it's Sara."

"Sara, how are you? Or the way you get around, should I say, where are you? Are you keeping well? I know you want to save the world, but care has to start at home, you know."

As always, his easy friendliness relaxed me. "No, I've gone for the soft life for a while." Not that anything had been soft with Rick. But I couldn't think about that—him. "I'm working on a cruise liner in Hawaii. Simon didn't mention it?" Typical that Simon wouldn't have kept his father up-to-date.

Derek snorted. "That boy and I are not on speaking

terms at the moment."

My ears burning, I held my breath. Simon worked with his father at Derek's law firm. "Oh?" I didn't want to pry, but hell, I wanted to *know*.

"He told me he's divorcing you, Sara. I'm sorry about that. Don't get me wrong; I'm not sorry for you."

I slumped in the chair. I'd always thought Derek and I got on well.

"I'm not sorry for you, because you can do far better for yourself than that useless piece-of-crap son of mine. I'm sorry for me because being married to you was the only thing keeping him on the straight and narrow. Now we've got all kinds of problems." His voice muffled for a moment as though he covered the receiver to speak to someone else in the room. Then he came back, tinny but clear. "Sara? I'm so sorry, love, but I have to go right now. Can I call you back in an hour or two?"

"Y-yes, sure. I'll give you my cell." I read the number from the screen of my mobile, still unfamiliar with it, said goodbye, and hung up. Then sat there staring at the phone on the huge polished desk. What had Derek meant?

My cell beeped, startling me from my thoughts. Text from Jay.

—*Thought you said ten at the diner instead of your suite?*—

I checked the time. Crap. Already half past.

Chapter Twenty-Three

Rick

I knew Sara would be mad as hell with me for turning up to the breakfast with her co-workers, but when I'd called Jay and basically spilled my guts in a most un-British fashion, he'd taken pity on me and told me where they'd be.

But now it seemed Sara might stand us all up. After arriving early, I'd sat drinking horribly insipid tea and making small talk with Jay and Melanie for the last forty-five minutes, my gaze permanently fixed on the door. If she bolted when she saw me, I'd damn well chase her down. What had that worthless husband of hers said to make her turn like this? Any other time, I'd have been pleased her reaction proved my theory correct; married women were safe. They hightailed it back to their husbands after they'd had a bit of fun. But now—now I was not willing to accept that as a possibility. Besides, the only bit of information I'd been able to glean from Marty was that Sara was most definitely not returning to Simon. Other than that, my security officer's lips had remained tighter than a fish's bum.

The bell over the door pinged, but I didn't need the alert. Sara stood outlined by the morning sunshine. The first time I'd seen her in casual clothes instead of her uniform. Or next to nothing. The next to nothing obviously won, but tight jeans and a fitted tee certainly displayed her ample curves gloriously. Fortunately, the table was high; otherwise, I would have propelled it into the air with my instant erection.

I started to rise from my seat as she approached, then thought better of it. Fortunately, my companions didn't stand either, though probably not for the same reason. Except for bloody Jay. Judging by the way his face lit up, he still had it hot and hard for Sara.

She made her way directly to us across the tiny room, though she glanced over her shoulder, back at the door, before speaking to me. "Why are you here?"

Melanie, who'd been simpering and acting in a cutely obsequious manner, gasped. "Sara!"

Sara spared her a glance and a smile for Jay. "Hey, guys."

She hadn't smiled at me. Only Jay. My hands formed into fists on the table.

Then she looked back at me, those amazing eyes sparking with anger, not passion. "Didn't Marty explain that you need to stay away from me?"

"Away from your room, actually."

"Lexical semantics."

"You know how I love to play word games with you."

Her lip twitched, the frown between her eyes smoothing. "Only with words, then?"

Jay cleared his throat overloudly, and Sara shot him a grin. Damn, I wanted that grin for myself. But at least she wasn't mad with me.

Or maybe she was—though the way she chewed at her lower lip before speaking didn't look like anger. More like...concern? "Rick, you don't understand. It'd just be easier if you stayed away from me."

"Maybe I'm not interested in easy."

"Really?" She quirked an eyebrow, the last of her reserve melting. "I'll try and keep that in mind." She turned to her co-workers. "Sorry, guys. Have we ordered? I want carb-heavy. And coffee. Lots of coffee."

"Oh, but carbs are so fattening," Melanie chimed in.

"Indisputably," Sara said. "Not that you need worry. But they also happen to be a damn fine way to numb emotions."

What emotions? Had I hurt her? I'd tried to give her an out if she wanted to return to her husband, but I'd been unable to pull it off, calling to check on her every few minutes like a lovesick teen. If she'd said she was leaving with Simon, I would have spent everything I had to buy the bastard off.

The waitress approached, poured coffee, and started writing down our orders. Sara went for pancakes with a side of bacon. She didn't dither about it, didn't apologize, and didn't pretend she was taking it home for a mythical dog. She simply ordered what she wanted with no care for anyone's judgment. Damn, I loved that.

I dragged my gaze quickly back to my menu. There was that word again. *Love.* Why had it kept popping up over the last couple of days? I'd noticed she ended her text with a kiss, but I couldn't book onto the next cruise and follow her like a puppy—not that I had anything against dogs, but because I had paperwork to get done. She'd said her rotations were ten days. If I waited a week and a half for her to return, could we be more than a one-night stand?

Jay unsurprisingly ordered the big breakfast. He handed his menu to the waitress, then turned to Sara.

"So, mate, what is it you're eating yourself into a catatonic state to avoid? Well, besides the endless YouTubes of you running out of the interview?"

Sara glared at him. "A true friend would pretend that'd never happened."

"Never said I wanted to be your *friend*."

Melanie interrupted. "Leave her alone, Jay. She doesn't need your teasing. In fact—"

I pretended not to notice, tapping my teaspoon on the side of my cup as she angled her chin very obviously toward me.

"Seems she doesn't need anything from you."

"Ain't that the truth." Jay sighed melodramatically. "So then, our Sara, what is it that sees you eating a shit-ton of carbs?"

Sara toyed with the edge of her napkin, seeming unusually at a loss for words. She kept glancing at the window. "Seems this is my farewell brunch. I'm not going back on the ship."

My heart kicked, and it had nothing to do with the weak tea. Had she preempted me? She'd already decided she'd stay here, with me. Damn, I should be mad at her assumption, but as always, her forthrightness charmed me. If ever a woman could take the bull by the horns... Lord, I wanted her to take me by the horn. Again.

"I've lost my job."

"What the heck?" Jay slammed his cup down on the table. "What do you mean? Because of the interview? Raynalds isn't an unreasonable man; I can't see him making that call."

"No." Melanie's baby-blue eyes filled instantly with tears. "You have to come. You're my roomie."

Sara passed a hand across her eyes. Did I imagine

that it trembled slightly? "It's not the captain. At least, I don't think so. Seems my husband saw fit to tender my resignation."

"Your what?" spluttered Jay.

"Your husband?" If Melanie's eyes grew any larger, she'd suffer ocular dislocation.

Sara waved down the chorus. "We're practically divorced. But he turned up here to finalize some paperwork. Amongst other things."

For the first time, her words seemed evasive. And I loathed hearing "my husband" trip off her tongue. "What other things?"

She shot me a glance, her expression almost…wounded. "Nothing important. Ah, food. That makes everything better. The good news is breakfast is on me. Do you like the way I didn't tell you until after you'd ordered? Didn't want any caviar on my tab."

"I don't think they serve—oh." Melanie caught on to the joke late.

Sara tapped the other woman's plate with her fork. "It's okay, Mel. I knew you'd be egg white omelet. It was these other two big boys who concerned me."

Her words, the insinuation, thrilled down to my groin. Damn, I wanted to show her just how big she made me.

Seeming oblivious to the effect she was having on me, Sara continued innocently. "And I have the money to repay you, Rick. Simon came through on that at least."

Every mention of the man had the hackles on my neck lifting. "There's no need, Sara. I told you that."

"And I told you it was only a loan. No strings attached. How's your bacon? American stuff is totally different, huh?"

No strings? Was that code? I should be able to tell myself that I wanted her no strings. I wanted that luscious body naked in my bed or, hell, even naked in an alleyway where I could press myself up against her. But no strings? I was beginning to suspect I wanted a chance of far more than that. "It's certainly not like kippers on toast."

Melanie pushed her plate of insipid egg whites away, patting her flat stomach as though the few mouthfuls could possibly have filled her up. "So what are you going to do, Sara? Ask the captain for your job back?"

Sara stabbed several pieces of pancake, drowning them in maple syrup. "I might go begging. But not this tour. I have to square things up with Simon and get him off my back."

"Off your back?" I jumped on the phrase. "What do you mean? Is he giving you a hard time? I thought he was all for the divorce."

"Wow, a barrage of questions and I've not even finished one cup of coffee." Sara laughed, though her eyes remained somber, and she seemed distracted.

I didn't want her to have to worry about anything. Not when I had enough money to make any kind of problem go away. "No, seriously, what's the issue?"

Sara lifted one shoulder, then winced. The wrong shoulder. "Nothing. Just regular divorce manipulations. You know how it is." She cast a glance around the silent table and then mumbled, "Well, nope, maybe none of you do."

"Oh, I'm divorced," Jay drawled. "But can't say there was any drama attached."

"Not me," Melanie chimed in.

"Nor me," I said. "So spill. How does this divorce business work?"

Sara cast a glance over her shoulder, as though worried she'd be overheard. Her gaze had constantly flicked to the café windows, even though they were so heavily painted out with advertisements it'd be near impossible to see in. She was skittish, and that made me more determined to get to the bottom of what troubled her.

She signaled for a refill of coffee, waiting until it was poured before speaking. Either she was buying time to order her thoughts, or she hoped we'd start another conversation. "It's just the usual stuff. Simon wants to take everything in the divorce. There are certain things I'm not prepared to surrender."

I almost sighed out my relief. As usual, nothing that couldn't be fixed with money. "I'll hire you an attorney. The best Australia has. You'll get more than your share."

Melanie joined in. "Oh, that's fantastic. It'll all be cool, Sara."

Sara scowled at me, and my blood ran cold. Bloody hell, what had I said wrong this time?

"Fixing it all with money again?" she sneered. "Thanks for your offer, but I'll represent myself if it gets that far."

She seemed to have more of an aversion to the trappings of wealth than I did. "What? You can't risk doing that." Her stubbornness and reluctance to accept a favor would see her lose everything, no matter how little that was.

Sara set her cup down with dangerous care, her tone low and icy. "I *can't*? Why not? Or do you hold to the belief that an attorney who represents herself has a fool for a client?"

"What the hell?" Jay blurted exactly what I was thinking.

I tried to tread carefully, but the words tumbled out, thick with my confusion. "What do you mean? You're a cabin steward."

"Yes. But I'm also an attorney."

Just when I thought she had nothing left to shock me with. She was in the legal profession? That certainly explained a lot. And raised a hell of a lot more questions. "You didn't mention that."

"Why would I? I'm not defined by my job, Rick. Are you? In any case, I assumed Marty had told you."

Marty had known? Why had he kept it under his hat?

Melanie interrupted eagerly. "You stand up in court and get the scumbags put away and stuff?"

"I can, but I don't. I'm not currently a trial attorney. More of the boring-paperwork, corporate-law type. That's why I'm here hanging out with you guys. To see what the real world is like for a change."

The information hadn't disturbed Jay's appetite. He mopped up his egg with one last piece of toast and pushed the empty plate away with a satisfied sigh. "Well, got to admit, I did not see that one coming. How come you're not going back to law if the cruise deal is over? Not that I want you to," he added quickly. "Though the idea of you in a suit and heels does hold a certain interest."

Sara screwed up her face at Jay. Just as bloody well, because I wanted to punch him. No one should be sharing my instant fantasy.

"Well, this whole divorce thing kind of came out of the blue only about, ah, twenty-four hours ago. I was planning on sticking to this lifestyle a bit longer, then maybe going back to the Solomon Islands to do some more volunteering with the law reform commission."

"And that's law? Or working in hospitality?" Melanie seemed to be having trouble getting her head around it all. Bless, I wasn't the only one.

"Law. But right now, I can't afford to get back. I have to get this divorce mess cleaned up and get a job."

"But you're not going back on the ship, and you're not about to leave Hawaii?" I had to be certain.

"Ship, no. Hawaii, also no, simply because I don't have the cash to leave until I sort Simon. I'm going to have to run up an account at the Backpackers and hope I can work this out quickly."

"You can stay where you—" I winced as she leveled a glare at me. There I went, splashing cash around again, trying to fix the world. Bugger it, in for a penny, in for a pound. "Does the Backpackers have doubles? I've a hankering to try the lifestyle."

Again, that twitch of the lips. Sara tilted her head. "The place is full of free spirits indulging in wild sex and unfettered love."

"Thought you weren't much into spirits? Tend to send you to sleep at the wrong moment."

This time she rewarded me by tracing her tongue across her full upper lip, on the pretext of catching the cream from her coffee. "Two out of three ain't bad."

Jay's chair scraped as he stood up. "That sounds like our cue. Plus, the air's getting a bit thick in here for me."

"Oh no, not yet," Melanie said. "We still have hours before we need to be aboard."

"I didn't say we were boarding, just that we were giving these folks a bit of privacy. Rick, good luck with the mermaid, man. And Sara, you'll definitely be here when we get back from this roster?"

"Sure will. I'll see you both in ten days, okay?"

I was sure as hell going to read hope into the fact that Sara didn't try to prevent her friends from leaving. Or correct Jay's assumption that we were a thing.

Jay bent down and kissed her—only on the cheek—and shook my hand. Melanie started sobbing and hugged Sara.

Sara patted at her back. "The shipwrecked sailor watch is all on you now, Mel. Try to haul out a good one, okay?"

The pair departed, and an awkward silence descended over the table.

I stared into the bottom of my teacup for a moment, then realized I didn't want to look away from Sara's face for that long. "Sara, I'm sorry if the way I try to help you comes across as, I don't know…entitled? It's not how I mean it. It's just I have ready access to money and I've no idea how to make anything better without it."

"Oh, you can make things better for me," she almost purred. "But first, you have to realize one thing." She straightened, her tone suddenly firm. "I'm not a damsel in distress, Rick. I don't need rescuing. I can take care of my own shit, and I don't need you or your money."

I winced at the harshness of her words, but she relented.

"I don't *need* you. But I do want you to make good on your promise."

My voice damn near cracked. "Which promise?" I hoped she was talking about the same one I'd texted about, not that I'd forgotten something important. All the blood rushing from my brain to my dick made it pretty hard to remember anything.

She leaned closer, her lips against my ear. "To fuck me. Now."

Despite the bulge in my pants, I shoved my chair back and stood. "How are you at sprinting?"

"I suck." She grinned, letting me know the double entendre was deliberate, and stuffed a wad of cash in the check folder.

I had to shove my hand in my pocket to stop myself from automatically paying the bill. That, and it meant I could try and bend my rock-hard cock back to less-obvious proportions.

Tried and failed, because Sara stood, her breasts pressed against me as she stretched on tiptoes to plant a kiss on my lips. A short kiss, a sweet kiss.

A kiss that meant so much more than it should.

Chapter Twenty-Four

Sara

Despite my dislike of athletic pursuits—wait, was sex considered an athletic pursuit? In that case, despite my dislike of *most* athletic pursuits—we made good time back to the hotel, though Rick's firm grasp drawing me along certainly helped. A skateboard would also have been welcome.

A few shops short of the hotel, I dragged Rick to a halt. "We can't be seen together. And your room, not mine, okay? He knows where mine is."

"But why can't we—"

"You're wasting time. Which floor?"

"Seventh."

"Okay, give me five minutes. I'll be waiting for you at the elevator on the seventh." My heart was pounding like a teenager at her first concert. If the elevator wasn't working, I'd have enough adrenaline to sprint up the stairs. Finally, *finally*, Rick was going to fuck me. No foreplay required, I was ready for him. Had been since the moment I saw him waiting in the café, the second I realized he was still interested, that he felt our affair as unfinished as I did.

The ride up in the elevator alone was exquisite torture as I recalled our ride together the previous day. At least it gave me time to check my reflection, run my fingers through my hair.

Regardless of my directions, Rick didn't give me five minutes head start. More like two. But I couldn't help grinning like a loon as the elevator door opened and my spike of fear that it might be Simon disappeared. To hell with my husband. I couldn't control him—nor could he know where I was or what I was doing. Never mind what I planned to be doing in a few seconds. I intended to rip those clothes right off Rick Winchester. I knew what lay beneath, and I was going to have some of it. No, *all* of it.

Rick glanced up and down the corridor and then reached for me. Pulled me against him before kissing me, almost savagely. "When you wouldn't answer my calls, I thought you were going to take off on me."

I grabbed at his hair and tugged his mouth back to mine, talking against his lips. "No way. I'm a big believer in promises. I want my wish fulfilled."

"Then your wish is my command." One arm around my waist, he half lifted me from the floor as he rushed me down the corridor. "Lord, the things I want to do with you. I'm so glad you're not back on the ship today; there wouldn't be enough hours." He keyed the door, then thrust it open with one shoulder. "I feel I should carry you across the threshold."

"You can if it gets us to the bed quicker." Hopefully, he wouldn't try, though. I'd hate for him to damage something important, trying to lift me.

He grinned again, his eyes sparkling as he covered my mouth in a hungry kiss, walking backward as he dragged me into the room.

From the corner of my eye, I caught a flash of movement and stiffened, jerking away from Rick.

He must have read the shock in my face, as he whirled around. "Marty! What the bloody hell are you doing in here?"

"Same as I spend most of me life doing, lad. Watching out for you. It'd help if you answered your phone once in a while."

Rick looked guilty. "I turned it off while we had breakfast." He pulled me against his side and gazed down. "I'd reached who I needed to."

"Well, seems you two have it sorted, then?" Marty searched me with a long look. "Thought you'd determined to stay away from my lad?"

I bit at my lip nervously. This felt ridiculously like being caught making out by a boyfriend's dad. "Simon doesn't know where we are. I figured we could have a little time together."

"What's bloody Simon got to do with it?" Rick's body stiffened against me. And not the bit I wanted stiff. "Dammit, Marty, why so many secrets? And come to think of it, why didn't you mention Sara's an attorney?"

The older man pinched at his nose. "Didn't know my job description included chief snitch among the duties. Besides, seemed to me it was irrelevant. No matter what I told you, it wouldn't have changed your feelings any, would it now?"

Rick shook his head adamantly. "Not a jot."

Wait, feelings? What feelings?

"Anyway," Marty continued, "as I've set my mind at ease that you're safe—odd how that only seems to happen when the gel's around, isn't it?—I'll be getting back to Elizabeth."

"Eliza—dammit, man, what is with you calling my mother by her first name all of a sudden?"

I covered my chuckle at Rick's very British outrage. "I doubt it's all of a sudden. Can't you see they have a thing going on?"

"They have a what?" He sounded horrified. "No, you've got it wrong, Sara." His arm tightened around me. "Marty has three girlfriends. Not to mention a houseful of ferrets."

"Girlfriends?" Marty snorted. "You mean Doreen, Maureen, and Anna?"

"Whatever you bloody call them, man. That's not the point."

Marty squared his shoulders, fists balled as though ready for a fight. "No. The point is when I say I'm taking Doreen down the pub for a pint, it means I'm takin' my bloody greyhound for a walk and getting a drink on t'way." His accent thickened with each word.

I wriggled from Rick's grasp. "And the other two? Maureen and Anna, was it? They're also greyhounds?"

"Too bloody right," Marty growled. "And if the lad here weren't so wrapped up in saving the world, he mighta realized that."

"They're dogs?" Rick seemed slow on the uptake, finally kicking the door shut behind us. "But my mother?"

"Aye, lad. That one's a little harder to explain, I'll give ye that. We've been friends for a long time, you know. Right back from before she first met your father. She's a mighty fine woman, and she needs someone to lean on. It's not right she's left to struggle alone while your father's here but not here." Marty's eyes were soulful. "And I am right sorry for that, lad. I'd not hurt your father for anything, but he's well beyond being hurt. And your mother, well, she's a lady of passion. She needs someone."

Rick raised his palm. "Hell, man, for the love of all that is holy, stop there. I don't need any more information. Good luck to you, is all I can say. At least, in light of what I intend to do next week, I know you're not after Mother's money."

Marty scowled. "Would you ever have thought that of me?"

Rick regarded him silently for a long moment. "Never. You know you've been more father to me than any man alive."

Marty cleared his throat phlegmily and shuffled a little. "Well then, I'd better be off. Was thinking of picking up your mother one of those flower necklaces they have here, given that she likes orchids."

"Leis," I supplied.

"Oh, please don't," Rick murmured alongside me. "This is my mother. None of your wordplay." He suddenly chuckled. "Flowers, Marty? I thought they were reserved as your great buy off."

"Only works with your generation, lad. Elizabeth likes little trinkets. Right, I'm off, then."

I moved into Rick's embrace as the door closed behind the guard. "What do you mean, 'buy off'?"

His hands framed my face as he stared down into my eyes, a smile playing at the corners of his mouth. "Marty seems to believe that whenever I want to move a, uh, partner along, all he needs do is present her flowers from me. Sort of 'here you go, thanks for a jolly good time, see you at the polo, then, ta-ra.' "

"Ah, I see. But he told me earlier that you wouldn't allow him to bring me flowers."

He drew me close and kissed me slowly and deeply.

The kiss wasn't passionate; it was…something else. "Sara, I will never buy you flowers."

"It takes some skill to make that sound romantic, Richard Winchester. Nicely done." Though I joked, my mind tripped and stumbled over his words. Was he teasing? More clever wordplay? Or…something more?

"Oh, you want skill, do you?"

"Only your best attempt."

His hands slid down my arms, thumbs brushing my nipples. "Hmm, let's see what I can dredge up. That expensive education ought to be good for something."

Still shivering from the contact with my nipples, I moaned as his mouth found the side of my neck, his tongue firm and hard, stroking the sensitive flesh. "Oh, God, yes. Just like that, Rick." What was it about this guy that drove me so crazy? Flirting with Jay had been fun, but Rick was so much…more. I had to have him. The thought of him leaving caused me physical pain, but perhaps having him thrusting inside me could exorcize that. "No foreplay." My voice came out overloud and demanding, but, damn, I needed to control this. "No foreplay, Rick. I just want to fuck you. Now."

"Are you sure?" His hands were under my shirt. "Because I'd happily play here for hours." He removed one hand and slid it to my butt, nestling his fingers in the crease. "And did I remember to mention how simply spectacular your arse looks in jeans? Makes me want to bite it. In fact—" He spun me around and dropped to his knees, then sank his teeth into the denim-covered mound. Groaned with his mouth full, then pulled back. "Clothes off, Sara. I need your clothes off. Now."

When had I lost control? Yet I ripped off my tee, revealing my lacy bra, my breasts almost spilling over the top.

Rick stretched to grope a breast as he bit at my bum. "Sara, you're killing me. I want to touch and taste and feel everything at once. I can't get enough of you, and it's driving me crazy."

He surged back to his feet and turned me to face him. Well, turned me so that my breasts faced him. He gazed at them with such adoration I had trouble believing he'd already seen them naked several times. "You're an absolute fantasy come to life, you know that? I don't just mean all this." He waved a hand up and down my frame. "But you're a total package. This awesome body, your smart little mouth, your outspokenness, your work ethic, your intelligence, and—"

The phone rang in my jeans pocket, and I startled. Generally, the vibration was quite pleasant, but right now, I didn't need any extra stimulation. "Sorry," I muttered, digging it out. Darn, I wanted to hear that one last bit of my fabulosity itemized. And then take this suave, clever, hot-as-hell, totally irresistible man to bed and screw his brains out. I glanced at the screen as my thumb moved to terminate the call. "Oh! I have to get this. I'm so sorry." I didn't wait for Rick's nod but keyed the screen. "Hi, Derek?"

Derek's voice was tinny, betraying the miles. "Sara, I'm so sorry to have rushed out on you earlier. Pouring oil on more troubled waters your husband has created."

My husband? How about his son?

"That's fine. But, Derek, you said you're no longer on speaking terms with Simon. May I ask why? Though, before you say anything, I should caution you that I'm asking because I'm trying to sort out the terms of our divorce."

"Let me guess. The bastard's trying to stiff you?"

Before today, I'd never heard Derek speak ill of his son. Rick moved behind me, easing me farther into the room.

Tiny goose bumps followed the trail of his fingers across my back. "Well, that'd be one way to put it. I have to say I never expected this from him. He arrived in Hawaii saying he'd rethought the divorce. That he wanted to stay married."

Rick's hand tightened on my back, and I could feel him holding his breath.

"When I declined, he said he'd take everything."

Derek sighed heavily. "Another bit of his nonsense. Ever since he took up with that flighty young thing who seems to have nothing but marshmallow between her ears—and probably in her breast implants—he's been burning through money. Trying to impress her, I suppose. Not that that's anything new, he's always had a taste for being flashy. But before you left, he had a dual income to do it on. With you taking care of all the bills, there was never a chance of the creditors coming after him."

Derek's chair creaked, and I could imagine him reclining wearily back into the deep olive-green leather in his elegant office.

"For a while, there was talk young Emma's family has money. But it seems they're too smart to allow her to get her hands on it until she's grown up a good bit. I'll put it plain, Sara. Simon's broke. I've bailed him out twice, but now I've cut him off."

"What?" I clutched the back of a nearby chair for support. Simon couldn't be broke. Money was everything to him. It funded his lifestyle and, more importantly, proved his worth. He had such disregard for anyone who wasn't wealthy he couldn't join the ranks of the impoverished. "Oh, Derek, that's awful. And I feel kind of responsible."

"Oh no, you don't," interrupted my father-in-law. "Don't you go there. Simon's always been a greedy little bastard. He lives beyond his means, and now he'll reap the punishment. Maybe it'll pull him back into line. I told him I'm cutting him from the firm, but of course, I won't. He has to earn the money somewhere to dig himself out of this hole. And say what you like about him—not that you've ever said a bad word, Sara, though I rather wish you had spoken up—he's a damn fine attorney. He'll earn his way out."

I'd ignore the side helping of guilt that came with Derek's disclosures. "So that's why he's trying to clean me out in the divorce? Because he actually needs the money?"

"Clearly." My father-in-law's acerbic tone had strengthened as he got the story off his chest. "But don't you let him screw you over. You've provided for his lifestyle long enough. No reason for you to provide for his girlfriend. They're both capable of holding down a job."

Rick had guided me around the chair and then pushed me gently into it. Now he handed me a glass of water, then stood, rubbing at his chin, clearly unsure whether he should leave or not.

I reached for his free hand and threaded my fingers through his. "That's the problem, though. I signed a watertight prenup."

Derek harrumphed. "You mean the one he presented you with two days before your wedding?"

271

Yeah, I clearly remembered being blindsided by it. All the arrangements for a lavish function made, guests invited, dress purchased, and Simon had laid down the paper as though it were a gift. "Yes. That one."

"I can't advise you against my son, Sara. That wouldn't be ethical. But I suggest you do some homework on that prenup. You're a good lawyer. You'll find what you need. Simon's trying to hoodwink you. I wouldn't put it past him to throw a little extortion into the mix."

Lucky Rick couldn't hear the other end of the conversation. "Oh, we've already been there."

A low groan rolled through the phone. "Really? I was hoping he'd at least be above that. What's he done?"

"I have a, ah, new relationship." Heat crawled up my neck. Rick's fingers tightened around mine, his thumb stroking the back of my hand. "Simon's trying to manipulate that."

"Well, don't you let him. You're every bit as smart as him, and you have a damn sight more integrity. You be sure to get what's due to you."

Still, I didn't like to think of Simon being put in such a position. I'd have to negotiate with him. "Thank you so much, Derek. You have no idea how much you've helped me."

My father-in-law's stern tone softened. "Just you be sure to keep in touch. There's always a bed here for you when you come home."

I clicked off the cell and stared at the screen for a moment, digesting the news.

Rick dropped to his haunches in front of me. First thought to flash into my mind was *why do I have my pants on*? Closely followed by *lucky I'm sitting, because just looking at this man makes my knees go all kinds of weak.*

He ran a hand from my knee to my thigh. "Everything all right?"

I needed to curb my habit of immediately insisting I had everything under control, of needing to prove I could take care of it myself. I covered his hand with mine and lifted it to my mouth. Kissed his knuckles. "It's more than okay."

My tongue traced down the side of one of his fingers, and the flare of desire in his eyes kindled the heat in my loins. I needed these jeans off now. Screw the thigh-chafing, I should have worn a skirt while he was around.

Rick wound his arms around my butt, pulled me to the very edge of the chair, and bit at my mound through the jeans. He had to be able to feel the heat emanating from me. Another two seconds and he'd get a damp patch, to boot.

His hands slid up my back, then deftly unhooked my bra and freed my breasts. Fingers working on my nipples, he thrust his face into my groin with far more force than he'd used when I was naked. And, damn, it was so fucking good.

Now I was torn. I wanted to race to the bedroom, to strip naked and feel him thrusting hard and strong within me. But I also wanted him to continue with exactly what he was doing right now...and maybe experience all the other treats he'd alluded to. Would we ever have enough time for everything I wanted to do with him?

But first, I had homework to do. "Can you wait an hour?"

"No," Rick growled. "But I will. As long as you

remain at least semi-naked and allow me to continue visually worshipping you while I wait."

I smiled but started scrolling screens on my phone, my brain instantly clicking into work mode.

Inspired by Derek's hints, even without my laptop, the search didn't take long. Simon didn't have a leg to stand on. He couldn't take my gran's house. And though I was willing to tell the world how I felt about Rick who, despite his teasing, had respected me enough to sit silently beside me as I worked, I now had far more effective ammunition against my soon-to-be ex-husband.

I finished writing the last of my notes, carefully copying from the screen, then tossed my phone onto the couch. "Now, Mr. Winchester, where were we?"

Rick grinned, dropping from the chair to his knees and edging my thighs apart. "I believe I was—"

Loud thumping at the door interrupted his words.

Chapter Twenty-Five

Rick

I had my head between her thighs, her breasts swinging free above me, and bloody Marty was banging at the door. The only banging I wanted happening was in the bedroom. "Not now," I bellowed, my voice muffled by Sara's leg.

The thundering knocking came again, an urgency to the tattoo. I closed my eyes for a moment. Breathed in Sara's musky scent. "Will you excuse me for a moment?"

She giggled. "You're such a gentleman. Chuck me my tee on your way over?" She pointed toward the door where she'd shed the garment. Shame she hadn't dropped her jeans in the same move. I'd be that one step closer to nirvana.

I scooped up the shirt and tossed it to her, then paused with my hand on the doorknob to make sure she had it on before I let Marty in. Those breasts weren't for Marty's eyes. He had Mother's. Yeah, that was a thought to settle my cock down to more manageable proportions.

Sara sorted her wild ringlets and gave me a thumbs-up.

As Marty pounded again, I dragged the door open. "You'd better be reporting a disaster of colossal import—" It wasn't Marty. It was Simon fucking

Prescott.

A waft of cardamom, ginger, and pineapple billowed into the room. I knew the smell. The man had expensive tastes.

I squared my shoulders, blocking Prescott's view. "What do you want?" The British gentleman deserted my tone entirely when the occasion called for it.

He glared at me, then shifted from one foot to the other, craning to see beyond me. "Why don't you ask my fucking wife? I've no doubt she's in here. You realize she's fucking you over?"

Sara's hand pressed into the small of my back. "Let him in, Rick." Her voice sounded weary, as though she'd not wanted this confrontation. Hardly surprising.

And Prescott seemed drunk, weaving blearily, though it was barely past midafternoon. He shoved past and tried to whirl around to face us but lurched against the TV unit instead. "I warned you, Sara." He shook a finger in her direction.

I moved closer to her, sliding an arm around her waist but angling slightly across so I could protect her. Even had Prescott not been drunk, I could take him down. Hell, I could take an elephant down to defend Sara.

He took a step closer, but instead of retreating, she also edged forward.

"What the hell, Simon?" Sara snapped. "What do you think you're doing here? And why are you drunk?"

"I warned you," the man reiterated. "I warned you not to make me look a fool, but here you are, whoring around before I've even left the country. Now it's your fault that lover boy's life is about to get all fucked up."

"*I'm* whoring around?" Sara didn't seem the least

disconcerted by the aggression in her husband's tone, and I had a sudden flash of the force to be reckoned with that she'd present in court. "Tell me, why didn't Emily-Elinor-Ellen—whatever her name is this week—accompany you? Couldn't you afford her ticket?"

Prescott's eyes cleared for a moment, and he made an effort to pull himself upright. "Of course I could. But I wanted us to have a private opportunity to settle this in a reasonable manner."

"No, you wanted to blackmail me, Simon. Which happens to be illegal."

He scratched at his neck, the sound rasping across the room. "Speaking the truth is not blackmail, Sara. If you were a better attorney, you'd realize that. Everyone knows you're scamming. Even Winchester here isn't stupid enough to believe you just happened to turn up in his life."

"No, I'm not," I drawled deliberately slowly, my voice soft. I'd long ago learned that to make an irate person pay attention, you lowered your voice, forcing them to listen. "I'm quite sure she researched me in Burke's Peerage before she flung herself into the abyss."

"Don't play me for a fool, Winchester," he sneered. "It's your arse I'm trying to save here. I meant *after* she'd rescued you. When she was suddenly moved to declare her love for you."

"Unfortunately, she's done no such thing." I caught Sara's glance up at me and hoped I hadn't overstepped the mark. But, damn, I was getting pretty close to sure about this business. I could happily give up every single thing in my life, but not her. I needed to get to know her a whole lot better.

Sara tugged on my hand, silencing me. "The concept

of selflessness means nothing to you, does it, Simon? You think it impossible someone would do something decent just for the sake of it."

"Let's say I'm a realist." He shoved spatulate fingers through his salt-and-pepper hair as if to tidy it, though, despite his state, not a follicle lay out of place.

Damn, I wanted a chance to do more than ruffle it for the bastard. But this was Sara's fight; I had to respect her strength and ability.

"And I realistically explained to you what would happen if you didn't follow my directives."

"I'm years beyond following your directives. I'm also not giving you an uncontested divorce. I'll fight you for every damn cent. You may care to think on that and remember that all I originally asked for was my gran's house. You wouldn't give me that, and now you'll lose big time. Half your cars, Simon. Half the house. All of Gran's house. Half the shares. Just adding that up in my head, it seems I come out with more than you do."

"I told you, the prenup means you've lost it all."

"That prenup isn't worth the paper it's printed on. Someone very kindly steered me toward the precedents that will see the agreement thrown out of court. You're very fond of precedents, aren't you?" Sara had taken a few steps toward him, her arms crossed, seeming not in the least daunted by the man who towered over her diminutive frame.

I felt like I should be on the sidelines, cheering on the tiny Amazon.

"I know you're a good attorney, Simon. It'll only take you minutes to discover what I have, but I'll save you the time. Remember how you coerced me to sign the prenup? Well, precedent has been set with a very similar case. The bride was presented an ultimatum only days before the wedding, where she was informed that she must sign the prenup or the ceremony would be called off. Sound familiar? That prenup was thrown out of court. The documents have no legal validity if they're signed under duress."

He swung his head bullishly. "You can't prove duress."

"I'd say the date on the document and the sworn statements of my bridesmaids would be enough to do so. That's assuming you want all your dirty linen aired in a courtroom. We both know how the media will love that."

"What the hell do you want money for, anyway, Sara? I thought you'd decided to go all fucking tree-huggy, vegetarian hippie, and had no use for it anymore?"

"Oh, money has its uses. I've never disputed that, only how it's used. All your money will go to the orphanage in the Solomons. I don't need it for myself. I can earn what I require to survive."

"Earn it flat on your back, you mean." Prescott jerked his chin at me.

Jesus, the gall of the bastard. In a flash, I understood Sara's anger at my offer of money.

My fists balled, but she had the situation under control, her tone level and matter-of-fact. "I'm not interested in Rick's money. In fact, it's something of an issue."

I didn't like to hear the word *issue* being applied to me in any context.

Prescott slumped against the cabinet, his head in both hands. "But how, Sara? How can you manage without money?"

Her tone gentled, as though she explained to a child, though her words still sliced at the man crumbling before her. "Do you mean how can I manage without the obscene wealth that you find necessary? It doesn't matter how much you have, what toys you buy; you'll always want more, need more, desire *things* to prove your worth. Yet you'll still feel empty. Cheated. Because you don't understand, Simon; only poverty can provide any meaning to wealth."

Good Lord. She'd hit the nail on the head. That was exactly the concept I'd been unable to articulate all these years, the verbalization of my core belief.

I needed this meeting over. I wanted Sara alone. Not so I could fuck her. So I could talk to her. Here was someone who would understand everything I strove for.

As though she read my mind, she turned on her heel and headed for the door. "Anyway, are we clear now, Simon? You can run to the media with your fabrications, but be certain that I shall be quick to retaliate with the factual accounts of your debt and blackmail attempt." She swept the door open and gestured at the hallway.

Prescott's mouth flapped open twice, then he shuffled across the room, his shoulders hunched, his face drawn and haggard. The debonair lawyer had been replaced by a middle-aged drunk. At the door he paused. "But…*Sira*?"

"*Sira* died a very long time ago, Simon. Probably around mistress number three." She didn't say the words harshly; in fact, they seemed to contain a little melancholy. But she shut the door in her husband's face.

Then she sagged against the frame, the bravado of the courtroom leaving her in a rush. "Too early for a drink?"

"Not really. But being British, I'd probably recommend a nice strong cup of tea."

She smiled slightly crookedly, her eyes betraying her sorrow. "Sounds topping. Is that right?"

"If you lived about a hundred years ago, maybe. I'll brew you a cuppa."

"You know how to do that?"

"Shall pull the silver spoon out of my mouth to do so."

I noted the effort it cost her to push herself from the door, the glance she cast at it, as though afraid Simon lurked outside.

I moved past her to open the door, then glanced up and down the corridor. "All clear." I put the snib on to reassure her, though I'd far rather show her how much I cared with a more physical display, preferably involving my fists and Prescott's smug face. "Sit. I'll make the drink." Besides, I needed a moment to collect my thoughts. To work out just what I wanted to say to her.

Because this had become so much more than a brief holiday affair.

This woman's actions had rescued me from the ocean, but her words were what parted my sea of doubt.

I tapped the teaspoon on the side of the cups, then carried them into the lounge. Handed one to her. "There you are. Tea. Mighty curer of all ills. Used to drown ex-husbands. Though I can't say I agree with that famous singer."

She lifted her eyebrows as she clutched the cup in both hands, steam partially obscuring her face.

"You know, the one who said, 'I'd rather have a cup of tea than sex.' "

"Oh, hell no. I wouldn't even say that about coffee.

And I do love coffee." She closed her eyes for a moment and blew out a long breath.

She was exhausted, but I had to set this straight. Set us straight. "Sara, what you said before—"

"Which what? I think my mouth was working overtime. Actually, it feels a little strained now." She clicked her jaw from one side to the other, her eyes teasing me.

No, I couldn't think about that mouth right now. It was time to slap all my gilt-edged cards on the table. "What you said about only poverty being able to provide meaning to wealth. Is that your true belief?"

She lifted one shoulder, wincing a little. "Of course. That's why I used my money to go to the Solomons. That's why I'll return there after Hawaii. You have to see these things to learn about them, to understand them. It's not enough to flip fifty bucks a month to sponsor an orphan; that's not investing in the issue or making a meaningful change. It's paying nothing more than lip service to a huge problem so you can put up a Christmas card from your sponsor child and have all your friends see that you've 'done the right thing.' There's so much more that we could be doing. Should be doing."

"I understand that. Completely. But that drives you to dislike people who have wealth?"

"I try not to hate on anyone, wealthy or otherwise." She dropped her gaze, scraping a nail across her jeans. "It's not the money, but the inequality that frustrates me."

"I'm at fault for having inherited that 'inequality'?"

"Not at all. But I do believe that you're responsible for what you do with your wealth. I'm frustrated by the way those with money—no, *some* of those with money—use it to further the gap between themselves and those without."

If she kept saying things that agreed so perfectly with my vision, my damn heart was going to burst from my chest. "You'd endorse the somewhat unpopular royal view then?"

She lifted an eyebrow. "Don't tell me you know the British royal family?"

"I'm not a name-dropper. But I will paraphrase something I heard. In order to effect change, it's necessary to get off our phones, get out into our communities, and take actual action. And I agree entirely with both that sentiment and with you." I blew across the surface of my tea, but I was trying to calm my mind by creating a storm in the teacup. "Problem is I'm yet to work out how to convince Mother of the purity of paring back."

She frowned. "What do you mean?"

I considered her for a long moment. This was it. All in. "If I had no money to my name, would you feel the same way about me?"

"No."

I'd swear one of Mother's ponies just kicked me in the gut. "No?" My shock ricocheted around the room.

Sara set her cup aside carefully, her brow furrowed. "I'm only human, Rick." She looked up and held my gaze. Obviously unaware that she was so much more than *only* anything.

Her hand waved, as though she'd draw the words she wanted from the air. "Sure, I can get mad at Simon for splashing around his cash and his obscene desire for money. But I can't pretend I don't appreciate the things money can buy. The gorgeous suite you put me up in.

The clothes you wear. Your awesome cologne. Not one of those things is necessary, but they sure as hell are nice. Addictive. And impossible without money."

Wait...did her words hold a glimmer of hope for me?

Yet I didn't want her to desire me for my money. In fact, that was the precise opposite of what I needed. And not where I'd thought she was going at all. Fuck, had I just dug myself a grave?

She pinched her lips together, gaze sliding from mine for a moment, then she impatiently shoved her hair behind her ear. "But you see, the thing is, for the last year I've been trying to change my desires, my ideas about what I *need*. To be better, do better. Now I want my money to buy happiness for others. I want my work to actually count for something."

Her gaze nailed mine, her back straightening as though she presented her final argument. "So no, if you didn't have any money, I wouldn't feel the same." She rubbed a hand across her chest, as though it ached, and took a deep breath. "If you had no money, I'd be more...secure, I guess, because I'd know that what I feel for you is pure and unadulterated. That it could *only* be love that keeps us together, not my avarice."

I'd thought I was drowning, but she'd thrown me a life preserver. And she'd said the word. She'd said it before I'd even worked up the courage.

I put my cup on the table and stepped back. Shoved my hands into my pockets and paced to the window overlooking the sun-drenched bay. Then back again. I could barely restrain my excitement and keep my eagerness tamped down in an appropriate manner. Hell, when I was around Sara, appropriate was the last thing I wanted to be. "Look, do you think you could repeat all that while I record it, and I'll play it to Mother?"

Turning to follow my agitated movements, Sara lifted her hand in question. "What does your mother have to do with anything?"

My turn to try and explain what had been a gut feeling, practically inexplicable, for so long. But the clarity of Sara's vision would help me find the words. "A few years back, I came to much the same conclusion as you; those with money have a mandate to help those without. So I qualified as an engineer and learned several languages. I pretty much sucked at both. Neither came naturally to me; I had to work at them, hoping I could use them to do some good. Since then I've traveled, volunteering for Engineers Without Borders."

I blew out a short, exasperated breath. "But it's not enough." The familiar frustration roiled within me, but for the first time, I knew for certain I'd taken steps along the right path. "Unfortunately for Mother, I've realized that my beliefs are incompatible with owning a vast estate and strings of polo ponies. No matter how hard I work, my money can do more than I will ever achieve through labor alone."

I crossed the room and dropped to my knees in front of Sara, laying my hands on her thighs, her warmth soaking into my palms. "I have a moral obligation to use my inheritance in the best way I can."

I took a deep breath, tightening my grip on her legs. Marty had done his best to comprehend the scheme and had supported me regardless, but Sara was my kindred spirit. She'd intuitively understand my reasoning. "I've had papers drafted to transfer the bulk of my family's assets, along with a good chunk of cash, to the various not-for-profits I support. If I sign, my estate won't be left precisely penniless, but our standing among our supposed peers will be substantially reduced." With each sentence, weight lifted from my shoulders, as though I'd already cast aside the harness of unwanted privilege.

Sara leaned forward, placing a palm on each side of my face, her eyes wide and astonished. "You plan to give everything you have to charity? That's—amazing. I don't have any words."

I certainly didn't want to stop her smart little mouth from working. Or from doing any of the other things I suspected it would do so well. "Oh, don't think too highly of me; *everything* would be rather an exaggeration. But if I do this, I will have to work for a living. Which will doubtless leave Mother somewhat appalled." Yet perhaps not as shocked as I'd spent months anticipating. I assumed I had Marty to thank for gradually warming the frozen cockles of Mother's aristocratic heart. Not that I wanted to think about how that defrosting had been achieved.

Sara ran her fingertips down the side of my face, deliberately rasping the dark stubble. "So that's what Marty meant about you having a death wish? He thinks your mother will knock you off for squandering the family fortune?"

I turned my face to her palm so I could kiss it. Darted my tongue out for a quick taste, drilling into the valley between her fingers. She giggled, lust deepening the emerald blaze that led from her pupil.

Even in the midst of sharing my secrets, I was entirely aware of my desire. I forced myself to keep talking instead of giving in to the urge to persuade her to my cause with my mouth, my lips, my hands. Various other portions of my anatomy, which were quite convinced they could do the job.

"Don't be daft; she won't soil her hands. She'll employ an enforcer." I flashed a grin in case Sara took me seriously. "No, I'm reasonably sure she won't go quite that far, though I fully expect to be excommunicated from the family. Marty's death-wish comment would be because I've spent years dragging the poor sod around some rather unprepossessing countries, trying to run from the lifestyle that seems inherent with my title. If I'm being completely honest—as I will always be with you—taking risks like working in Palestine, or searching for mermaids in the middle of a hurricane, were avoidance tactics. I was procrastinating on making this final move."

Sara slid down to the floor, also kneeling. She looked up at me, her palms pressed to my chest. "And now that you've caught the mermaid? What's your game plan?"

Caught the mermaid. Did she mean it? And if she did, would I ever be able to hold on to her? Lord knew I was willing to spend a lifetime trying. "Now, hopefully with some encouragement from a person whose integrity I greatly respect, I intend to sign the documents and then front Mother. Break the news of her virtual impoverishment—which she will spend in the arguable comfort of an exceedingly luxurious cottage. Doubtless accompanied by Marty and his furry harem."

"Sounds cozy." Sara's lips were inches from mine.

I'd take her proximity as tacit approval of my plan.

"Though I can't say it holds any appeal for me," she continued. "I've developed something of a liking for cramped cabins and tents." Her fingers traced my jaw.

"Tell me, have you ever been to the Solomon Islands? Because they need engineers. And lawyers. Living expenses only, you won't get paid…although I'm sure other compensation could be negotiated."

"Can't say that I've been there. I'd potentially be interested but would probably need a guide. Any recommendations?" Much as I loved her banter, I needed to kiss Sara now. I ached to be closer to her, to be wrapped around her. To be inside her.

For years, I'd been willing to risk my body, but I'd always guarded my heart. Now I was ready to open up.

"I think I could hook you up with someone to show you the way around." Eyes dancing, she took my hand. Placed it on her chest, above her heart, then drew it slowly down to cup her breast. Her nipple hardened instantly against my palm. "See? You take directions rather well."

"And this other compensation you mention?" I rasped my fingers over her nipple, the fabric of her shirt rustling beneath my calluses. "Would you be the person to speak with about that?"

"I would, indeed. I'm reasonably certain I'll be able to come up with something that will entice you."

She licked her lips suggestively, and I gritted my teeth together, willing down the erection that threatened to burst the zipper on my trousers.

"However, if I'm to provide you a character reference for this position, I think you have a promise you first need to make good on."

Though my heart beat furiously, I reluctantly removed my hand from her breast. "Ah. About that. I'm sorry, Sara. I know I promised. But I've changed my mind."

Chapter Twenty-Six

Sara

Shock immobilized my face. My mouth barely moved as I stammered, "Y-you don't want…"

Rick traced his thumb across the bow of my lips as though he memorized the shape. Like he'd never have another opportunity.

How had I read this so wrong?

Oh yeah, that was right. Practice.

He stood, drawing me to my feet. I wanted to resist, but too many warring emotions in too short a time had drained me, leaving me weak.

Instead of walking away, he stood close, his hands comfortable on my hips. "Do you remember, in the boat, I asked why you were there? Now I know." The laughter had dropped from Rick's eyes. He was intent and serious, his accent crisp as he enunciated carefully. "You came to rescue me. But not only from the ocean. I was drowning in my own cynicism and on the verge of allowing rationality to overrule passion—in every facet of my life. Now you've shown me that what I want to do is not only right but entirely possible."

Yeah. I'd always talked too much. Like, great he was a philanthropist and all, but that was not going to help alleviate the deep, hungry ache in my lower belly.

Never mind the one higher. In the center of my

chest. The one that had nothing to do with my injuries. Not the physical ones, anyway.

A tiny frown cut Rick's forehead. "I'm terrified I'm going to scare you away, but I promised you complete honesty." His eyes seemed to beseech me, his throat working silently for a moment. "I've searched for you so long, without ever understanding what it was that I sought. I needed you so desperately, without ever being aware of the lack. So the thing is, Sara—" He heaved a deep breath. "No. I don't want to fuck you. I want to take you to my bed and make love to you."

All sound and movement stopped. I'd swear even my heart froze.

Then I took a step back.

Grooves of disappointment carved his cheeks, but he didn't remonstrate or try to reach for me, restrain me, stop me. He'd allow me to be free. To make my own choices.

My fingers wound into the hem of my shirt, and I drew it over my head, releasing my breasts. Unsnapped my jeans, then shucked them with a little wriggle to free my hips. Stood there, dressed only in my panties. My face heated instantly, my heart pounding as though I'd never been exposed to him before. But this time was different. This time, I offered more than just my body.

"No one's ever made love to me, Rick."

His pupils were blown out, darkened with lust. Or with something more. Something I'd never seen before. "It would be my honor to be your first."

I wanted to tease him about being so correctly British, but, God, what he said, the way he said it, was always so perfect.

He closed the space between us, one hand sliding up

to cradle the back of my neck as he guided my mouth to his.

The kiss lacked our previous frenetic urgency. As my lips opened beneath his touch, his tongue brushed over mine and we explored each other, slowly, carefully, as though memorizing tastes and textures. This time, his lips not only teased; they promised.

As the kiss deepened, I pressed closer, my palms resting on his pecs.

Rick stooped, one arm around my back, the other behind my knees, and lifted me.

He didn't even grunt.

This guy was earning more brownie points than he'd ever be able to cash in. Unless I allowed him a lot of time.

And I couldn't think of a single reason not to.

He strode into the adjoining room and lowered me to the bed as though I were fragile.

He could be right; I felt like I'd somehow shatter if I didn't feel his naked skin against mine immediately. "Your clothes," I ordered. "Off. I want all of you, Richard Winchester."

"Oh, you're going to get all of me, right enough." His gaze was direct.

I knew he meant the words literally.

As had I.

Body and soul.

He stripped, revealing the deliciously taut, sinewy body I'd happily ogle for hours. The bed sank beneath his weight as he knelt, easing my thighs apart. He settled between my legs, his warm breath whispering across my core.

I chose to think his groan was pleasure rather than relief at setting me down, but I tangled a hand in his short hair, restraining him. "Not this time. I want you inside me, Rick. I need you to fill me. To connect with me. Completely."

"I will. I promised, remember? But foreplay comes first… You know, it's kind of suggested by the prefix."

His jaw grated against my palm as my fingertips traced the groove in his cheek. "We don't have to play by any rules, Rick." Not anymore. "I'm not into the bases, remember, and we can always go back. And forth. And back."

Amusement flared in his eyes. "Hmm. I never did master the waltz. You may have to show me your moves."

He shifted up the bed—*up me*—and I quivered with laughter as his tongue dipped into my navel, like he was determined to steal a taste despite my ban. My tummy probably wobbled like jelly. And I didn't damn well care, because Rick made his adoration obvious.

His skin stroked a delicious friction across mine, like a rough towel on a summer's day, his pecs crushing my nipples as he kissed his way between my breasts and up the side of my neck.

Anticipation shivered through me, goose bumps pebbling my flesh as his teeth found the hoops in my ears, the tiny spikes of pain as he tugged hardening my nipples with the memory of the last time he'd touched me this way.

And where his hands had gone next.

Biceps straining as his weight rested on his forearms on either side of my head, he lowered himself until his hard torso pressed against every inch of me, his muscular legs forcing between my less-than-muscular thighs.

No way could he miss how wet I was for him.

His gaze rested on my bruised shoulder. "I hate seeing you in any measure of pain. And I should say I'm sorry about this—" His lips barely brushed the lilac flesh. "—but I'd be lying if I did. Because, if you hadn't jumped into the ocean, I'd not have met you."

"You're trying to insinuate I threw myself at you? That's hardly a gentlemanly accusation."

A devilish grin flashed across his face. "I'm gentleman enough that, if you care to do it again, I promise to catch you."

"How about *you* throw yourself *on* me, and I'll do the catching?" Being able to smell and touch him, knowing that soon I'd greedily accept everything he had to offer, was foreplay enough. I wanted him. Now. Though undeniably exquisite, the wait was also excruciating.

"Enticing proposal." His index finger followed my hairline, down my cheek, across my lips. "I can't tell you enough how much I love your smart mouth."

"Uh-huh. And here I was, thinking you were going to give me a good rogering. Instead, you're already on about oral."

"I'm more than willing to give rather than receive."

"*Such* an altruist. But I do believe in fair turnabout."

His tongue traced the edge of my lips, tickling. "Then I shall gladly wait my turn. But first, I believe you had a request?"

My levity dropped as I linked my fingers around the back of his neck, pulling him closer. The rich scent of his aftershave filled my lungs. His weight on me felt warm and secure and so *right*. "I do. Make love to me, Richard Winchester."

His lips curved into a slow smile before they

descended on mine.

He tasted like tea and salt and something indefinable, something I didn't ever want to forget, something I needed to save forever, pressed between the pages of my mind.

His mouth consumed me, hungry and demanding, and I moaned as his cock prodded my swollen pussy lips, both demand and promise in the padded steel.

I wanted him deep inside me, yet confusingly, I wanted to make this tantalizing moment last forever.

He could have taken me right then, but Rick adjusted his position, pressing his rigid length along my slick channel, the head of his cock nudging my engorged clit with every breath either of us took.

I moaned.

He grinned, assertive and self-assured, and God help me, I loved the look on him.

"You like that?" he murmured.

I nodded, not trusting myself to speak.

"And this?" Taking his weight on one forearm and knee, he fisted his cock and guided it along my slit, dipping a little deeper with each pass.

Sweat beaded his brow, and I knew the effort he took not to plunge into me.

On each upstroke, I quivered as his domed helmet brushed the trigger point at the top of my pussy. On each downstroke, I moaned, arching my hips, trying to force him to enter me.

"Uh-uh," he cautioned. "I said I'm making love to you, remember?"

"This is teasing, not making love," I ground out.

"Don't I know it." He shifted to take my nipple in his mouth.

The feeling of him suckling, rolling my other nipple between his thumb and forefinger, was enough to get me off. My thighs quivered uncontrollably, and I pushed at his shoulders. "Why are you determined to torment me? For God's sake, just get it in. I've been hot as hell for you for days!"

He lifted a quizzical eyebrow. "You don't like what I'm doing?"

"Of course I bloody do. But I'm terrified that we'll only get so far, and somebody will knock at the door or the earth will shift or Kilauea will erupt or some damn thing. We don't have a great record with foreplay, remember?"

He turned down the corners of his mouth, wrinkling his forehead as though he considered the matter. "You know, you could be right. And really, you're the only thing I want exploding around here. But I do have a solution."

"Fabulous. Care to share?"

The lines feathering from his eyes deepened as he grinned. In a swift, fluid move, he drew back and then sank his cock into me.

"Fuuuck!" My feet slammed to the mattress, and I arched my back, trying to force him deeper, even though he filled me so completely.

"Rather thought I was," he said, though his words were even more clipped than usual, his chest heaving against mine. "Sara, you feel so damn good around me. Even better than I'd imagined."

I needed to say something funny, probably something about fantasies and mermaids, but no way in hell could I think of anything. My entire being was focused on him. Not only the feel of him—thick, hard, and firm—within me, but his touch, the length of his body pressed against mine. The roughness of his callused hands, so at odds with the rest of his appearance, caressing my curves with each long, languorous plunge.

His mouth finding my ear, he urged my legs farther apart and ground into me. "I can think of so many ways I want—and plan—to take you, and I know missionary is so terribly British and potentially boring—"

"So not boring." I gasped.

He blew out a sharp breath, closing his eyes for a second and holding still, buried within me. No. Not still. Dear God, he wasn't pumping, but his cock twitched inside me, a flickering movement, vibrating against the G-spot I hadn't even known I possessed, and holy hell, he was going to make me come.

His eyes opened, and he resumed his slow rhythm. A sexy, lazy smile spread across his face as he thrust deep and then ground his hips against mine, a practiced move that stimulated my clit each time. My hips jerked toward him as though he played me like a puppet on a string. "Good. Because this way I get to see all of your gorgeous body. Touch you. Kiss you." He did so, proving his point. "And you know what's best of all?"

Yes. The hold and twitch. No, the almost-withdrawal-and-graze-the-clit move. No, wait, the deep pump. "All of it," I panted.

"Flattering." He shook his head. "But best is, in this position, I get to watch when you come, beautiful Sara. I get to bury both my cock and my tongue deep inside you as you explode into a storm around me."

I lifted my hips, wriggled my hands beneath his arms, and dug my nails into the hard muscles of his shoulders. "That works both ways." My teeth found his lower lip, seizing the tender flesh, goading him from his deliberately slow pace.

He grunted and thrust fast and deep.

I spread my thighs as wide as I could, almost screaming as he withdrew and plunged back into me.

The pressure swelled and mounted within me, the need for release centering every sensation on my core, the world narrowing to just this moment, just this lust and longing and *elation* he pounded into me.

He shifted onto his knees, and I scissored my legs around his waist. Urging him on with cries and moans, I tried to return his thrusts, unable to match his pace as he slammed into me, our flesh slapping together as he drove me higher and higher.

The fireworks built within me, effervescence roiling in my groin and sparking through my chest.

His gaze never left mine. "Keep your eyes open, Sara," he commanded. "I want to see you come."

"Not alone." I gasped. I needed proof that he wanted me as much as I wanted him.

His thumb found my clit, circling, then pressing each time he drove into me. "Then come with me, Sara. And stay with me."

"Oh, fuck! Yes!" His demand tipped me over the edge, every need and sensation coalescing into a moment of pure clarity as my back arched up to give him everything, my body screaming for release, clawing to the pinnacle, then swooping in a dizzying freefall as he groaned my name, his strong hands holding me close as he spurted hot and thick inside me.

I knew exactly what I wanted.

And it was him.

My body trembled and quivered as Rick slowed,

lowering himself on top of me, still embedded deep within me. Sweat sheening both of us, he was panting nearly as hard as I was.

My hands tracing the muscles of his back, I found words first, though they were broken and breathless. "You know *make love* is an odd expression, right? There's no implication of whether the words infer a singular act or plural." I licked at the salt on his neck and then buried my face in his shoulder, inhaling his sweat and manliness. I was strong, an independent woman. And I'd ask for what I wanted. "I should warn you, as a lawyer, I require specificity."

Rick drew back, his chest heaving, and waited until I met his gaze.

I knew whatever he said next would be momentous. Life-changing.

And I was ready for it.

"The implication was most definitely not intended to be singular." His voice dropped lower, deep and commanding, his accent lending a certain precision to the words. "We Brits are notoriously bad about expressing our emotions, but if you want specifics, I'm more than happy to provide."

His gaze caressed me, his fingers tracing the contours of my face. "Sara Grant, I intend to make love to you every day, for as long as you will permit me."

He kissed me, deep and long, though I could never have enough. Then he drew back, his voice softer than silk, stronger than steel, more certain than the dawn of a new day.

"You, my love, are my once in a lifetime. My perfect storm."

Epilogue

Sara

With my eyes closed to fully maximize the enjoyment of the last of the day's balmy sunshine, I could hear the childish squeals and giggles long before they drew near.

A lazy smile curved my lips as a shadow fell over me, a baritone whisper of "Shh, don't wake your mama," greeted by quickly stifled four-year-old laughter.

"Maman, Maman, reveille toi!"

The perfect French took me a moment to translate, then I slit my eyes open. "I'm awake, I'm awake," I mumbled.

"Il est temps de s'habiller!"

My daughter's faithful steed craned his head back to look up to where she perched astride his broad shoulders. "Okay, you might have caught that, but I have no idea what she said," he grumbled.

My French wasn't good enough to follow Sophia's excited chatter, but I knew her excitement related to a certain dress she'd chosen for herself, layered tiers in the soft shades of a Hawaiian sunset. "Soph, could you tell Uncle Jay what you said—but in English this time?"

Her hands clutched under Jay's chin, Sophia planted a kiss on top of his shaved head. "I said mummy needs to get dressed, silly."

"Silly, am I?" He grasped her waist and swung her down.

Her sandal-clad feet hit the balcony deck amidst a flurry of squeals and giggles.

She clung to his leg like a limpet. "No, Uncle Jay. Not silly. I luff you."

Often, Sophia's French and German superseded her grasp of English. Well, as far as I could tell; I lagged sorely on two out of three.

As Sophia plopped onto the edge of my deck chair, I stretched, then rubbed both hands across my face, chasing away the last of my languor. "It feels so good to relax."

"The way you lot carry on, I'm not surprised." Jay nudged his chin behind me to the plate glass windows of *The Spirit of Ohana's* premier suite. "You do remember it was an easier life cleaning cabins, right? I'm sure Captain Raynalds would be happy to offer you another position. I know I would." He quirked a brow, but we both knew he was teasing.

"I have very fond memories. But despite this being the nicest place we've stayed for years, I wouldn't change a thing about my life." As I spoke, Sophia nestled into the crook of my shoulder, her curly hair tickling my chin, her hand stroking across my belly as she crooned softly. I pressed my lips to her head, then looked up to meet Jay's dark eyes. "I can't believe Captain Raynalds is doing this."

He shrugged. "Well, seems you're still something of a rock star in his books. Doesn't hurt that you manage to maintain a fairly high profile. And I guess he couldn't offer you anything less than premium accommodation, considering the precedent."

Yeah, that profile. Bane of my life. Seemed that our choices made disappearing into obscurity more difficult than it should have been.

"What are you doing with my women?" growled a mock-angry voice.

As always, excitement thrilled through me, my toes curling, anticipation tingling my fingertips at the tone, the air of possessiveness that I knew came only from love.

"Babysitting your rug rat, man." Jay stooped to pinch Sophia's cherubic cheek. "I only get uncle duties for ten days, so got to make the most of it."

"Fair enough." Rick placed a tall drink on the table alongside my reclined deck chair. "Virgin mai tai for the….well, for you." He winked at me.

Yeah, so not a virgin anymore. Neither my heart nor my body.

"Really?" Jay's groan was a deep rumble. "You two should be over this stuff by now."

Nope. Never.

He heaved an exaggerated sigh. "C'mon, Sophia, the boring grown-ups need some alone time. And Auntie Melanie said she's going to fix your hair."

Jay held out his hands, and Sophia deserted me, fairly leaping into his arms and snuggling against his neck. She'd only met him once before, but they'd bonded instantly. Maybe because she'd discovered such a source of strength and love in her father, she expected the same adoration from all men. Jay surprised me, though. He seemed almost wistful when he was with my daughter.

Rick bopped Sophia's nose with his fingertip and gave her a kiss. "Okay, you be a good girl for Uncle Jay."

She pouted. "I always good, Daddy."

He smiled. "Yes, you are. You're my angel. Well, except when you're naughty. But I love you then, too. Always and forever, right, princess?"

Always and forever. That had become our signature, the words the three of us said to one another each night.

As Jay carted our gorgeous daughter off, Rick bent over me, his lips seeking mine as hungrily as they had from our first days together.

His sinewy, tanned forearm leaned against the mound of my stomach, and he chuckled. "Junior's complaining."

"Mmm. You're squashing him." I shouldn't tease. When we'd first discovered I was—unexpectedly—pregnant, Rick had been scared to touch me for weeks. Only when I reminded him of his promise—to make love to me every day—had he picked up the courage again.

"You know, I didn't think you could ever be any sexier than you were when I met you." His gaze roamed my bikini-clad body. "But now, with even more curves—" His huge palm cupped my swollen breast, his thumb gentle on my engorged nipple. "You're amazing. And growing my baby." He shook his head in disbelief.

"What happened to kids being a narcissistic perpetuation of self?" I teased for the hundredth time.

"No narcissism here. I don't want a clone of myself; I want the world to be blessed with your genes. I do wish that you'd take things a little easier, though, Sara."

Tempting. Life had been crazy over the last three years. A good kind of crazy. So many countries, so much work.

"We could cancel the next trip. Stay here a bit longer and relax." Rick sounded like he was pleading.

I traced my finger down the cleft in his cheek.

"You're just trying to avoid Elizabeth. You know she and Marty are desperate to see Sophia again."

"Hmm." He didn't sound convinced. "They came last month."

"And the month before."

"That should be enough."

Rick's relationship with his mother was...unusual. She'd accepted the change in her financial circumstances—though she was still, as he pointed out, very far from impoverished—with perfect aplomb and appeared entirely happy living with Marty since Rick's dad had passed two years earlier. Rick, however, seemed to expect her to backflip at any moment and wasn't able to accept the doting, though somewhat rigid, grandmother figure she presented, uncomplainingly traveling the world to wherever we were stationed.

My fingers traced patterns on his naked chest over his heart. "Well, we have to go next week. I'll not be able to travel much beyond that."

As if to signify agreement, a tiny foot or fist thrust a lump up in my belly. Rick bent to press his lips to my stomach. But his hand tracked lower, brushing my bikini pants.

I gurgled with delight, parting my legs to ease his access.

Suddenly stern, he drew back. "No."

"No?" I wasn't accustomed to his rejection.

"No more hanky-panky."

I grinned at his very British term. "Never?"

"Not until I've made an honest woman of you."

I sighed, pretending annoyance. "Guess Sophia's right, then. I'd better get dressed."

"Not on my account. You can wear rags or a

ballgown, and I'll love you regardless."

He had seen me both ways, many times. "I think Captain Raynalds would probably prefer if we presented nicely, given that he's invited the press."

"Hmm," Rick rumbled. "If I'd known it'd take a press presence to convince you to accept, I'd have manipulated this years ago. You do realize, though, that we'll have to recreate the event for Mother and her cronies when we get back to the UK?"

"Don't be mean. You know she's wanted this for you for years." Though I'm sure Elizabeth's dreams hadn't involved me, a divorced, pregnant Australian with a penchant for living rough, she was carefully cordial toward me.

"I'm sure she could indulge her fantasy by dressing up Maureen, Doreen, and—what's the other one called?"

"Anna."

"Yeah. That."

"Grumpy old man. You give Marty a run for his money." I kissed Rick. Long and lingering. Possessively. This man was all mine.

As my hands hooked around the back of his strong neck, his lips searched mine, taking and giving with equal eagerness. This man knew how to kiss, how to drive me wild simply by breathing against my lips, how to ratchet up my insatiable craving for him with the slightest movement, his thumb brushing the rim of my ear as his tongue gently probed.

As always, he'd tease until I was moaning and desperate for him.

And as always, I'd desire him with an unquenchable thirst.

He drew back eventually, his pupils dilated with a

look that I'd come to learn was so much more than lust. "Go and get dressed, my love. It's time for me to make you my wife."

My breath suddenly ragged, I nodded.

As Rick helped me to my feet, I gazed across the blue Hawaiian ocean. Above the mountains of the Na Pali coast, the evening sky swirled with pink and lavender, the exact shades of Sophia's flower-girl dress.

Still, the rugged landscape stirred longing within my soul.

But I knew I'd already discovered my greatest adventure.

I was living it.

This man.

This life.

This family.

Always and forever.

A word about the author...

A professional counselor by trade and author of best-selling rural fiction under Léonie Kelsall, her "real" name, Laney Kaye writes hot merman and shifter romances, and laugh-out-loud steamy romcoms, perfect for spicing up your day (or night!)

~*~

Find Laney Kaye online at:
https:www.leoniekelsall.com